Rumors, Ruin and
the Duke

RUMORS, RUIN AND THE DUKE

The Lost Lords Series

Karla Kratovil

TULE
PUBLISHING

PROLOGUE

June 2, 1826

THE DUKE OF Hartwick glanced down again at the missive that had just been delivered. As he tried to decipher the cryptic message it contained, he paced the plush carpet.

> *I have the information you are seeking. Please allow me to ask your forgiveness in person. Meet me on the south side of St. James Park at midnight. Look for my coachman. Be careful not to be followed. ~Galey*

A thousand questions raced through his mind. Galey was one of his father's oldest friends; what did he know about the circumstances around his family's deaths? What could he possibly need to apologize for? Why the clandestine meeting? Why not just meet in a private room at the club? Or visit him at his home? *Very strange indeed.* And how did Galey even know about his inquiries? Could Hart finally receive answers to the suspicions that had eaten at him for years?

The thief who killed both his father and older brother five years ago, and thrust him into the role of Duke of

Hartwick, had snatched away the two men he admired most in the world. He had been quietly investigating the circumstances surrounding their deaths ever since to no avail. Hart knew deep down in his soul that the two had been dead long before their bodies had been found shot through the chest in a hack on the Strand. If Lord Galey had any information that would help Hart discover the true cause of their demise, then he would meet him anywhere he wished, under any circumstance.

The low rumble of music and voices filtered through the door and beckoned him back to the party. Lucy would be waiting for him. Exiting the quiet of his study, he strode down the corridor and approached the doors to his ballroom.

Two footmen flanked the double doors. "Good evening, Your Grace."

"Tell Mr. Kent to have the carriage brought around in thirty minutes."

"Yes, Your Grace." One of the footmen scrambled off to find Hart's coachman.

The other opened the massive, gilded door that led into the ballroom.

Hart walked into the crowded room. Music from a string quartet and the rise and fall of conversation assaulted his ears. The ballroom of Hartwick House was illuminated by hundreds of candles. Guests danced across the intricately pattern wood floors; some mingled along the edges, sipping wine and spirits, and many spilled through the open French doors onto the large stone veranda in search of cooler evening air. He scanned the crowded ballroom for Lucy. He had promised her a dance, and even with the urgency clawing at his gut, he wouldn't go back on a promise. He flipped open his pocket watch; it was only eleven. Where was the birthday girl?

Then he spotted her standing next to his great-aunt Trudy. The two of them stood next to an open glass-paned door that led to the outside. Lucy's cheeks were flushed pink from the heat. She took a sip from the glass she held, and her nose wrinkled in distaste. He chuckled. Moving toward them, he snatched two glasses of champagne from the tray of a roving footman. Today marked Lucy's twenty-second birthday.

Lucy's father, Captain Middleton, had been a good friend of the family, and when he and his wife died, Hart's father had been designated as the young girl's guardian. Hart had unofficially been looking out for Lucy since his father's death, but really, watching out for Lucy had been his job for years. A job that should have been an easy one. He sighed; nothing was easy when it came to Lucy Middleton.

His father had sent him to smooth things over at Ms. Bolen's School for Young Ladies of Quality countless times over the five years Lucy had attended. And each time she had promised to behave better. Since her time at school, she had been living with Aunt Trudy, and the shenanigans had continued as Trudy sponsored Lucy's foray out on the marriage mart. He grudgingly gave Lucy credit for her spirit. Nobody pushed around her or her friends, for that matter.

But she should have been safely married off by now … and not his problem anymore.

Thank God for Great-Aunt Trudy. The old girl had taken Lucy into her home and under her care when Hart's world had been flipped upside down. Lucy acted as Trudy's companion and the two got along famously. Not that Trudy was the ideal chaperone, more likely to join into the trouble than put a stop to it. Hart plastered a smile on his face as he approached the two ladies.

As always, Lucy looked beautiful. A blue ribbon weaved through the chestnut curls piled high on her head. Her dress fell in a waterfall of shimmering blue silk that complemented the startling blue of her eyes. Those eyes were fixed on him, and her pink lips turned up into a smile. "Hart!"

Hart nodded. "Good evening, Aunt Trudy, Lucy. Enjoying your birthday celebration, brat?" He handed a glass of champagne to his aunt, then plucked the lemonade from Lucy's hand, and replaced it with the sparkling wine.

"Very much, Your Grace." She raised an eyebrow. "So, I'm allowed wine now?"

He shrugged. "Today is your birthday. It's no time for tepid lemonade."

The grin she flashed him was blinding. She took a swallow of champagne. "Delicious."

"Hartwick, where have you been all evening?" Aunt Trudy trilled. "You are the host, and I have seen nary a hair on your head since the receiving line."

"I received an important missive and needed to take care

of crafting an immediate response."

"Bah, you are the most eligible bachelor here. You have been hiding. Don't bother to deny it." She waggled a finger at him.

He held up his hands in protest. "Truly, I had business to take care of, Aunt. Your accusations are unfounded. You know how much I like to flirt." He winked at Lucy, making her smile behind her glass.

"Well, perhaps before the flirting begins and ladies begin swooning at your feet, you can claim the dance you promised me," Lucy said.

"Indeed, I did not forget." He transferred their empty glasses to a passing footman and held out a hand as the music changed.

Lucy laid her hand in his, and they strolled to the center of the room. The waltz began. He pulled Lucy into his arms. "So, who here tonight does Auntie have her eye on for you?"

Lucy's nose wrinkled again as she glanced up at him. "Colonel Harrington. But I won't have it; he's even older than you."

Hart twirled her out with one hand and clasped the other to his chest in mock horror. "You wound me and all men of maturity with your derision."

Her unladylike snort of laughter caught the attention of couples around them. "Ha! You mature?"

He slid a hand back to her waist and gave a playful squeeze. "Shush, you. You're one to talk, you naughty thing."

Lucy's lips turned up into a small smile, which meant she was secretly pleased by his comment. Her gaze caught his as they moved across the parquet floor, and Hart recognized the flirtatious gleam in her eyes. She was incorrigible. He was far from immune to her beauty. But Lucy was under his protection and, by honor, off limits, not to mention that he was far too old for a girl so fresh-faced. The ten years between them made him feel positively lecherous. So much so that a year ago, he had sent Aunt Trudy and Lucy off to the continent on a grand tour just to have her out of his hair and off his mind.

"He is a terrible bore, and he looks at my person as though I am a present he can't wait to unwrap." She fluttered her eyelashes. "Perhaps you can scare him off for me with one of your stern ducal glares."

Hart frowned. Despite her light tone, a tightness around her eyes spoke volumes to her discomfort. "I have something important I must attend to tonight, but I will have some words with the Colonel next time I see him at the club. He is far too old for you. What is Trudy thinking?"

"Perhaps she is tired of me." Then Lucy shook her head, her sapphire earrings catching the candlelight as they swayed. "No, that's not it. I am a delight."

Hart laughed as Lucy intended. But as the music stopped, he lifted her chin with one finger, so she was forced to look at him. "I know that you think you no longer need someone to watch out for you, but if you ever need help, I want you to know you can count on me. I will always protect you."

Her expression softened. "I know." She turned and laid her hand on his arm as they headed back to where Aunt Trudy stood chatting with Lady Hathaway. "Where are you off to? You know Aunt Trudy will not approve of you slinking away to meet one of your mistresses during the party."

"One of my mistresses?" He raised an eyebrow. "How many do I have?"

She shrugged. "I imagine a small harem perhaps?"

"As enticing as having my own harem sounds, tonight's outing is strictly business."

THE NIGHT WAS thick with fog as Hart stepped down from his carriage. The mist wrapped around the light poles across the street and covered the trees in the park like a ghostly blanket.

His coachman, Thomas Kent, tilted his head toward the only other conveyance on the quiet street. "That is Lord Galey's coach down there. I recognize Jack Davies, his coachman."

"Thank you, Thomas. Just wait here." Hart walked the fifty yards down to the other town coach.

Galey's driver scrambled down from the box. "Good evening, Your Grace." He pulled open the door.

Hart climbed into the carriage. Two matching oil lamps

illuminated the interior and the tense features of the older man seated on the velvet squabs. Hart settled himself across from Galey and nodded. "Galey."

"I'm glad you agreed to come, Hartwick." He turned to his coachman. "Take a walk, Davies."

The man nodded and shut the carriage door. Hart sat back and folded his hands in his lap. This was Galey's show; he was here to listen. Galey took out a handkerchief and blotted his brow. The silence stretched. Hart wished to shake the man, to demand he tell him everything he knew about his father and brother's deaths. Was Galey toying with him? Would he demand something first in payment for the information?

"Thank you for meeting me." Galey cleared his throat. "What I am going to tell you has long weighed on my conscience."

Hart again waited silently.

"But you must understand … what I mean is that the people who are responsible for the murder of your family are very powerful."

He sat forward. "Murder? Do you know that it was not a random robbery?"

Galey nodded. "Your father's betrayal was not taken well. He chose to support your brother instead of sticking to the agreement." He shook his head. "I never thought that was so wrong. We all are just trying to protect our own, aren't we?"

"I don't understand. What are you getting at? Who did he betray?" Hart shook his head. None of this made sense.

The older man straightened, and his gaze snapped back to Hart. "They have ears everywhere. That's why no one could see us meet tonight. But I can't live with this guilt anymore. It's not right. Henry was always a good friend." His handkerchief came out again. He mopped his brow once more.

Hart was losing patience with the man. "Galey, what happened to my father and brother?"

"They were killed. For not following the plan—"

Next to him, the window shattered.

"They know!" Galey gasped.

A small earthenware jar sailed through the broken window and landed with a thud on the carriage floor. Hart stared at the lit fuse burning bright in the dark. His brain finally comprehending the danger, he flung open the door and vaulted onto the cobblestones. Turning, he reached out a hand. "Quick—"

The blast knocked him backward onto the hard pavement. Searing pain raced over his arm and chest. The smell of burning fabric filled his nostrils. Flames surrounded him. He flailed at them with his hands, but he could not fill his lungs with enough breath to call for help. Then he heard yelling and the heavy fall of footsteps. He was enveloped in black cloth that smelled of horse. The flames were extinguished. As the heavy cloth lifted, he tried to focus on the face above him. When he blinked, a sharp tearing agony tore through his right eye. His scream rent the air, and his vision dimmed as he slid into unconsciousness.

CHAPTER ONE

One year later

T HE MOONLIGHT ENTICED Lucy to step outside the ballroom. Night air, fresh and cool, skated over her overheated skin. The dancing inside was in full swing. Not a soul lingered on the veranda. Lucy fled down the steps that led down to the gardens. Her gaze scanned the great hedges that cast long shadows across the manicured lawn. Realizing she was alone, Lucy glanced backward at the lights spilling from the house. There were plenty of young debutants for men to dance with; no one would miss her. She followed the moonlight through the opening in the boxwoods and into the center courtyard that featured a large stone fountain.

She came to a stop and turned her face to the sky. What a beautiful night. It was a shame she must attend these social functions. Tonight would be a perfect night for stargazing. The scent of jasmine filled her nose, and she drew in a breath to savor the sweet smell. In the next moment, that breath left her in a sharp gasp as a pair of arms banded around her from behind.

"Miss Middleton, didn't anyone tell you young ladies

should not be found unchaperoned in the gardens?"

She closed her eyes. *Fitzwilliam*. Blast the persistent rogue. "Unhand me immediately, or you will certainly regret the consequences," Lucy growled.

The man who stood behind her, pinning her arms to her sides, chuckled into her ear. "Miss Middleton, how could I possibly regret the consequences of being caught in a compromising position with you? That is exactly my objective. You are what I want. And I always take what I want."

"And if I don't want to be taken?"

"That is inconsequential, my dear. You will marry me. This will ensure that you will. Don't worry; you'll enjoy it as much as I will." He licked the shell of her ear.

Lucy choked on her outrage. Fitzwilliam really didn't know how to take no for an answer. The despicable bastard thought he could coerce her? *Unbelievable!* She lifted her foot and stomped down hard on his instep with her heeled dancing shoe, his grunt of pain satisfying. His arms loosened enough for her to turn and thrust the heel of her hand sharply up at his weak chin. He stumbled back a step. She hiked her skirts up and delivered a swift kick between his legs like her father had taught her. Fitzwilliam crumpled to his knees with a wheeze.

Lucy sent him a look of disdain as she smoothed her skirts. "I told you that you would regret the consequences. Do not come near me again."

Fitzwilliam's eyes burned like hot coals as he stared up at her from the grass. "You bitch," he hissed. "You will marry me. And mark my words; I will punish you for this."

A sharp sliver of fear pierced her chest. Lucy filled her lungs with cool night air. He couldn't make her do anything. Although this had been a close call. She had not realized he'd followed her from the ballroom. A foolish mistake on her part to wander outside to the gardens by herself. But she had so desperately needed some fresh air. *Stupid.* She turned on her heel and strode away.

Her footsteps crunched on the pea gravel of the path. At the break in the hedge, she paused to glance around. No one was in her vicinity. Although she could see people further down the veranda. She quickly made her way through the shadows to the last door, which led into the ballroom. Spotting Aunt Trudy, she slowed her pace as she made her way to her, smiling at people that she knew. She let out a breath of relief as she stepped up to Trudy's side.

Aunt Trudy looked her up and down with her shrewd blue-grey eyes. "What's happened?"

"Whatever do you mean?" Lucy replied.

"You are clearly flustered. And your dress looks wrinkled."

Lucy smoothed her gloved hands down the peach silk of her gown. Damn him to hell. She stepped closer to Trudy and opened her fan in front of her mouth. "I was ambushed by Lord Fitzwilliam, whose intention was to compromise me so that I would consent to marry the snake."

"He did what?!" Trudy raised her own fan to cover her shocked expression.

Lucy nodded. "He came up behind me and pinned me against him. He spelled his intentions out very clearly."

"Well! And I thought he was halfway decent. I hope you took care of him."

Lucy nodded. "But I fear he will only be more of a problem now. He was incensed."

Trudy let out a long sigh.

She tucked her arm through Lucy's. "Time to go home. We will figure something out."

THE NEXT DAY, Lucy joined Aunt Trudy in the morning room for breakfast. The older woman sent her a bright smile. "Good morning, dear."

"Good morning, Trudy. You are up early." Lucy sat down. A footman poured her tea. The fragrant smell of orange blossom wafted pleasantly from her cup.

"Yes, I can't seem to sleep well anymore. Age ruins that for you. My rheumatism made me ache."

"Do you have enough salve? Do I need to order more?"

"Yes, dear, that would be nice. I could use a fresh jar." Trudy picked up a folded newspaper from next to her plate and slid it across the table. "You might be interested to read the scandal page today."

Lucy raised an eyebrow. She picked up the paper. The *Piccadilly Press* was Trudy's favorite of all the scandal rags. She claimed it was not all gossip but that it also contained insightful articles. But Lucy didn't believe her for a minute. Trudy lived for the gossip. Glancing over the gossip page, she immediately saw Fitzwilliam's name in bold print.

> *Last night at the Jackson's ball, Lord Fitzwilliam was seen hobbling in from the gardens quite disheveled, according to one witness, a bruise blooming across his chin. This author would like to know who he was fighting with. And who won said scuffle? My bet is on the other fellow, as no one else was reported to look worse for wear. Unless you consider the perpetual unkemptness of Lord Wentsforth when he is in his cups…*

The article continued a running diatribe of comments on the appearances of guests at last night's event. Lucy looked across at Trudy with a grin. Nobody had seen her! And Fitzwilliam would be mortified at the press.

Trudy took a sip of her tea, her eyes serious. "You shouldn't be smiling. His pride wounded, Lord Fitzwilliam will be looking for retribution. What did you do to him last night?"

"Just what my father taught me. He gave my mother and I both lessons in defending ourselves against those who were bigger and stronger. Life can be hard for a woman when your husband is always at sea." Lucy tried to wipe the grin from her face, but her lips still twitched as she remembered his groan of pain when she had kicked him in his manhood. "Fitzwilliam is a bully and a brute."

"No doubt. And I am glad you are safe. But he will not be easy to shake off. Especially with wounded pride at stake."

Lucy's glee drained away. Trudy was right. Lord Fitzwilliam had been hunting her all season. She had politely turned down his offer of marriage. But he was persistent, even after she had refused his invitations to the opera and to the races. She had avoided him at social functions, hoping someone else would catch his eye. Instead of his attention being flattering, his persistence made her skin crawl. Last night's behavior confirmed what her instincts had been telling her about the man.

Trudy picked up a cream-colored card and waved it back and forth. "Luckily, I know just who can help you. He's back."

"Who's back?"

"Hartwick, of course."

Lucy set her cup down with a clatter. Hart was back in town? "How long? Is that from him?"

Trudy shook her head. "I left instructions to the staff to inform me of his whereabouts. He arrived in London two nights ago."

Hart was back in London. Her heart beat an unsteady rhythm in her chest. What had brought him out of his self-imposed exile? Would he come to see them? *Don't be foolish.*

"Doesn't matter. He won't help. He made it very clear that he wanted to be left alone when he threw us out of Belstoke Manor last summer."

"He was wounded and lashing out. He didn't mean the

things he said, my dear. I'm sure he regrets what happened."

Lucy stared down at her half-empty cup of tea. Did he? She doubted it. "If he did regret his words, then we wouldn't have to hear of his return to town through the servants."

Trudy would never fully understand the pain he had caused Lucy by ejecting them so abruptly from his life. Not one word from him for the last ten months. No responses to her letters, which she had filled with news and tidbits of her life, her attempt to entertain and distract him from his melancholy. And he had shut out not just her and Trudy, but all his friends. Even his closest confidants like Lucius Grisham, had written to her concerned about Hart's worrying silence.

She stood. "Please excuse me. I think I will go work with my quarterstaff."

Lucy stalked down the corridor to the music room. She shut the door with a snap. Crossing the empty room, she pulled open the instrument closet and retrieved her quarterstaff. The weight of the carved oak staff provided an immediate balm to her jumbled emotions. Lucy toed off her slippers and headed to the opposite end of the long room. The windows had a view of the back gardens. Shaded by the large oak trees outside, this room was always cool in the spring and summer months.

Neither she nor Trudy were at all musical. So, Lucy had turned this room into a training room when they returned from Italy last year. Unorthodox perhaps, but Lucy had no use for the vapid pastimes of a gentlewoman. Stitching bored her to tears, and she had no talent for painting or music. She did love to read and often read aloud to Trudy in the evenings. But when she was upset, like now, what she really liked to do was fight.

A large, heavy, sand-filled bag hung down from the ceiling in the far corner. Nearby, under the window, a long chaise stretched out, its turquoise velvet a cheery focal point in the largely empty room. Lucy leaned her staff against the wall and swiftly undid the small pearl buttons on the front of her dress. She stepped out of the simple cotton day dress with its tight-fitting sleeves and carefully laid it across the chaise. Stretching her arms above her head, she twisted her torso gently from left to right, her chemise swirling around her knees. Next, she rolled her shoulders. Lastly, she tipped her head to the left to stretch her neck, then repeated the movement to the right. Usually calming, this morning the simple stretching routine did nothing to soothe her. Lucy snatched up her staff.

She placed her feet wide and used her staff to strike the bag with a satisfying thump. Twisting, she landed another blow with the opposite end of the staff. She let out a long breath as her memories from last summer flooded back. On the awful night of the attack, she had paced the hallway outside his room. Not allowed inside, she had relied on Trudy to tell her the extent of his injuries. The surgeon, Mr. Madewell, had stayed for days to supervise his care. Staving off infection had been his top priority.

Trudy reported that large ribbons of skin had been

burned across Hart's shoulder and along his right side, leaving the skin there waxy and pink. Over the first few days, blisters had formed and then burst. Burns also snaked down his right arm, singing off the dark hair that had covered his forearm. But the worst injury had been to his eye. Shards of crockery from the homemade bomb had lacerated the right side of his handsome face. The surgeon had carefully removed one of the slivers from the corner of his right eye.

They'd had to keep him dosed with laudanum the first fortnight lest the pain had him thrashing and moaning. After the first week passed with no fever, she and Trudy had made the decision to move him to Belstoke Manor, the ducal country seat, to remove him from the grime and disease of the city.

Lucy had spent two months watching and waiting for him to surface out of the worst of the pain. It hadn't helped that three weeks into being at Belstoke, Townson informed her that Hart refused to take any more laudanum. Stubborn fool. Lucy had taken to distracting him from his discomfort by reading Shakespeare, acting all the parts with different voices. She started with *As You Like It* and moved on to *A Midsummer Night's Dream*, thinking that comedy was what he needed. But one day, he had asked her to read from *Hamlet*, saying it matched his mood much better.

Lucy beat against the bag in a familiar rhythm. *Thump, thump, twist, thump.* She increased her pace, taking her frustration out on the heavy bag. Often, she would picture it as someone specific. Today, it should have been Lord

Fitzwilliam, but all she could see was Hart. His cold expression and rigid posture when she had confessed how much she cared for him. That day, at the manor, she'd walked into his bedroom to find him pacing back and forth in front of the fireplace. Agitation stamped across his face.

She had hurried over. "Hart, what's the matter?"

His gaze swung to her in surprise. "Nothing." He came to a stop. Then he ran a hand through his hair; his lips pulled down into a grimace. "What am I going to do with myself now?"

"What do you mean? You will do as you always have."

He huffed, then slumped into a nearby chair. "I certainly cannot, not with this ruined face and body. I'll scare small children as I walk down the street. Actually, I will probably trip over them as I try to navigate the city streets with only one working eye. This morning, I ran into the door jamb twice just trying to enter and exit the dressing room."

"It will take time to adjust. You must allow yourself grace while you recover."

A loud snort was his only response.

She approached and sank down to her knees in front of him. "Hart, you will be fine. Life might be different, but you will adjust." She smiled at him. "You might have to give up your harem."

His lips twisted into a self-deprecating half-smile. "I doubt they'll still want me." His gaze shifted from her to stare at the empty fireplace grate.

"I still want you." She took a deep breath in. Marshaling

her courage, she placed her hand on his knee. "I love you. No scars can change that."

Hart abruptly stood, jostling her back onto her heels. "No, Lucy, save your affection for someone worthy of it. You could choose anyone. Your whole life is ahead of you." He stepped past her to pace to the fireplace.

She scrambled to her feet. "But I want you."

His broad shoulders rose and fell with his rapid breaths. Then he turned to face her, his features set in a cold, distant mask. The bright pink scars across his cheek like claw marks added to the harshness of his expression. "Lucy, you are acting like a child. We could never become romantically involved. I wouldn't allow it."

His words sliced through her. A child? Was that how he still viewed her? Nothing but a responsibility, a burden?

Hurt and embarrassment fueled her already raw temper. "I'm acting like a child? You are the child, moping around here as though your life is over. Worried about your good looks being damaged. Not one ounce of gratitude that you are still alive."

"How would you know how I feel," he roared. "Get out."

Seeing the pain flash in his eyes, she immediately regretted her words. "I'm sorr—"

"Get out!"

The door to the room swung open and Trudy stood in the threshold. "What in god's name is going on in here. I could hear you bellow as I walked down the corridor."

"I want you both to get out of my house," Hart shouted. "I don't need your pity or your coddling." He turned his back to them and placed his hands on the mantel. "Go home. Leave me alone."

Thump, thump, twist, thump. Lucy continued her assault on the sandbag. Tears she didn't want threatened the back of her eyes. *Dammit!* She planted the staff on the floor and panted, trying to catch her breath. It still hurt. Even though she understood that he had been lashing out. The problem was that she couldn't convince herself to stop loving him. She had tried all year. Flirting with gentlemen at balls, dancing in other men's arms. Logically, she must marry. Trudy wouldn't be around forever; she was seventy-five years old, for goodness' sake. And being Trudy's companion was not a plan for her life. She must marry. But certainly not to the likes of the despicable Fitzwilliam. She only wanted one man. But he didn't want her.

Hart would never see her as a woman. Only as the girl he had been tasked to watch over. Lucy's only saving grace had been the distance he had put between them the past year. It had hurt, but it had also made it easier to not think about him. And now he was back in town and back in her thoughts. She pushed a damp tendril of hair from her brow. Well, she refused to be the first to reach out. If he wanted to see her and Trudy, he would damn well need to darken their doorstep.

Unfortunately, the next edition of the *Piccadilly Press* the following Thursday forced her to take action. Lucy sighed as she stood outside Hart's townhouse in St. James Square. The day was lovely, the weather sunny and warm. In contrast, her thoughts were thunderous. She hated that she must ask for help. She hated that he would probably not be happy to see her. She hated him. She bit down on her lower lip. Well, she hated that he had not come to see them this past week. *Blast it, girl, just knock.* Lucy grasped the brass knocker and hammered it twice against the dark green door.

CHAPTER TWO

HART SLAPPED THE newspaper down on the polished table. He took a sip of his tea and contemplated the words on the page. Lucy was getting married. Good for her. But Fitzwilliam? What a spineless jackanape. The man had no discernible skills except spending his father's money at the tables. What did she see in him? And why hadn't he, Hart, been contacted about the contract? Everyone knew Lucy was under the protection of the Duke of Hartwick. He shook his head. Didn't matter. He would make sure Fitzwilliam couldn't get his hands on Lucy's inheritance. Then his duty to see her safely married would be done.

The morning sun glinted off his glass of juice. Hart reached out and twisted it back and forth, watching the refracted light make a pattern on the table. Someone as vibrant as Lucy should never shackle herself to a man as pedestrian as Fitzwilliam. Of course, it was none of Hart's business whom she chose. He had much more important matters to take care of while he was in town. He had stewed long enough over the letter that he had found in his father's desk at Belstoke. Finding and exacting revenge against whoever had murdered his family was his purpose now.

Two hard raps of the door knocker echoed down the hallway. Who could be calling on him? No one knew he was in town. He closed his eyes and sighed. *Trudy.* He was a fool to think Aunt Trudy hadn't heard of his arrival from the servants. But the imperious voice that rang out in the next moment was not that of his great aunt.

"Mr. Townson, I don't care if he is not receiving. He will receive me. Now kindly step out of my way."

The door to the breakfast room swung open, and there Lucy stood like the first blush of spring, fresh and pretty in a gown of pale green. Her cheeks were pink from the crisp morning air, and a few of her tousled mahogany locks had escaped their pins. She likely walked over from the Portman Square house; Lucy always eschewed riding in a carriage if the destination was walkable. She froze in the doorway, looking adorably uncertain for a moment before she schooled her features into a polite mask.

Hart stood. "Hello, Lucy."

"Hello, Hart."

Torn between the pleasure of seeing her and regret at his behavior the last time they had been in the same room, Hart stood silent, his brain refusing to function properly. The silence between them stretched out uncomfortably. Finally, he swallowed the dueling emotions that clogged his throat, and his manners kicked in.

He gestured to the seat across from him. "Please come in and join me. Tea?"

Lucy hesitated, and he thought she might turn and flee

his presence. Would he blame her? Hardly. Neither his visage nor his disposition had improved much over these last many months, but at least he could try to act the gentleman. He offered her a smile. Lucy let go of the door handle and entered the room. She slid gracefully into the chair and nodded.

Glad to be able to sit down, he drank in his fill of her beauty, which he had been denied for almost a whole year. Her gaze scanned over him as well. He ignored the urge to run a hand over his hair, which he knew was a long, wild mess these days. And how long had it been since he had shaved?

A footman poured Lucy tea. "Thank you, Timothy." She gave the man a smile, but it faded as she turned her piercing blue eyes back to Hart. "You have been back in town for a week." Her statement flatly laid out her disappointment.

"I did not think you or Trudy would want to see me."

She pressed her lips together into a thin line as though she were keeping herself from replying.

Then she sighed. "Trudy would love to see you. It's very bad form to not have called on her immediately, considering your long absence from our lives."

The reprimand stung, partially because he knew she was right. He should have gone to see his aunt. And partially because she quite deliberately did not include herself as someone who wanted to see him. He regretted that he'd hurt her that day when she had told him of her tendre for him, but it had been for the best. She was getting married and moving on with her life as she should. Severing her schoolgirl attachment to him had been the right thing for her future.

"I apologize. I will go see her. I promise."

Lucy nodded. She studied him over the rim of her teacup. "Why are you in town, Hart?"

He thought to dissemble, but as she narrowed her eyes, he decided against it. He cleared his throat. "I have found a new lead to what caused my father and brother's deaths. I'm here to follow the thread."

"Are these the same people that tried to kill you?"

He nodded. "I believe it is all connected."

Lucy leaned forward, her hands clasped together tightly on the table. "Then you must give the information over to an investigator. Someone whose job it is to catch criminals."

"No, this must be investigated delicately."

"But, Hart, we are speaking of criminals. You must think of your own safety. You have the ability to hire someone to handle this. All the resources that are at your disposal—"

"This is personal," he bit out.

"I see that nothing has changed. You still have no use for other's opinions." She shook her head. "Clearly, you mean to do some personal damage. Some sort of revenge."

He took a sip of tea and tried to compose his expression. None of this had to do with her. "I am simply going to follow the lead and ascertain if it's true." He gestured to the newspaper in front of him. "I read that felicitations are in order."

She sighed, and her lips thinned into a slash of frustration. "That is why I am here. That piece of gossip is a lie. I need your help."

"What do you mean? A lie?"

"Fitzwilliam doesn't know how to take no for an answer," she muttered.

Hart leaned forward. "Lucy, tell me what happened."

"Last week, he assaulted me at the Jackson's ball. I was stupid and took some air in the garden. He came up behind me and grabbed me. He made it plain that he wanted to be caught in a compromising position with me so that I would have to accept his proposal."

Bastard! Hart clamped his lips together. "He had already asked for your hand?"

She nodded. "And I had already turned him down. Well, I don't like being coerced, so I used my defensive moves and hurt him so he would let go. Then I hurried straight back to Aunt Trudy."

He couldn't stop his eyebrows from raising in surprise. "What defensive moves?"

"Father taught me several moves that can be accomplished in skirts. My mother, too. He wanted to make sure that we could defend ourselves from drunk sailors in port when he wasn't at home to protect us." Her lips turned up in a wicked smile. "Turns out they work on overzealous lords as well."

Hart leaned back in his chair. "I approve. And I would very much like to see these moves of yours someday. But how would this incident lead to your engagement?"

She huffed. "Trudy warned me I had stepped too hard on his manly pride. He sent that tidbit to the paper without ever speaking with Trudy or me. Perhaps he thought I would be too embarrassed to set the record straight? The trouble is, I don't think there is anything I can say to make him stop harassing me. This is why I am here. I need your ducal clout. Can you please make him go away?"

"Certainly. I'm appalled at his tactics. Do you want me to shoot him?"

"Yes!" Her laugh melted the tension between them. "I mean, no, not actually. Just scare him off."

"He did not see me about the marriage contract, so there is no engagement as far as I'm concerned. I will take care of this immediately." He gestured for the footman to approach. "Have Mr. Townson send a summons to Lord Fitzwilliam."

Lucy sighed and her posture relaxed. "Thank you, Hart. I may have defensive moves, but as a lady, I have no offensive ones. Why is it that men think they can just make all the decisions? Just take without permission? That's what he said. He was used to taking what he wanted."

Hart curled his hand into a fist. How satisfying it would be to wrap that fist around the man's throat. The thought of Fitzwilliam's greedy hands touching Lucy made him see red.

"Hart, you look positively thunderous. Don't kill him. Trudy would be very cross with you."

"And you? Are you still very cross with me?"

Again, the silence between them stretched. "I-I'm hurt at the way you cut us out of your life. And not just us, Grisham told me the same. No letters, nothing." Her shoulders drew up tight again, and he chided himself for reminding her she was angry with him.

He nodded, accepting her words. Incapable of fixing the damage he'd done to their friendship, if it had even been that. His self-subscribed role as her protector had not allowed even that level of intimacy. She needed his help, and that sent a surge of warmth through his battered chest. He would always watch out for her safety, for her happiness, but he could accomplish that from the shadows. She sat here lovely and so fierce and full of life. She didn't need a moody bastard like him returning to her life.

Lucy let out a small huff. "Hart, what have you been doing this past year?"

Raging, drinking himself into short bouts of fitful sleep, fighting against ghosts, crawling his way out from a deep hole of melancholy. The only thing that motivated him to pull from his own dark thoughts and set the liquor aside was his newly formed obsession to gain justice for his family. Everything else in his life was ruined. This was his new purpose.

But he could never explain any of that to Lucy, so instead, he said, "Healing."

Her head cocked to one side, then she shook it as she rose to her feet. "Fine, then I will leave you to it. Good day, Your Grace."

He rose as well and watched her stride toward the door. She paused as the footman opened it for her, but she didn't turn around. "Thank you for taking care of Fitzwilliam. I do appreciate it." Then with a swish of her green skirts, she was gone.

CHAPTER THREE

A N HOUR LATER, Viscount Fitzwilliam slithered into Hart's study. "Good afternoon, Your Grace."

"Please sit." Hart pointed to the chair across from him. He knew the exact moment the viscount got close enough to see his scars. Fitzwilliam's steps faltered for just a moment before approaching and taking the seat. Hart leaned forward, placing his hands together on top of the gleaming mahogany desk between them. Letting the man take in the entirety of his ruined face. Hart watched his Adam's apple bob above the linen at his throat. It was almost comical the way Fitzwilliam's eyes widened dramatically. Almost.

"I had no idea you had returned to town, Your Grace."

"I expect that is true, considering that you did not come to gain my permission for the gross falsehood that you had printed in today's paper." Taking advantage of Fitzwilliam's discomfort, he lowered his eyebrows into a glower.

"Ah … but it is true." Fitzwilliam lips curled up into a sickly-sweet smile. "We have become quite enamored of each other this season."

"That is not what the lady says."

The man's smile faded. "You have spoken with her?"

Hart nodded. This weasel would pay for trying to take advantage of Lucy. The faded yellow-green bruise along the man's jaw did give Hart some satisfaction. Lucy was definitely a spitfire. He would have loved to see her give the rogue blow to the face and good tongue-lashing as well.

Fitzwilliam recovered smoothly. "Well now, I know she is a bit reluctant to get married. The tidbit I passed to the paper was just a little nudge in the right direction. We would make an excellent match. I planned to call on her today and convince her our marriage would be a mutually beneficial arrangement."

"And how did you plan to convince her? Like you did at the Jackson's ball?" He held up a hand as the man opened his mouth to reply. "There will be no arrangement between you and Miss Middleton. I would never give my consent for her to marry a man who assaults a woman in order to gain her acquiescence in any matter."

"But it was just a misunderstanding. You know how women are. They sometimes need to be convinced of the right course of action. Lucy is far too self-governing for a female. She just needs a firm hand. I assure you she and I get along famous—"

The nerve of this weasel. Hart rose to his feet. He slammed his hands on the desk, and he leaned forward menacingly. "You may be assured that by the end of today I will own every outstanding marker you have." Fitzwilliam blanched and shut his mouth with a snap. "Come within fifty feet of Miss Middleton or if I hear of even one foul word besmirching her reputation, I will call in every one. I am guessing it is no small amount based on your desperate attempts to get your hands on Miss Middleton's dowry."

The viscount's mouth opened and closed like a fish caught on land. "But what will people think if it is called off?"

"Not my problem. Now get out of my house."

Red-faced, Fitzwilliam rose to his feet. "You are as monstrous as you look." Then he stormed out of the room.

Hart crossed over to the bar cabinet and poured a healthy two fingers of brandy into a cut crystal glass. What a fucking day. Between the minefield of a conversation with Lucy this morning and the ridiculous posturing of the viscount just now, he had about as much interaction with people as he could take. Monstrous indeed. The man hadn't even been able to see the irony in his own statement.

But his day was not over yet, because Lucy was correct; he should have visited Trudy by now. He swallowed down the liquor and carefully closed the cabinet. There was no more time for wallowing at the bottom of the bottle. He'd done enough of that in the last year. Dulling his emotions along with his physical pain. Now, he wanted to feel every piece of that pain. He would channel all of it to finding the man who had killed his family. Hart crossed to the bell pull.

Moments later, Townson opened the door. Tall and thin as a rail, the butler had not a hair on his head except for two dark, bushy eyebrows. In Hart's opinion, Townson's ability to put people in their place with one disdainful look down his long, hawklike nose was the man's best attribute. Townson had kept everyone at bay for the past year when Hart simply hadn't the mental strength to face the pity in the eyes of his family and friends. His butler had been his frontline defense ... except for today. Hart briefly wondered how Lucy had made it past the man.

Townson raised an eyebrow in question. "You rang?"

"Have Mr. Langford come see me this afternoon at two and have the carriage ready at three."

"The town coach or the phaeton?"

"The coach. I am going to see my aunt."

A brief gleam of satisfaction flared in the man's eyes. "Very well, sir."

Hart had a sinking feeling that Townson had decided his time in exile was up.

Hart straightened his shoulders. "And bring me my correspondence kit. I have some letters to write."

THE HUSTLE AND bustle of the city was much the same as it had always been. Hart stared out the window of the town coach as it made its way to Portman Square, where Trudy and Lucy lived. Perhaps it was him that had changed because everything felt so foreign. The noise grated his ears, and had women's hats grown in size this season? As the ladies of Mayfair promenaded down the street, it seemed to him that their wide-brimmed hats laden with flowers and ribbons were particularly ridiculous.

He smoothed a hand over his hair, which his valet trimmed this afternoon. It was still long enough to swoop over his right eye and cheekbone if he let it fall forward but shorter in the back, so he didn't so much resemble a shaggy dog anymore. His great aunt would be brutally assessing and not mind giving her opinion on his deportment. She had been telling the dukes of Hartwick what's what for three generations. The coach pulled to a stop in front of Trudy's charming townhome. The gleaming whitewashed front of the house was interrupted by a bright yellow front door. Two marble columns flanked the steps to the entrance, and bright colorful flowers spilled from the window boxes.

He slapped his hat on his head and made his way up to the door. It opened as he arrived in front of it, and he was ushered in by Trudy's butler.

"Good afternoon, Your Grace." The man held out his hand for his hat and accessories.

"I'll just keep this." Hart gripped the smooth brass head of his walking stick.

The butler nodded. "Lady Weatherby is expecting you in the Rose Room."

"Thank you." He followed the man up the stairs and to the right down a richly carpeted hallway papered in a soothing blue damask. Hart let out a long breath. He was safe here in Trudy's home. The quiet sumptuousness of her house soothed his nerves, which had been jangled ever since he forced himself to leave the house today. They walked all the way to the back of the house. The last door on the left was his aunt's personal sanctuary. She sat by the window, her embroidery hoop in her lap.

"You've finally come to see me."

"Good afternoon, Aunt Trudy." Hart gave a deep bow. "I apologize for my tardiness in visiting."

Trudy's sharp eyes raked over him from top to bottom. He resisted the urge to fidget. "I suppose I'm too pleased to see you looking so well to be angry. Come sit." She turned to the butler, who still hovered by the door. "Have the tea cart sent in."

Hart sat across from her. "You are also looking well, Trudy. How is your health?"

"Just fine, young man. How is yours? Still drinking yourself into a stupor every day? Wandering the halls of Belstoke Manor at night like a ghost?"

Hart blinked at her, his shock muting his tongue.

"Did you think I wouldn't keep tabs on one of my only remaining relatives? My favorite nephew?"

"Who has been—never mind. No, I am no longer drinking and haunting the manor."

"So, you have emerged. Tell me, what has brought you to town?"

"Some business matters," he replied.

"Typical. The appropriate response would have been to repair relationships with important people in your life, but I guess that would be asking too much of a man. Go on and ask me what you came to. Let us get business matters out of the way first."

How did she know he planned to steer the conversation toward his father's associates? He planned to be subtle, but Trudy was, as ever, too shrewd. "Aunt, do you know what this is?" He pulled out the small wax seal stamp from his pocket and handed it to Trudy. "I found it in Father's desk among his correspondence. This symbol was stamped on the pages of a letter sent to him as well."

Trudy peered carefully at the carved seal. She shook her head. "Something about it is familiar, but I cannot put my finger on where I have seen this symbol before." She looked up and met his gaze. "Why do you ask?"

"Why would father seal letters with anything other than the Hartwick seal? The letter he received, which was stamped with this same symbol, was angry and threatening. It made no sense; the author was upset that father was going pull out of some deal, but what the deal entailed was not made explicit. It contained threats of retribution." Hart ran his thumb over the gold seal. "The words on the page felt personal. I suppose a business venture gone bad could raise the same emotions. Dangerous emotions."

Trudy frowned. "I am sorry I can't remember. I will think on it, though."

A servant entered with the tea cart, and Trudy set aside her embroidery hoop on the table next to her. Once the tea was poured, she took a sip and eyed him carefully over the rim. "Lucy told me that you looked shaggy and unkempt. She feared you were still not well. But I can see she was overreacting."

He pushed his hair back from his face and sat up straighter under her perusal. "She was not. I had Niles shave me and trim my hair just this afternoon. I hadn't been worrying overmuch about my appearance while at Belstoke. But when Lucy barged into my breakfast room this morning, I was reminded that appearances matter."

"And how do you feel? What is the status of the eye?"

"I can only see blurry shadows and changes in light. At low light or at night, it is fully useless." His sharp frustration with losing his sight in the eye had dulled over time as he learned to maneuver using the cane to feel out possible obstacles in the blind spot he now had on the right side.

"I'm sorry to hear that. I hoped it would heal. But it is not the worst impediment."

Hart snorted.

"You still have one working eye, do you not?" Trudy challenged.

He shrugged. She sounded like Lucy, chiding him for feeling sorry for himself. Which he'd done plenty of the past year. "Yes, and I can see your look of worry clearly with it. Aunt Trudy, I'm fine. I promise."

She nodded and set her cup down. "Moving on to pressing matters. I'm in need of your help with a family matter."

"Is there something the matter with Fred?" Hart asked. Trudy's son lived with his very large family in Dorset. Although a jovial man and an excellent father, Fred was a bit dimwitted. He was next in line to inherit, and Hart highly doubted that his cousin could handle the running of the dukedom. That had been reason enough for him to hang on when things had felt particularly dim. After all, Hart had a duty to uphold as the Duke of Hartwick. At least until he sired a proper heir.

Trudy waved her hand dismissively. "No, he and his brood are all doing fine. Who I mean is Lucy."

"Aunt Trudy, Lucy is not in our family."

"What a thing to say! That girl has been my companion for four years. She is more precious to me than anyone else besides my Fred. I want to see her safely settled before I die. That could be any day now."

Hart stifled a smile. All the Barclays were prone to the dramatic. "Aunt Trudy, I thought you said your health was just fine."

"At my age, my health is as mercurial as the weather. You can never tell when I will up and keel over. Lucy must be married. Because of the portion left to her, she is at risk from predators like Fitzwilliam, as you well know. And as head of this family, it is your responsibility to match her with an appropriate husband."

"I took care of Fitzwilliam today. He won't be bothering her again."

"Good. I knew you would. Now, I need you to find her someone decent, not too old, athletic, not a gambler, and someone with some spirit, no dullards."

"I have only been in town one week after a yearlong absence and you want me to pull a young, decent, non-gambler, non-dullard gentleman out from my back pocket for Lucy to marry?" What did Trudy think he was, a magician? Even when he'd been active in society, the only gentlemen he'd been friends with had been reprobates. Certainly not anyone he would allow to get near Lucy.

"Don't be silly. I have a list." She reached into her embroidery bag and drew out a piece of folded parchment. "I need you to vet the men on this list. And let me know who we are left with to introduce to her."

Hart reluctantly took the list from her. It contained at least a dozen names. A quick glance through made him snort in disbelief. Most were unacceptable. "I can tell you right now most of these men don't meet all the criteria. Has Lucy seen this list? Surely, she has opinions about who her future spouse should be."

"Oh, she has opinions all right. But her most ardent opinion is that she does not want to marry. We will have to figure out who to put into her path." She pointed an elegant finger at the list. "But she cannot know we are doing it. It must appear that she has made the choice."

Hart ran a hand down over his face. This was not a good idea. Trudy did not know about the private things that had been said between he and Lucy. How badly he had smashed to bits Lucy's heartfelt declarations. He should have rebuffed her feelings more gently. Nevertheless, she hadn't needed his desperation and despair in her life any more than he needed her kind pity. So, he had sent her away.

He looked down again at the list of prospective husbands

for Lucy. She deserved to have someone to take care of her, someone who would be able to return her affection. "All right. I look through the list, cross off the ones who I know are trouble, and investigate the ones I don't know enough about."

"And help me introduce the gentlemen we think are good candidates to Lucy in an inconspicuous way?"

"Aunt, I have no plans to jump back into society. No one wants to see this face across the dining table. And with this blind spot I cannot twirl around the dance floor without risk of bumping into people. I would hardly make a coveted guest these days."

Before the explosion, he had always been on every guest list in town. His over inflated reputation as a rake had not outweighed the allure of his title or his good looks. Every woman in London had wanted their chance to capture a duke as a husband. But Hart had never minded the hunt. He always enjoyed the company of women. Of course, now, who would he find that would be willing to marry a scarred and damaged husband, even if he was a duke.

"Nonsense. The scars are not so bad. You simply look like a war hero."

"Except that I am no war hero."

"You are a duke. No one would dare insult you."

"To my face," he muttered.

"You have the connections to help introduce Lucy to the right suitors. Besides, having been away for the past year has only made you more interesting. Mysterious. Lucy deserves to be settled safely. This innuendo that was printed in today's scandal sheets will damage her reputation unless it is corrected immediately. Only a respectable marriage can save her now."

Hart nodded tightly, already regretting his part in this. He had his own investigation to pursue. He did not need to add matchmaking to his list of to-dos.

CHAPTER FOUR

LUCY SIGHED. WHY was she here? She had every intention of hanging on to her anger. She'd planned to let him rot in his bad decisions. She really had. But then this morning, as she took her morning constitutional, she had somehow ended up in front of his house. She handed her gloves and parasol over to Mr. Townson. "Where is he?"

"This way, Miss Middleton." Townson turned and led her up the grand staircase to the first floor.

The house was the same as it always had been. Simple, elegant furnishings throughout. Tasteful landscapes dotted walls papered in muted tones of beige and gold. Perhaps because the house had lacked the presence of a duchess for so long was the reason the décor felt so staid and dull. When Lucy had her own home, she would fill it with color, fresh flowers, and interesting pieces of art collected from her travels.

Townson stopped in front of Hart's study. "One moment, please." He knocked and then slid inside, leaving her in the corridor.

Since when did she need to be announced? It wasn't as if she were a stranger. Lucy crossed her arms with a huff. This was a bad idea, but someone had to look out for him. He'd looked terrible last week. Unkempt, his hair a wild, long mess only partially concealing the spiderweb of thin white scars that snaked from his temple across his cheek and disappeared into the stubble covering the lower half of his face. But the scars weren't the most distressing part about his appearance.

It was the bleakness in his eyes that had been hard to see. Hart had always carried himself with a certain self-possessed swagger. His gaze always cool and confident. Many thought him arrogant or intimidating, and it was his due as a duke. But Lucy knew if one looked closely, they could see the ever-present twinkle of humor in his eye or catch the slight quirk of his lips when he was amused. His cynicism led to a dry sense of humor and to his fait accompli outlook on life.

She tapped a foot on the floor. What was taking so long? As though her impatience could be felt through the door, it opened, and Townson held it wide for her to enter. Lucy entered the room cautiously. Hart stood behind his desk tugging down his cuffs. When he glanced up, wariness radiated from the deep, misty grey of his eyes. He had cut his hair, and although still too long for current fashion, the dark swoop of hair across his forehead suited him.

"Good morning, Lucy. I didn't expect to see you again so soon."

Lucy wandered slowly through the room toward the large mahogany desk that dominated the space. She ran her fingertips over the back of an upholstered chair, which sat along with its pair in front of a large fireplace. The perfect spot for brandy and smokes. As she looked around the room, she again noted that nothing had changed since this room had belonged to Hart's father. "Everything in this house is the same as it always has been. Won't you ever redecorate to suit your tastes?"

"This was never meant to be mine, so I guess I never put much thought into how I would like it to be." He watched her as she moved closer. "I guess I will leave it up to my future duchess to do with it as she pleases."

Lucy continued to wander through the room not ready to have to answer the inevitable question of why she was here. She stared up at a hideous stuffed boar's head mounted on the wall. "Are you planning to marry then?"

He shrugged. "Well, I must. It will just be a matter of finding someone to tolerate me."

"You are fairly intolerable," she teased.

Finally, she came to a stop in front of the desk. Hart stood stiff and still as though he didn't know how to act. She tilted her head; how strange. Who was this new man? And what had he done with the old Hart?

Curiosity had her asking, "Care to go for a stroll with me?"

"I don't think so. I have a lot of things to do." He waved a hand at the papers strewn over the desk.

"I won't take no for an answer. You are far too pale and thin. Have you eaten this morning?"

Hart's glance slid to the left. She followed his gaze to a

tray laden with slices of ham along with toast and jam that sat on the side table. "I became engrossed in the ledgers, and I forgot to eat."

"I see." She pursed her lips. "First a walk in the sunshine and then food. Let's go work up an appetite."

His mouth opened then closed, and she wasn't sure she had convinced him. But then he came around the desk and snatched up a walking stick that leaned against the end. Townson was standing guard right outside the door as they left the room. His bushy eyebrows raised high when Hart said, "Get my things. Apparently, we are going for a walk outside."

Once outside in the bright sunshine, Lucy's mood improved tenfold. She was just helping a friend in need. This was not more than that. He clearly needed someone to look out for his health. She would assure herself he was recovering, then she could leave him alone with a clear conscience. For a moment, she tipped her face to the sky so she could feel the sun on her cheeks.

Then she pushed open her pale blue parasol. "Shall we hoof it to Green Park?" Looking down at his walking stick, she frowned. "Or do you need to stay closer to home? Have you hurt a leg? I don't remember your leg being one of your injuries."

"No, the legs work just fine. It's the eye. The stick is to help navigate my blind spot."

Lucy nodded and came to stand on his left, the opposite side of his bad eye. "I knew you would figure out a way to cope. You're not one to give up."

He harrumphed from next to her.

They set off down the street. Whatever trouble he had with the right eye, it didn't impede his stride, and Lucy was glad she didn't have to slow her normal pace. Next to her, Hart was still stiff, his frown set in place.

"You needn't look so grim. People will think you don't enjoy my company."

He glanced her way. "Sorry. I haven't been out in public at all since the accident. My manners are rusty."

"And who's fault is that?" She arched an eyebrow.

They walked for several blocks without speaking. She watched Hart's shoulders relax incrementally. By the time they turned into the park, his demeanor had relaxed enough that he began to resemble himself again. The silence between them was not uncomfortable. Lucy enjoyed walking next to him, letting the warmth of the day soak into her bones. It had rained every day the last week, but today the sun shone down and made everything in the park look lush and green. Small white and yellow butterflies fluttered around a flowering rhododendron.

Lucy laid a hand on Hart's arm. "Look." She pointed to the bush.

He stopped and stared at the butterflies. "I wouldn't have noticed them."

"Today is a beautiful day. You have been cooped up too long. Take in all this green." She gestured widely with one hand. Then she squinted up at him. "You really do look terrible. But at least you cut your hair."

One corner of his mouth turned up. "Don't hold back the truth."

"I won't. You have been wallowing, ignoring your friends, and I'm still cross with you." She reminded him, and herself as well.

He reached out a hand to touch the delicate petals of a flower and a dozen tiny butterflies scattered up into the air. Lucy laughed in delight at the beautiful frenzy of yellow and white wings. Hart turned his head to stare at her.

Feeling self-conscious, she pushed back a stray wisp of hair that fluttered with the breeze. "What?" she asked as Hart just stood there.

"Why did you write? You kept sending letters even after I sent you away."

She shrugged. "I guess I thought you could use some diversion from your sulking."

"I did. They helped."

"You read them?" He had never replied. She assumed her letters had moldered in a pile on his desk.

"I read every one." His searching gaze trapped hers.

All her old feelings fluttered wildly in her stomach like the butterflies rising from the bush. But she ruthlessly pushed them down. She refused to let those tender feelings surface. His rejection had hurt too much. She began walking down the path.

Hart followed her. His walking stick tapped against the pea gravel as he strode to catch up. "I visited Trudy like you told me to. She has opinions about you getting married."

"I know that she would like to see me settled."

"But you don't wish to be married?" He glanced over at her.

"You see what sort of fools I must deal with in polite society. Fitzwilliam isn't the only fortune hunter trying to get under my skirts." What she didn't want to tell Hart was that, in truth, she got very little attention.

As the daughter of a navy captain, she was far too low on the social ladder for most titled men to consider her for a wife unless they really needed the large dowry Hart's father had gifted her when she became his ward. Hart would of course be well aware of this. The thought of his pity was unbearable.

"Actually, I have a beau. But I haven't said anything because he doesn't yet have enough money for us to marry."

Hart's head whipped around to look at her. "Who is he?"

Who is he ... who is he? Lucy scrambled for a name to give. "Gregory Murdoch. He is a solicitor. He works for the firm of Jackson & Worth."

"Where did you meet him?"

"My very good friend, Violet, is the daughter of the Earl of Blackpool, and Mr. Murdoch handles their accounts. I met him at a luncheon where we cultivated a friendship. But you must promise not to tell Trudy. I don't want her meddling."

Hart snorted. "A solicitor? I believe Trudy has higher hopes for you."

"I am the daughter of a navy captain and a vicar's daughter. Marriage to a solicitor makes perfect sense. It makes far more sense than marriage to a peer."

She needed to change the subject before she dug herself any further into this lie. Although it hardly mattered, Hart would never meet her fake beau. They certainly did not run into the same circles, not that Hart ran in any circles these days. She glanced sideways at his profile. His brow was wrinkled as he frowned down at the ground.

"You must know Trudy has plans for you as well. She is most certainly scheming to have you matched now that you are back."

"She can scheme all she wants. It won't do her any good. I'm not fit to be a husband to anyone right now. That is not why I am in town."

Lucy let out a long breath and switched her parasol to the left side as they made a turn, and the sun changed positions. "Yes, that's right, your investigation. How is that going?"

"Frustratingly slow. At Belstoke, I found a letter in my father's desk that contained several explicit threats. Apparently, he was going pull from a business deal. But the specifics of the deal were not spelled out in this letter. The threats of retribution were clear, though. This week, I have been going through ledgers and correspondence from the year the letter was dated to see if I can find what business ventures my father was invested in. I haven't found anything as of yet. But I am barely halfway through, and unfortunately, my left eye tires quickly without the help of its pair."

The words were out of her mouth before she could think it through. "I could help if you tell me what you're looking for specifically."

"You don't have to offer."

"I know." She stopped so she could face him.

His posture was again stiff. His expression closed off.

"Why won't you accept help?"

"I don't need your pity."

"Yes, that's just it. I pity the rich, handsome duke." She rolled her eyes. "Fine, forget I offered." She strode away down the path.

Why did she continue to try and help him? She should leave him to his own devices. He was a grown man who wished to be left alone. Why couldn't she get that through her thick skull?

His gruff voice called out. "Lucy, stop. Yes, I can use your help."

She turned.

His hand flexed around the gold top of his walking stick. "I'm sorry."

She couldn't stop the smile that spread. "All right then, first food. Then we will get to investigating."

CHAPTER FIVE

"THIS IS THE letter that I found." Hart slid it across the desk.

Lucy nibbled at a slice of cheese as she peered down at the letter. He watched her take tiny bites, savoring the salty parmesan. She was engrossed in the words on the page as she next reached for a strawberry from the platter of food that sat on the desk between them. He couldn't pull his gaze away from her lips as she took a bite of the ripe red fruit. A tiny dribble of juice escaped, and her tongue darted out to lick it from the corner of her mouth. He bit back a groan. His groin tightened. God, it had been too long since he had a woman's lips around him. He tore his gaze from her mouth and tried to wait patiently while she finished reading the letter.

Lucy's head popped up. "What's this?" She tapped her finger on the bottom corner of the page. "I don't recognize this symbol."

"I don't know. It is the same symbol from the wax stamp that was among my father's correspondence kit." He reached into the top drawer to his right and pulled out the gold-plated stamp. Flipping it to show Lucy the seal. "It's not something I recognize, and it's not the ducal seal." He laid his right hand out so she could see the crest on the top of his ring.

Lucy's brow furrowed. One finger reached out and drew a path along the scars on the back of his hand, light as a feather, to the cuff of his shirt. "Do they still hurt?"

He was too startled by the soft touch to pull back.

He shook his head. "No, not there. But the ones along my shoulder and upper arm have tightened the skin so much that when I move it certain ways, it hurts quite a bit. I fear my range of motion in the right arm will never be the same."

She pulled her hand back and picked up the seal from the table. "It must mean something if your father also used the same symbol to stamp letters. I think we should start by sorting that large pile of correspondence by just the ones that have this stamp."

Glad that she was not going to keep asking about his injuries, Hart pulled his hand back, then took a section of the stack next to him and handed her a portion. Lucy was right; the stamp had to mean something. Why hadn't he thought to look for more letters with it? He delved into the stack and began flipping through to look for the mysterious symbol. There were many letters stamped in the bottom right corner with the stamp, and the pile between him and Lucy began to grow.

"Eat something," Lucy said.

He glanced up.

She raised her head from the page she was reading. "Eat

something. Don't think I'm not paying attention."

Without breaking eye contact, he reached over for a piece of bread and took a large bite, chewing with exaggerated movements for her benefit. He meant to tease her for being so managing but was surprised to find that he was hungry. He polished off the roll. Picking up another, he layered it with a piece of ham this time. Hart caught Lucy's smile as she lowered her gaze to the page once again.

He hadn't much of an appetite for anything except perhaps liquor the past year. His apathy for the business of living had kept him in a stasis of sorts. He glanced at the woman across the table from him. Lucy's impertinent highhandedness was just what he needed to pull him back to the land of the living.

They worked in silence for a while, sorting the pile of letters into two; letters with the stamp and those without. Hart began to read through the ones that had the stamp. Some were just newsy, filled with the type of conversation in which old friends catch up. Some were more purposeful, letters arguing about the merits of various bills up for a vote in the Lords. All were from men Hart knew to be friends of his father. Names he recognized, men he knew.

He picked up another letter. It was an ardent note about a bill to support pensions for widows of servicemen. Hart traced the large loopy signature of Lord Galey. Galey had been a good man. One who had tried to follow his conscience and paid the price with his life. How had their meeting been discovered? Hart frowned down at the symbol stamped next to Galey's signature. The how didn't matter as much as the why. Why had his father and brother been murdered? He must know the truth. He had already paid such a heavy price; it couldn't be for naught.

"These are all from the same six men," Lucy commented.

"Yes, these were my father's friends. But none of these men would want to kill him. They were all like family, almost like uncles to me and my brother."

"But what of the unsigned letter, the angry one that contained the threats of retribution if he pulled out of the deal? Logically, because of the stamp, it should be one of these men."

Hart nodded. "But which one? And what deal? It had to be about money. Only money could kill a friendship."

"I agree. I would suggest looking through your ledgers from that year or the previous one. See what, if anything, your father had invested in outside of the normal running of the estate." Lucy stood. "Well, I must go. I should have been home an hour ago to accompany Trudy to the milliner shop. She will be wondering where I am."

Hart rose from his seat as well. "Fredrick will accompany you home."

"Not necess—"

He held up a hand. "It is necessary for my peace of mind. You shouldn't be out walking alone."

"What I was going to say is that it is not necessary because my maid, Helen, is here. Please have Townson fetch her from the kitchen. I am perfectly aware that I cannot walk around London unchaperoned." Lucy crossed her arms across her chest and shot him a glare.

The movement pushed her breasts up, stretching the fabric of her dress tight across them. Hart watched them rise and fall as she let out a disgruntled huff. What was the matter with him? He should not be thinking about her breasts or the smooth skin of her throat, or her full pink lips.

He cleared his throat. "Um, yes, of course." He crossed the room to ring the bell.

The light floral smell of her perfume filled his nose as he passed her. Her presence filled his senses, bringing them back to life. He wanted to pull her against him and feel the curves of her figure, burying his nose in her hair, find out the taste of her skin. Good Lord, it had been far too long since he had a woman if just being in the proximity of one had him lusting inappropriately over Lucy.

The door opened. Townson appeared in the threshold. "How can I be of help, Your Grace?"

"Can you send Helen upstairs please. Miss Middleton is ready to leave."

"Certainly. Are you finished with the food tray?"

"No, he is still eating." Lucy interjected. She turned to him and winked. "Now be a good boy and finish it all."

Her laughter filled the room as he sputtered. *Brat.* Before he could say anything at all she sashayed out the room.

CHAPTER SIX

"**Y**OU TOLD HIM what?" exclaimed Violet.

"Vi, really!" Lucy grabbed her best friend's arm and pulled her further down the hall, so they weren't standing right outside the ladies' retiring room. They slowly walked back toward the ballroom. "It was the first name that came to mind. You have been talking about how handsome Gregory Murdoch is nonstop."

"Well, he is. And whenever he comes to the house to meet with my father, he always has a charming smile and a smoldering look to send my way." Violet sighed. "A terrible flirt, that one. Don't worry, I just like looking at him." They crossed the marble tiles of the hall, their heeled slippers echoing in the two-story foyer. "I can't believe the duke is back in town."

"Yes, and he is changed. Brooding is an understatement. I just didn't want him to think that I have spent the past year pining for him."

Vi sent her a sympathetic look from under her sooty lashes. "I understand. He doesn't need to know that you have been longing for his affections. What will you say when Mr. Murdoch never comes to propose though?"

"Bah, Hart won't be around that long. And he doesn't socialize with solicitors."

They entered back into the din of the ballroom. The ball was the typical crush. A string quartet played in one corner, and the painted floor was packed with dancers. Potted trees softened the edges of the room and framed conversation areas. The back doors were open to let the night air in, but instead of cooling off the interior of the ballroom, it simply allowed couples to sneak out into the gardens. Lucy had learned her lesson. She would stay safely inside and with her friend.

Violet opened a fan painted with bright pink flowers. "I'm sure your right. Oh look, there is Addie."

"I wasn't sure if we would see her at all this month. Her mother must be feeling better." Lucy waved as their good friend, Adeline, walked by with her parents and older brother.

Adeline whispered in her mother's ear, and her mother glanced their way. With a pat on Addie's arm, she released her into the crowd. Adeline hurried over.

Lucy gave her a swift hug. "Addie, we are so happy to see you out."

"Mother is having a good week. I'm so excited to be out of the house. Tell me everything that is happening!" Addie pushed her spectacles up her nose.

Violet leaned in to kiss Adeline's cheek. "Lucy has an imaginary fiancé."

Adeline's eyes widened. "What?!"

"That's what I said," Violet leaned toward Adeline. "And the duke is back in town."

"Really?" Adeline turned to Lucy. "Have you seen him?"

Lucy huffed and opened her own fan to help block her comments from being overheard. "Yes, I have. I needed his help with discouraging Lord Fitzwilliam. I'm sure the innuendo that was printed in the *Piccadilly Press* was planted by him."

Both her friends nodded in tandem.

"Not that Hart would have come to see Lady Weatherby or me if I hadn't gone to see him first." She was still hurt by his indifference.

Her best friends knew better than anyone how infatuated with Hart she had been. Hart had always been so charming, always easy to talk with. When she was young, Hart and his brother Robert had seemed larger than life. Both had been kind to the lonely orphan their father had taken in, but Hart had stolen her heart with his irresistible grin. But now she was an adult, and Hart was changed. She needed to put aside her old infatuations. She briefly closed her eyes. Why oh, why had she told him she had a secret fiancée?

"And how is he? Has he recovered from his accident?" Violet asked.

Lucy grimaced. She knew her friend meant well, but the ballroom was no place to discuss Hart's injuries. "Well enough," she answered vaguely.

Addie looked back and forth between Lucy and Violet. "But what does this have to do with the faux fiancé?"

Lucy felt her cheeks heat. "Well, Hart … the duke, I mean, was asking about whether I was planning on settling down. He had this terrible look of pity on his face like he didn't think I ever would. And I don't know, I just said it. I told him that I had a beau who was a solicitor but that he didn't have enough money saved for us to marry so we weren't telling anyone our intentions yet." She shrugged. "When he demanded to know who, the first name that popped into my head was the solicitor that Violet is always mooning over, Mr. Gregory Murdoch," she whispered.

Adeline covered her mouth with a gloved hand and giggled. "Mr. Murdoch is handsome. He works for my father as well."

Lucy's stomach flip-flopped. She placed a hand to her belly. "You don't suppose his firm works for Hartwick?"

"Highly unlikely." Violet shook her head. "The duke's holdings are vast. He probably has a firm that works exclusively for him."

Lucy relaxed. Vi was right. There was no way that Hart would ever meet Mr. Murdoch.

HART OFFERED MR. Langford the list of men that Trudy had given him with one addition, Gregory Murdoch. "I need to know the finances, vices, and rumors about these men."

Mr. Langford folded the paper and slid it into his pocket. "Yes, Your Grace."

"Did you bring the ledgers I asked for?"

"Yes, Your Grace." His man of business reached down for his briefcase. "Is there a particular question I can answer for you?" He pulled out three ledgers and placed them on Hart's desk.

"No, I don't even know exactly what I am looking for. I will know it when I see it."

"Very well, sir." Langford pulled at one end of his long, wiry mustache.

"That will be all, Langford." Hart scowled as the squirrely little man hurried to the door.

Langford's nervous energy put him on edge. This was exactly why he had spent the last year cocooned at Belstoke. Having to endure people's reactions to his scarred face was demoralizing.

Hart turned to the ledgers sitting on the desk. He should sit and start looking through them, but he was far too restless. He crossed to the window and flipped back the curtain. The gas lamps on the front gate illuminated the street in front of his Mayfair mansion. Not a soul stirred in the square. His neighbors, no doubt, were already out for the evening. It seemed like another lifetime when he would have been dressing in his evening clothes and heading out for a night of revelry with his friends.

What were Danvers, Comstock, and Quincy up to tonight? Had any of them succumbed to the parson's noose in the last year? Probably not. The only one of them that had any decency had been their friend Grisham. Hart knew that

Lucius was happily tucked away in Marbury with his new wife. He was glad Grisham had got out of London and the lure of its many vices. Lucius deserved to be happy. The lads were probably at Brook's having dinner and wine before deciding which proper social function to grace with their presence. Had Danvers got his sister married off?

A carriage drove by, interrupting his thoughts. Perhaps he should just bite the bullet, get dressed, choose one of the many invitations he had received, and get out of the house. Everyone wanted to get a good look at him and, fuck it, he might as well get it over with.

Hart strode to his desk and picked up the stack of invitations left by his secretary. Flipping through them made his stomach feel sick. There were several dinner invitations and two invitations to balls, a handful of notes to meet for drinks, and one charity function. He chose an invitation at random and threw the pile down. Exiting his study, he headed for the stairs.

Townson hurried over to his side.

"Tell Thomas to get my carriage ready. I'm going out."

CHAPTER SEVEN

THE CARRIAGE PULLED up in front of the Bruton Street house. Hart peered out the window at the grand home of Lord and Lady Thornbury. He'd been to fêtes at their home before. Thornbury had been a good friend of his father's. So why did the acid taste of fear coat the back of his throat? Through the home's large windows, he could see people mingling. His dread continued to build. He ran a hand down his face, the raised lines of his scars now a familiar pattern under his fingertips. Why was he hesitating? He didn't care what others thought of him. He never had. Of course, it had been easier when opinions had always been favorable. Back when he had used his good looks to charm and flirt and used his title to stay aloof and unapproachable.

Now everyone inside would want to have a look at his ruined face and speak with him about where he had been, how he was doing… His hand began to shake at the thought of all those questioning stares, all the pitying looks. He clenched his fingers into a fist, but the tremors spread to the other hand. Beads of sweat popped out on his brow. A discreet knock startled him.

The door opened. Thomas stood waiting. "Are you ready

to go in, Your Grace?" His coachman studied him from underneath the brim of his cap. "Perhaps you would like to take a ride around the block first?"

Hart closed his eyes and tried to take in a deep breath and compose himself, but his body refused to respond to his command. Instead, his breath stuttered in his chest. His heartbeat drummed too fast. Dammit, what was wrong with him? Panic, sharp and familiar, thrummed. He needed a drink. The sharp burn of a brandy would ease the tension inside him. He should go home. It had been a mistake to think he could do normal things again.

"Your Grace?"

A swell of music and voices rose into the night air. Hart opened his eyes. Over Thomas's shoulder, he saw that the front door of the house was open. And illuminated by the glow of light from the interior stood Lucy. A liveried footman held out a hand and then escorted her down the front stairs. Her hair was intricately curled and studded with pearls. A pair of sapphire earrings swung gently from her ears; the pair he gifted her last year for her birthday. The hypnotic swing of the earrings and the familiar slopes and curves of her face enabled him to take in a breath past the tightness of his throat.

"Thomas?" Lucy called out as she reached the drive. "Is that you?"

Hart straightened in his seat as Thomas turned to face Lucy, effectively blocking the door opening.

His coachmen tipped his hat. "Good evening, Miss

Middleton."

"Good evening, Thomas. Is Lord Hartwick in there?"

The soft lilt of her voice brought his shaking to a halt. Hart brought out his handkerchief and blotted his forehead before replying. "Yes, he is. Thomas, it's all right."

Thomas moved aside, and Lucy peered up at him. "Hart, what a surprise. I would not have expected to see you here tonight."

He cleared his throat. "Um, well, I thought maybe it would be good to get out of the house, but as we arrived, I was having second thoughts. I may just go home."

Lucy's gaze ran over him. "Well, this is opportune. I was feeling unwell and was headed home myself. But if you can give me a lift, then my coachman will not have to make two trips, as he must return later to pick up Aunt Trudy."

"Of course, I can." Relief poured through him at having the perfect excuse to leave. "I'd be delighted to escort you home." He held out his hand.

Lucy quirked one eyebrow. "Delighted?" She put her hand in his, and he helped her climb into the seat next to him.

Thomas closed the door. Then the carriage rocked gently as he climbed into the box. In the next moment, they were off.

Lucy flicked back the curtain and watched the house as they pulled away. Then she leaned back with a soft sigh.

He frowned. "Lucy, Trudy knows you've left, doesn't she?"

She straightened. "Of course. I left her a note with a footman."

"You're not feeling well?"

She swiveled to face him. "If you must know, I am simply sick of being at these boring events. I saw my friends at the beginning of the evening, but inevitably, they must also go dance with men their mothers want them to meet. And Aunt Trudy kept parading me around. I swear we stopped to talk with every gentleman in attendance tonight." Her bottom lip jutted out. "I could not take another moment."

He shrugged. "You won't receive censure from me. I could not even force myself to get out of the carriage."

"Why didn't you want to go inside?"

"I'm not sure," he replied honestly. He couldn't put his finger on what caused his overwhelming feeling of dread. Except that ever since the accident, the feeling had been ever present. Haunting him at moments he least expected.

"Why did you want to attend this ball?"

"I need to speak with my father's friends. To start inquiring about the time period surrounding his death. Previously, I was reluctant to voice my suspicions that his and Robert's death was not a piece of bad luck. But the time for self-doubt is over. I can't find the answers I need sitting at home."

Lucy scrunched her nose. "I understand it must be hard to face the wolves when you've been gone so long."

He closed his eyes. He didn't give a damn about the wolves, or did he?

Now that his heart had settled back to its normal sedate

rhythm, he felt foolish for his panic. "I'm frustrated with myself. It's just the idea of everyone gawking, wanting to be the first to see how damaged I am. It makes me want to run." He shook his head in disgust. "I don't even know who I am anymore."

Lucy scooted closer. Her hand slid up to cup his ravaged face. "Hart, these scars don't change anything about who you are. You are the Duke of Hartwick. Intimidating, roguish, and far too charming for your own good."

The light touch of her fingers sent a tremor through him. Unlike the earlier ones, this was an all too familiar shiver of awareness. Hart pulled her hand away and guided it gently back to her lap. He had no business receiving gentle touches and kind words from this lady. Her affections were engaged elsewhere, as they should be. He didn't need or want to think about how good she smelled or how her soft touch left his skin heated. Or how having her near settled him like no glass of brandy ever could.

He scooted down the seat, putting a few extra inches between them. He glanced out the window into the dark night beyond. It wasn't late, perhaps half eleven. This used to be the beginning of his evening out.

"Everything has changed." He shook his head. How could he possibly explain? "The knowledge that someone killed my family, killed Galey for telling the truth about it, and almost killed me has been burning in my gut for the past year. Finding and punishing those who did it is the only thing that can stop this anger from eating me alive. It is the only thing that matters now."

Lucy's eyes widened, the deep blue almost midnight in the dim interior of the carriage. Her hand reached out to touch his arm. "Hart."

He flinched. She needed to stop touching him.

Her hand paused, then retracted.

She stared forward for a long moment. "I had a thought about that symbol on the letters. Where did your father go to school? Perhaps it is a fraternity of sorts from his school days."

"He went to Oxford. The place is famous for its secret societies. Thank you, Lucy. That is a brilliant idea."

Robert would have known what their father was involved in, business and personal. He had been the golden child, his father's confidant, his heir. It never bothered Hart much; after all he knew his place in the pecking order. And it had been impossible to be resentful when Robert had been such a good brother. Always taking an interest in his life, filling in the cracks caused by their father's disinterest. Letting him tag along with the older boys at Eton. And when their mother died, Robert had been the one to comfort him, let him cry and rage as little boys would. Christ, he missed Robert. Why had it been him? Why would anyone want to snuff out the life of such a good man?

They rode the rest of the trip in silence. Lucy sat unusually quiet and still. The carriage pulled to a stop. He turned to apologize for being so morose, but the carriage door swung open, and instead, he alighted to the street. Hart held out a hand. Lucy hesitated before laying her hand in his and descending.

He forced a smile. "Let me walk you to the door."

"That's not necessary." She pulled her hand from his the minute she stepped to the ground.

"Nevertheless." He took hold of her elbow and escorted her to the door.

As they paused in front of the cheerful yellow door, Lucy turned to gaze up at him. Her head tilted. "Hart, I want you to be careful until we figure out the why of all these deaths. I don't want you to become a victim."

He couldn't promise her that he would be safe. He had no way of knowing if the killer also wanted him dead or would once Hart started asking questions again. It was a risk he was willing to take to find out the truth. So, he simply raised an eyebrow and countered with his own question. "We?"

"You know very well you need my help. I am far cleverer than you." She patted his lapel. The front door opened. "Goodnight, Lord Hartwick." Lucy disappeared into the safety of her house.

He chuckled under his breath. She was right, of course. She had been the one to make all the conjunctures thus far. Not that he would ever admit it to her.

He walked back to the carriage, his dark mood lifted by Lucy's teasing. "Thomas, I am feeling much improved. Take me to the club."

CHAPTER EIGHT

H E CHOSE A chair in the back—not to hide—just to observe others without being noticed. The walk inside and across the large room had fetched enough scrutiny to make him sweat. Heads had turned, and conversations stopped as men stared. Many gave him nods and greetings, but those were a blur as Hart focused on getting to the pair of leather armchairs in the back corner of the main room. Composing his features into a haughty mask of indifference was as natural as breathing. For once, Hart was grateful to his father for his strong, if distant, example of how the Duke of Hartwick should comport himself.

As he settled back into the chair, a servant appeared at his elbow, causing him to jolt embarrassingly.

"What can I get for you this evening?"

"Brandy, three fingers." Why was he so damn jittery these days?

"Right away, Your Grace."

Hart finally took stock of the room. Brooks's main room was long and narrow. The green walls were lined with portraits of its founding members and large paintings of lush landscapes. Raucous laughter and colorful swearing travelled across the room from several large circular tables where men gathered to gamble away a pleasant evening. Along the edges were smaller clusters of chairs from which a low hum of conversation buzzed. Thick embroidered Turkish rugs covered the dark wood floors and muffled the constant murmur of voices. Hart had a membership at White's as well but had always preferred the lively energy here at Brook's.

His drink offered on a small silver tray appeared at his elbow. Hart took a large gulp of his favorite brandy. "Bring another along shortly." The man nodded and disappeared. Hart took a more measured sip. Who was here tonight? No one he knew. Some men he recognized but did not socialize with. Wait, no, he'd recognize that bald spot anywhere— Comstock. His old friend sat at one of the large tables, his back to Hart. The men were playing cards, a large mound of coins piled in the middle of the table.

The man across from Comstock nodded toward Hart. Comstock twisted in his seat to glance over his shoulder. His eyes narrowed. Then he rose, swayed a bit on his feet for a moment before steadying, and began to walk toward Hart.

Hart straightened and finished off his drink. His friend looked more perplexed than threatening. Hart took that as a good sign. "Good evening, Comstock."

Comstock came to a stop in front of him. "Hartwick, I didn't know you were back in town. And it's Galey now."

"Yes, of course. My apologies, Lord Galey. Won't you have a seat?" He gestured to the chair next to him.

Comstock hesitated but then sat down with a sigh. "I

really want to hate you. But you look like shit."

Taken aback, Hart said nothing for a moment. When he found his voice, he asked, "Why do you hate me?"

"Because you're alive, and he is dead."

"I did try to get him out of the carriage, but it all happened in a moment, and I was thrown back by the blast."

"Can you tell me what happened? Why were you in my father's carriage?"

Hart debated how much to tell him, but really, if anyone deserved to know the why of it, it was the man's son. He glanced around the room. Anyone could observe the two of them talking, but they had some modicum of privacy from being overheard. Besides, the time for discretion was over; he wanted answers, and he didn't care if people knew his suspicions.

"Your father asked me to meet him that night. He had answers for me surrounding the murder of my father and brother."

Comstock's eyes widened. "I thought they died in robbery."

"I have had my suspicions about it being not a random act of thievery. Then I received the note from your father. He never got the chance to tell me the exact details just that he knew who did it, and he couldn't live with the guilt of not telling the truth."

"I don't believe you." His friend shook his head. "My father was incredibly honorable. He would never be a part of any murder."

"I didn't say he was a part of it. He said he knew who did it, and they were incredibly influential. That they had eyes and ears everywhere. Then the window of the carriage was smashed, and a crockery bomb sailed into the carriage. Your father yelled, 'They know.' I jumped out, turned to reach for him, and then the whole world exploded." Hart reached for his second drink and drained the glass. "I'm so sorry I couldn't save him."

Comstock was silent for several long moments. Then he turned his gaze to Hart. "I know you would have if you could have." He gestured to Hart's face. "Is this the worst of it?"

Hart shook his head. "No."

Comstock nodded. He raised a hand at a passing attendant. "I'll have what he is having."

The attendant turned to Hart. "And for you, Your Grace?"

Hart nodded. When the servant left, Hart turned to Comstock. "I am going to find out who is responsible for these murders. I will have vengeance."

A smile cracked open across Comstock's face for the first time. "I have no doubt you will, Your Grace."

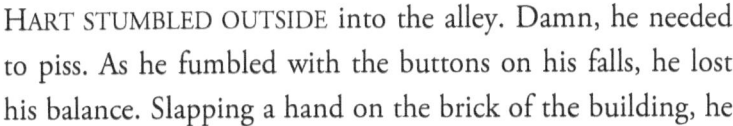

HART STUMBLED OUTSIDE into the alley. Damn, he needed to piss. As he fumbled with the buttons on his falls, he lost his balance. Slapping a hand on the brick of the building, he cursed his friend. He'd forgotten how much that bastard could drink. He laid his head against his forearm and drained his bladder. Buttoning back up proved to be just as challenging. Hart peered around blurrily. Now, where was his carriage?

"Good evening, guv." A gravelly voice came from behind him.

Hart tried to turn to face the voice but stumbled to the right. A sharp slice of pain seared his side. He yelped and jerked backward, his back hitting the wall.

"Stop moving, you," the voice grumbled.

A large, meaty hand gripped his shoulder. Through a haze of alcohol and pain, Hart stared down at the dark hair that covered the man's knuckles. This hand was going to kill him. This was how it would finally end. Damnation, Lucy had been right. He hated it when she was right.

Almost of its own volition, his hand found the cane resting against the wall next to him. He bashed the brass topper against the man's head. Only his aim missed, and he bashed the side of the attacker's shoulder instead. The knife the man held clattered to the ground though.

"Hey! Get off him," another voice yelled out.

Hart and his attacker both turned their heads toward the sound. A carriage had pulled up, and three men dressed in evening clothes were emerging from its dark interior.

The hand on his shoulder disappeared. So did the man attached to it, vanishing into the shadows like vapor. Hart placed a hand against the tearing pain in his side. Warm and wet; he was definitely bleeding. The three gentlemen who had saved him approached. Relief poured through him at their familiar faces.

Danvers was the first to speak. "Good god, man. Are you all right?"

Hart pulled his hand back and stared at the blood covering it. "I don't think so."

"Shit. Hartwick, is that you?" Quincy gripped his arm to steady him.

"It's him. Quick, get him back inside."

"No, get my driver. Don't want to make a scene." The idea of going back inside the club, bleeding all over the expensive carpets, was horrifying. He didn't want any more attention than he'd already endured this evening.

"Nonsense." He grabbed Hart's other arm. "We'll go in here at the back and shuttle you to a private room. The manager will call a doctor. I'm not putting you in a carriage injured." Danvers and Quincy muscled him back through the back door to the club.

"Jesus, Hartwick. I didn't even hear that you were back in town. Where have you been?" Danvers asked when they were safely in one of the many private lounges the club offered.

"Recovering," Hart wheezed out. Fuck, his right side throbbed.

Danvers's gaze raked over him. Then he reached forward to pull back Hart's jacket. His lips pursed together in a thin line. "I had no idea the extent of your injuries. No one did.

You just disappeared."

Hart batted his hands away.

"I just need to see how bad. Was it a knife?"

"Yes. Leave it. It's fine," Hart growled. He didn't want anyone touching him.

Quincy walked into the room. "The doctor is being sent for. Heyward went to tell your coachman what's happened. I ordered us a bottle of whisky."

The idea of more alcohol made Hart's stomach roil. He closed his eyes against the sensation. When he opened them, both men had taken seats across from him and were staring at him.

"What?" Hart said testily.

The two exchanged a look.

Danvers shrugged. "Nothing."

Hart sighed. He might as well get this over with. They wouldn't let it go for long. "Listen, the blast that killed Lord Galey also hit me." He gestured to the right side of his face. "This is from the shards of exploding crockery. And the burns cover much of my right side."

"Shit," Quincy muttered.

A sharp knock rang out, and the door opened. A servant hurried into the room with a bottle of whisky and four glasses on a tray. The man pulled out a folded towel and handed it to Hart. "Press this against the wound until the doctor arrives."

Hart unbuttoned his waistcoat and peeled it back to see the extent of the knife wound. His white shirt was soaked with blood, so there was no way to see how bad the cut was. He gratefully took the towel and did as he was told. It hurt like hell, but the throbbing abated somewhat. His alcoholic haze was quickly draining, leaving his head throbbing along with his side. Where was Thomas? He wanted to go home.

"Hart, when did you get back into town?" Danvers asked.

"Last week."

"You should have sent around a note. Lots has happened. We'd be happy to have a drink and fill you in."

"I'm not really ready to step back into society." Hart raised a hand, gesturing widely to his person.

"What? Because of the scars? We don't care about that. Besides, at least we'll have a chance with the ladies now that you're so ugly." Quincy guffawed.

Danvers joined in, jovially slapping Quincy on the back. But the two of them weren't laughing at him; they were just being their typical asshole selves. And far from being insulted, Hart laughed, too. Except laughing hurt like a damn bitch, and his laugh turned into a wheeze. Danvers poured him a drink, and against his better judgement, he threw it back.

CHAPTER NINE

The rumors are true! The reclusive Duke of Hartwick is back in town. And despite tales of his monstrous scars, back to his roguish ways it appears. He was seen stumbling, sloshed from Brooks, with his cronies well past the witching hour. And earlier that evening, outside of the Thornbury ball, seen luring a beautiful dark-haired debutant into his carriage. A woman reportedly engaged to someone else. It appears ruin seeks to ruin.

Lucy set down the paper with a huff. She glanced across the table at Trudy, who simply raised one eyebrow.

Lucy sighed. "Yes, it was me. I saw his coach in front when I left the ball, and he aided me by taking me home in his carriage."

"Aided you in your escape, you mean."

Lucy lowered her eyes and took a bracing sip of tea.

"Young lady, you may not leave a social event alone without telling me. I was worried sick." Trudy said.

"I left a note to be delivered to you."

"Coward. You well know I wouldn't have let you leave. There were several gentlemen there last night that I had not yet had the chance to introduce you to. Lucy, you are not even trying to find a husband." Trudy sighed. "I want to see you settled already."

Lucy had no response to the comment, which she had oft heard Trudy exclaim. "I haven't met any gentlemen that have remotely sparked any interest in me." She pouted just a bit. The only man she wanted did not want her. "Besides, it's my money. Why can't I just live as a wealthy spinster?"

"The money set aside for you by Hart's father is a dowry. Expressly earmarked for you to have a chance at an advantageous marriage. It cannot be used for any other purpose." Trudy reached out to pat Lucy's hand. "My dear, I will not always be here to watch out for you. The ways in which a gently bred woman must make her way in this life are limited and, frankly, in the hands of men. Now, your father was a good man who wanted to set you up for the best kind of future, which is why he asked the duke to be your guardian. You simply need to pick someone to share your life with. They are not all like Fitzwilliam. My own dear husband was kind and generous."

Lucy wasn't sure that it was really that simple. How could she tell the true worth of a man if all the courtship was so superficial, so contrived? She rested her chin in her hand. Dare she confess to Trudy that the only man she wanted to marry was Hart? Perhaps Trudy would just tell her how farfetched her dream was, or perhaps she was the perfect person to help her come up with a plan to woo him.

"Trudy, the truth is that there is only one man I want to

marry."

"I thought as much." Trudy plucked a ripe strawberry from the tray and popped it into her mouth.

"Do you know who I am referring to?"

"Oh darling, of course I do. And he needs someone to take care of him as well." Trudy ate another berry. "Hmmm, maybe Hart is the solution to our problem."

"Our problem?"

"Lucy, this article does not expressly name you, but nevertheless, everyone will know it is you. Reported to be engaged to another ... rumors like this can ruin your reputation."

"But I was never engaged to Fitzwilliam! And Hart has always watched out for me. Everyone knows his father was my guardian."

"It does not matter what's true. Only what people think is true. No man is going to court you if they think the Duke of Hartwick is your lover." Trudy's voice rose uncharacteristically high-pitched.

Lucy winced.

"There's only one thing to do." Trudy mumbled as she rose from her chair.

"What?"

But Trudy simply waved her hand dismissively. "Leave it to me, my dear." She left the breakfast room at a determined clip, leaving behind her signature scent of lily of the valley in her wake.

———◆———

LUCY WALKED AT her own determined clip toward Hart's townhouse. Her maid Helen at her heels. The wretched feeling in her gut would not abate after her conversation with Trudy. How dare that ridiculous scandal rag print so many lies. It seemed obvious that the true target of their poisoned pen was Hart himself and that her reputation was an unfortunate casualty. Why would they pick on a damaged man who was still recovering from a horrific accident? Creating lies about drunken behavior when she knew he had been on his way home last night.

Drops of rain splashed her cheeks. She glanced up at the gray sky and then pushed open her umbrella as the rain started in earnest. The foul weather matched her foul mood. By the time she arrived at the front door of Hart's house, her temper was at full steam. She couldn't wait to tell him about the article and share her righteous anger with him. Perhaps he could do something. Even buy the paper and fire the man who wrote the scandal section. Yes, that would be immensely satisfying. She knocked on the dark green door.

Mr. Townson answered the door himself. "Good morning, Miss Middleton."

"Good morning, Townson. I must speak with his grace." She shut her umbrella and stepped past the butler into the foyer.

"I'm afraid that he is not accepting callers at this time,

miss."

"Townson, must we do this every time I come to visit? I am not just any caller. He will see me. Now, where is he? Breakfasting?"

"No, miss. I'm afraid he is indisposed." Townson's eyes darted to the left, where Hart's formal drawing room lay.

Strange. Why would he be in a room expressly used for receiving guests? Who would he be entertaining at this hour of the morning? Lucy passed her umbrella and bonnet to Helen and then headed for the door. Mr. Townson hurried after her across the black and white tiles of the polished marble floor, sliding to a stop in his rush to prevent her from entering the room.

Lucy turned to face him. "Are you going to open this door and announce me, or shall I barge in?" She glared at the butler who looked so red he might be having an apoplexy.

She was in no mood for games this morning. She had important venting to do, and Hart must listen to what she had to say.

"Right then." She turned the knob and pushed the door open.

Inside, the smell of liquor and smoke hit her right in the face. Three men lay across various pieces of furniture. One man slumped in a chair, his long frame stretched out. His arm hung down over the armrest, a bottle of liquor clutched in his hand. Another man lay prone along the settee, one leg over the edge of the cushions and one planted on the floor. His sprawl was comical as he was dressed elegantly in evening clothes.

Then she spotted Hart. He lay in the chaise. His eyes closed, and was that blood staining his shirt?

"Dear Lord! Why is there blood on your shirt?" She hurried across the room.

Hart's eyelids popped open. He blinked, bleary-eyed, as though he was trying to focus. "Lucy?"

"Indeed." She glanced again around at the other two men, whom she had woken, as they clumsily straightened to sitting.

It was clear that the gossip rag hadn't made everything up. He had gone out drinking with his friends.

She put her hands on her hips. "And here I thought I would find you having a quiet morning with a cup of tea. Instead, I see you left me at my doorstep last night and then went out for a night of carousing with your degenerate friends."

"Hey," one of his friends protested.

Hart ran a hand down his face. "Lucy, could you please speak at a lower volume?"

"No, I cannot. Why is your shirt stained with blood? I told you to be careful until we could figure out what sort of danger is afoot. But no, you immediately go out and find trouble. What happened?!"

Hart rose to his feet. "Lads, I must ask you to go. Now."

The two men struggled to their feet and straightened jackets and cravats. One of them paused as he passed Hart. "Sorry, mate, didn't know you'd taken a wife."

Hart closed his eyes briefly. "I haven't."

Lucy crossed her arms and waited as the two men exited the room.

Hart turned to face her. "I'm fine. The wound has been stitched up." He tugged the two sides of his waistcoat together, covering his bloodied shirt.

She couldn't stop herself from moving closer. "What happened?" she repeated.

His fingers quickly fastened the buttons. "I was attacked in the alley behind Brook's. It's just a flesh wound."

"Attacked? By who?"

"Just some ruffian trying to steal my coin while I was taking…" He coughed into his hand.

Doubtful. Did he really think it a coincidence? "More likely someone hired to finish the job they started last year. Think about it. No one knows how much Galey did or did not tell you in that carriage. That makes you a liability for whatever secrets they are keeping about the death of your family."

Hart frowned. "Perhaps. It's hard to tell. He ran off when my friend's carriage pulled up behind us."

"Hard to tell. You mean because you were sloshed?" she scoffed. "I felt bad for you last night, but you were just beginning your evening of drunken revelry." She paced away from him.

To think she had been angry on his behalf for the lies she assumed the scandal rag had made up. But everything it said had been true. Her reputation was tarnished just by being acquainted with an infamous rake like him. To top it off, someone was trying to kill him, and he was too stupid to realize it.

She swiveled on her heel and strode back across the room, coming to a stop in front of him. "How could you be so reckless?" She poked a finger in his chest.

"How I spend my evenings is none of your concern." He crossed his arms in front of his chest.

"None of my concern? How incorrect you are, sir." Lucy pulled the torn-out page of newsprint from her jacket pocket and slapped it against his chest. Then she turned to leave. To hell with him. She was too angry to stay and watch him put two and two together.

"Lucy, wait. This is ridiculous. Luring young maidens into my carriage." He chuckled.

"Aunt Trudy didn't think it ridiculous. She said that everyone would know it was me. She was quite upset."

Hart moved to block her from leaving. "No one of substance reads these gossip rags anyway. You must ignore it."

He really didn't understand.

She clenched her hands into fists. "Everyone reads this paper. You read the false announcement of my engagement to Lord Fitzwilliam just last week."

"I'm sorry that your reputation was called into question because you were simply being a good friend." He reached for one of her hands, gently uncurling her fingers. "Our conversation last night did help me. In fact, because I felt much improved, I decided to go to the club and renew my investigation."

The warmth of his gaze held her in a thrall. His thumb brushed gently across the hand he held, and her breath caught in her throat. What was she mad about? Certainly not about the way it felt to stand so close to him. To feel petite against the breadth of his chest and to see his grey eyes turn molten. She took a step back. No, she must not get distracted.

"Well, um, we must have a plan to show that there is nothing untoward happening. Everyone knows that your father was my guardian. We must show that your interest is purely in helping me in my season."

Hart stared at her for a long moment before shaking his head. "Yes, of course. How do we do that?"

"I think it would be good if you escorted your aunt and me to a social function. Something respectable, something a brother type would do."

Hart nodded tightly. "Whatever you need. Let me know which function. Now if you'll excuse me, I need to clean up."

"Of course." She started for the door but turned back to send him a stern look. "And eat some breakfast."

HART ROSE FROM his bath and grabbed the towel off the nearby chair. He roughly ran it over his head to dry his hair. Then was more careful as he dried his torso, gently blotting at the stitches that sewed up the four-inch gash in his side. He walked out of the bathing room and across his bedroom to the tall mirror next to his bureau. The angry red mark under his ribcage stood out against the pale pink waxy burns that swathed his right side. Another scar to add to his collection. His lips pursed as he surveyed his disfigured body.

The smooth unnatural skin of the scar tissue twisted around his shoulder and down his arm. His right pectoral was similarly swathed by burns, the hair that should cover his chest refusing to grow through the thick scars. He ran a hand over the marks, tracing their winding path down his abdomen and around his hip bone. They were repulsive. Logically, he knew he should be glad to be alive. Glad that his body was still strong and capable. Except for the eye, of course. But whenever he looked in the mirror, he was reminded that he was damaged. His scars an outside reflection of his battered soul.

The horror of that night enveloped him. The flash of the explosion so bright. The acrid smell of smoke. The tearing pain in his eye, and later the agonizing torture as the doctor peeled away his charred clothing from burned skin. The weeks that followed were a hazy mix of pain and feverish nightmares that could only be dulled by laudanum. He had only patchy memories of gentle fingers across his brow and a sweet voice, which had soothed some of his terrible dreams. Hart shook his head to clear the memories he knew would suck him down into a spiral of despondency. He turned from the mirror.

Slowly, he raised his right arm up over his head, stretching the skin and joint while his body was still warm from his soak. Then he rolled his shoulder, his arm following the path in a circular motion that ached, but gradually released the tension that seemed a constant companion there. Hart moved through the stretches the doctor had suggested to keep the skin from tightening to a point where his right arm would be useless. He grimaced at the painful twinges as he pushed through the exercises.

Lucy had been right; he'd left whatever good sense he had in a bottle of brandy last night. Bad habits were so easy to fall back into. Especially with fucking friends like his. He shook his head. No, he shouldn't blame anyone but himself. His focus should be on his task to find out what happened to his father and brother. And those responsible were clearly not done trying to be rid of him. God, Lucy had been so angry. Magnificently so. Her blue eyes spitting fire as she pushed at him. Even hungover and covered in blood, his body responded to her.

Hart scraped a hand down over his face. His attraction to Lucy had been a thorn in his side for years. He should stay away from her, but now he would have to attend social functions with her as, what had she called it—a brother type. A dry laugh erupted from his chest. If Lucy had any idea how very un-brother-like his thoughts were, she would turn tail and run. No, more likely, she would just punch him ballocks.

CHAPTER TEN

"HE IS SO frustrating," Lucy complained to her friends as they sat in Violet's pretty receiving room having tea. She took a bracing sip. "He was attacked but then proceeded to get drunk with his friends?"

Violet and Adeline exchanged a look between them. "Dear, he and his friends were rather famous for their carousing," Violet said.

"Yes, I know, but he seemed so sad earlier in the evening. I've never seen him be so vulnerable. I guess I thought ... oh, I don't know what I thought. He needs to be careful, is all," she muttered.

"Do you think it was more than an attempted theft?" Adeline asked.

"Not necessarily," Lucy said carefully. She, of course, couldn't share Hart's suspicions about his family's deaths and his own accident. "But if he hadn't been sloshed, perhaps he could have heard the culprit approach."

Both ladies nodded.

"Men." Violet rolled her eyes.

"Well, he is going to escort Lady Weatherby and me to the theater this week, so we can all sit in the box and look respectable. Honestly, now that I have had time to think about the gossip that was printed, I agree with Hart; it's best to just ignore these things. Not that I would tell him that. Do you all think Lady Weatherby is overreacting?"

"Hmmm, my mother said she knew immediately it was you. But she had seen you leave the party by yourself," Violet said. "You should be more careful if you want to sneak out. I always fake swooning. It's a classic symptom and always guarantees that I am bundled into the carriage by my mother to be sent home."

"Violet! I can't believe you feign swooning. And here I always thought you had a delicate constitution," Adeline exclaimed.

Lucy grinned. "I knew. Your swoon is far too graceful to be real."

Violet took a sip of tea. "Ladies, you can use my trick if you like. It just takes a bit of practice."

Lucy chuckled. "Oh, Addie, I almost forgot." She reached beside her chair for her reticule. Pulling out the small drawing she had made of the symbol from the Hart's letters, she held it out to her friend. "Do you recognize this symbol? I think it might be Egyptian, and I knew you would be just the person to ask."

Adeline took the scrap paper and peered down at it for a moment. "It means protection. I believe. I can double check it against my book if you let me take it home."

"Yes, that's fine, thank you." Lucy pursed her lips together. Protection—interesting.

Violet leaned over to look down at the symbol. "I have seen that before."

"Where?" Lucy asked.

"In my father's study. Here, come with me, I will show you."

"Can we go into his study?" Lucy asked.

"It's fine." She waved a hand airily. "My father always spends his mornings at his club."

They followed Violet out of the room and down the corridor to the end. Violet opened the door to her father's study and swept inside. Adeline glanced over at Lucy with trepidation in her eyes. Lucy shrugged. They both cautiously crossed the threshold.

Violet turned. "Come on in, you ninnies. It's over here on the wall."

Lucy crossed to where her friend stood behind the large wooden desk.

But Adeline still hovered near the door. "My father would kill me if I entered his study. I don't think I have ever seen the inside of it."

"Don't worry. I sometimes come read in here. It's hard to find a slice of peace in this house. He doesn't mind at all."

Violet had four younger sisters and a younger brother. The household was often chaotic at best. Lucy turned to where her friend pointed. On the wall hung the very same symbol from Hart's father's letters molded in brass. Maybe six inches long, the metal symbol curved in a loop at the top, then stretched straight down with two arms coming off the sides bent downward at right angles. Interesting. "Violet, where did your father go to university?"

"Oxford."

Just as Lucy thought. Perhaps the symbol was some fraternity or secret society. But how many members used the stamp? Was it only between society members, or was it a badge that one was allowed to use for all correspondence once one had been part of the society? And how would they find out who was in the society? Did they have an official roster somewhere?

"Thank you, Violet. It's just as I thought. The symbol is maybe part of a fraternity of sorts from Oxford."

"Why are you wondering?" Violet asked.

"Oh, Hart was going through a box of old letters from his father, and he had seen the symbol next to his father's signature," she replied.

She couldn't wait to tell Hart that she had been correct. If they could find out who was a part of the society with the Egyptian symbol, they could narrow down possible suspects who had written the threatening letter.

DEAR LORD. HART looked so handsome in his evening clothes tonight. Lucy glanced at him as they settled into their seats in the theater box. He always had the dark, dangerous good looks of a pirate king, but with his longer hair and scars, that energy was amplified. What would it be like to be the object of his desire? To have those full lips devour her?

From next to her, Hart leaned close and gently flicked her dangling sapphire earring. "I see you still wear my birthday gift."

Her heartbeat raced at his proximity. "Yes, I love them."

Hart frowned. "I'm sorry I missed your birthday this year. I owe you a present."

She slid him a glance. "It's all right. I am just glad you are feeling better."

"Never turn down a gift, my dear," Trudy said with a smirk from her other side.

"She's right. I shall make it up to you," Hart murmured.

The curtain rose on the stage, and the orchestra began to play. They both turned their attention to the stage as the show started. *Othello* was not Lucy's favorite, but Trudy had insisted on parading her and Hart out in public so that everyone could see what an innocent relationship they had. She let out a sigh. What she wanted from Hart was far from innocent. What she wanted was to climb into his lap and kiss him senseless.

He would probably push her away. Hart had some self-appointed rule that she was off limits. She'd run the hurtful scene after his accident through her mind over and over. He had said she could do better than him, that she could choose anyone. Why didn't he want her to choose him? Was it really about his scars? Or was that just his excuse to keep her at arm's length?

Lucy chewed on her bottom lip, barely glancing at the

stage as she stewed. The soft candlelight flickered from the back of the box, casting long shadows across the dark red carpet in front of her seat. She tapped her slipper on the floor as she stared down at them. Hart's hand moved to her knee, stopping its bounce.

Then his lips were at her ear. "Cassio doesn't die here. He is only injured."

"What?" She furrowed her brow but didn't dare turn her head when his lips were so close.

"You looked worried. I fear you are damaging your perfect pout."

"Oh." Lucy ran her tongue over her abused bottom lip. "I was just thinking. Remind me to tell you what I found out about that symbol in your father's letters," she whispered back.

Out of the corner of her eye, she saw Hart nod and then shift back into his seat as he turned his attention back to the play. But his hand didn't move from her knee, and Lucy smiled into the dark as she enjoyed the warm weight of it through the silk of her skirts.

CHAPTER ELEVEN

A T INTERMISSION, HART stood and attempted to subtly stretch his shoulder. Having it in one position for the last hour had made it ache. Hell, it ached when he moved it, and when he didn't move it, it was a lose-lose situation.

Trudy stood and turned to the two of them. "Be expecting that people will come by to see us during the break. You two need to stand at least two feet apart at all times. No more holding hands in the dark."

"We weren't holding hands!" Lucy blushed.

Hart felt heat creep into his cheeks as well. It was true; they hadn't been holding hands. Although his hand resting on her knee probably hadn't been entirely proper. But Lucy had seemed so agitated. He had drawn soothing little circles across the silky fabric covering her knee every time her leg began to bounce again. Something was definitely bothering her.

"Aunt, I promise to be on my best behavior. Of course, I don't know if this one can." He jerked his thumb at Lucy.

"Really." Lucy huffed and walked to the back of the box. She snatched up a glass of champagne from the silver tray on a slim side table.

"Just teasing, brat."

Trudy gave him a stern look. She took his arm and walked to the balustrade. "Hartwick, who will you introduce her to this evening? Have you narrowed our list to appropriate candidates?"

Hart shook his head. He hadn't thought about the blasted list in days. None of those men were good enough for Lucy anyway.

"Well, then I'm thinking the Earl of Rawlings's son. He is a handsome boy, and I see he is here escorting his sister tonight. Adeline and Lucy are already acquainted. I'll send a note to invite them to come visit our box." She bustled off.

Hart glared out at the auditorium. Lord Rawlings's son was ... well, there was absolutely nothing wrong with him. He was three years older than Lucy, a perfectly appropriate age. But he was also rather bland, a typical cutout of a young aristocrat. Hart supposed that Viscount Danby *would* be a step up from her solicitor fellow. At least he would have a proper income to take care of her in style.

As he scanned the crowded theater, Hart caught the gaze of a woman who sat in a box one row down across the way. The last woman he ever wanted to be snared by in any way again. Lady Mirabelle's red-painted lips curled up into a friendly smile. Hart gave a small nod and turned his back to her, finding Lucy stood right behind him. She held out a glass of champagne.

"Do you know her?" Lucy peered around him, eyes narrowed.

"Yes, from a long time ago."

"Ah, she was part of your harem." Lucy took a sip of her wine.

"More like I was part of her harem. She led me to believe I was important to her, but in fact, she was married with a husband in the navy."

Lucy's mouth formed a small *O* of surprise.

He shrugged. "I was very young. It was a good lesson learned. I will never settle for being someone's alternative again."

The curtain that led to the corridor was pushed back. An elderly couple swept into the box. In the next moment, Trudy turned, with a sharp jerk of her head, beckoned them. He and Lucy dutifully walked over.

"Good evening, Lord Bartleby, Lady Bartleby." Hart greeted the couple.

"Good evening, Your Grace. Are you all enjoying the show?"

Trudy grasped Lady Bartleby's hand warmly. "Yes, indeed. Now that Lord Hartwick is back in town, he will be escorting our dear Miss Middleton to events this season. It was his father's wish that the duke see Miss Middleton safely settled in a good marriage."

"I see, yes, of course." Lady Bartleby replied. "Well, we just stopped by to say hello as we make our rounds. Please, enjoy your evening."

"Thank you." Trudy dipped her head. "You as well."

The couple exited as quickly as they arrived.

"That was laying it on a bit thick, wasn't it?" Hart said softly out the side of his mouth.

"There can be no subtlety when we are refuting rumors," Trudy replied in a firm tone.

Several more sets of elegantly dressed patrons filtered in and out of the box. Always with wide smiles and shrewd gazes skimming over the scars on his face, assessing his suitability to be allowed back into society. Hart rolled his right shoulder again and gripped the head of his walking stick, just barely stopping himself from pulling out his watch fob to check how many more minutes until intermission was over.

"Adeline, how nice to see you," Lucy exclaimed from next to him as Viscount Danby escorted his sister into the box. She took a step forward and kissed her friend's cheek.

"Good evening, Your Grace. May I present my sister, Lady Adeline Amberley." The viscount turned to the ladies. "Lady Weatherby, Miss Middleton, a pleasure as always."

"Please come in," Trudy replied. "There is perhaps more room at the front for you young people to converse." She waved her hand, shooing them. The curtain moved aside, and yet another grey-haired couple came through to greet his great aunt.

Lucy and her friend walked toward the railing at the front of the box. As he and Lord Danby stepped up beside them, Hart felt positively old and creaky standing next to the three younger people. They chatted about the latest race in which their friend had a horse entered. It felt like forever since he had attended an event at Ascot just to watch the race and have fun. Fun, what was that?

Lucy had increasingly overtaken his thoughts the past few days. He wondered what those plush pink lips would taste like. How her curves would fit up against him. Would she be soft and pliant in his arms? Her sapphire earrings swung to-and-fro as she laughed at something her friends said. Hart stared at the smooth column of her throat, imagining licking his way up to her ear and whispering, in great detail, all the things he wished to do to her. His cock twitched and Hart ruthlessly leashed his runaway thoughts. What was he doing? *Focus on the conversation, you filthy bastard.*

Lady Amberley glanced over at him through the round spectacles she wore before her gaze flitted back to Lucy. "I was able to look up the symbol that you showed me. It is indeed Egyptian. It's called the Knot of Isis. Isis was said to protect people from their enemies."

Lucy turned to him. "This was what I wanted to tell you. The symbol we found is for protection." Lucy smiled at her friend. "Adeline is quite the scholar of ancient civilizations."

"It stems from my interest in astronomy. Did you know that many of the constellations are named for ancient Greek and Roman stories about the gods?" Adeline said.

"I did not," Hart replied. "I had wondered about the symbol. I found it on a stamp among my father's correspondence supplies."

"Our friend Lady Blakely recognized the Knot of Isis as

well. Her father has the symbol hanging on the wall in his study," Lucy said.

That was interesting. Lord Blackpool had been a close friend of his father's when Hart was younger, but the two men had a falling out and hadn't been friendly in years. How did the Knot of Isis connect the two of them?

"Lord Danby, you attended Oxford, yes?" Lucy asked.

"I did."

"Do you know any of the school's student societies that use the Knot of Isis as their symbol?"

"What does it look like?"

"It's a bit like a cross, except the top is a loop, and the arms turn down at right angles."

Adeline took hold of her brother's hand and drew what Lucy described on his palm with her finger.

"Ahh yes, I have seen that before, but not at Oxford."

Lucy tilted her head to one side. "Where?"

"At a hel—um a gaming establishment just east of Drury Lane in Holburn. It's carved into the stone above the entrance."

Hart quirked his lips at the younger man's catch. A gaming hell in Holburn seemed an unlikely place to see the same symbol that a duke used to mark his correspondence. "Interesting. What's the name of the place?"

"The Blue Angel." Danby flushed as his gaze slid to the ladies.

His sister laughed. "It's fine, George. We know men attend all sorts of unsavory entertainments." She patted her brother's arm. "We're not naïve."

"Hmmm, my curiosity is piqued," Lucy said.

Hart raised an eyebrow.

"Not about the gaming hell. About why it has the Knot of Isis over the door."

"Me too," he murmured.

Danby turned to his sister. "We'd best head back to our seats."

She nodded and gave a small curtsy. "Good evening, Your Grace."

"It was a pleasure meeting you, Lady Amberley. Lord Danby."

After the viscount and his sister left the box, Trudy came to take her seat next to Lucy. "Did you have a nice visit with Viscount Danby and his sister, dear?"

"Yes, it's always a pleasure to see Adeline out of the house," Lucy replied.

"Her brother is very handsome, don't you think?"

"George? Yes, I used to have quite the adolescent tendre for him." She chuckled.

Hart frowned. *Handsome, bah.* He took his seat, and he kept his hands to himself as the gas lights were dimmed. After he dropped off the ladies tonight, he would take a ride to the Blue Angel. Perhaps someone would be willing to tell him about the Knot of Isis.

"No, ABSOLUTELY NOT." Hart glowered at Lucy across the dim interior of his carriage. Since Trudy had gone on to play cards at Lady Fenwick's house after the performance, he had agreed to escort Lucy home. Alone with him, Lucy had sprung her crazy idea on him.

"But I can help ask the right questions. And I'm very observant," Lucy replied.

"I am not taking you to a gaming hell. Absolutely not." He crossed his arms and then winced as his shoulder throbbed painfully.

Lucy pouted, her full bottom lip pushed out, enticing him to lean forward and nip it with his teeth. She was a far too tempting package, more than she realized. Not for a million pounds would he take her into a hell filled with drunken men.

Her eyes narrowed. "You should go home and have your valet wrap that shoulder in hot towels, then give it a massage."

"There's nothing wrong with my shoulder."

"*Pffft.* It has been bothering you all evening. Don't deny it. I told you I am very observant."

He sighed. Observant? Trouble was what she was. "It gets stiff easily when I am in one position too long. It will work itself out eventually."

"Martyr," she muttered. "I have some salve specially made for Trudy's rheumatism. It works wonders when massaged into stiff joints."

"Great, now I am in the same league as old ladies. Perfect."

Lucy stifled a giggle behind her hand. The carriage pulled to a stop in front of Trudy's house. "Why don't you come in for a moment, and I will fetch you a jar. It smells divine, not like old ladies. I promise."

He reluctantly nodded; he didn't want to make her cross with him again. He didn't have to actually use the stuff. They exited the carriage. "Thomas, wait for me here. I won't be long."

The front door opened as they ascended the steps to the townhome. Lucy gave the butler a smile as they entered the house.

She handed him her wrap. "Thank you, Harris. Lady Weatherby will be home later. She is playing cards with her friends."

The butler accepted Hart's hat and gloves.

"Harris, can you tell Mrs. Keely that I need a jar of the salve that I ordered for Lady Weatherby. Deliver it to the Blue Room please. We will wait there." She turned to Hart. "This way."

He hesitated.

"It is bad manners to leave a duke loitering in the entry." She headed down the hallway.

Hart either could follow her or stand there looking like a fool.

When they entered the room, it was unlit, and he paused letting his eyes adjust. Lucy crossed quickly to a table and lit a candle in a small hurricane lamp. The glow from it illuminated her soft features as she walked with it in her hand to light the tapers on a candelabra that sat on the low table in front of the sofa. Hart navigated carefully with his walking stick over to the seating area, trying not to trip on the side tables. He chose to sit in a wooden chair across from the sofa where Lucy had settled herself. Knees spread, he rested his hands on the top of his cane.

"I'd offer you something to drink, but we only have sherry. I know you don't care for it."

"It's all right. I am attempting to drink less these days. I fear my bad habits have been amplified this last year. I hope to remedy that."

"Has the recovery been hard? Physically, I mean." Lucy asked.

He shrugged. "At first, yes, but now the eye is just a nuisance. The shoulder is what still pains me. The physician said that the scarring from the burns has pulled the skin too tight and most likely is tugging on the nerves beneath. There is nothing that can be done."

"I don't accept that. There is always something to be done."

Hart smiled at her mulish expression. How did she always walk around with such certainty that life would work out the way she thought it should?

A small rap at the door was followed by Trudy's housekeeper stepping through the threshold. "I have the salve for you, miss."

Lucy rose and accepted the glass jar. "I'm going to send

this home with the duke to help with his shoulder. I'm sure Lady Weatherby would approve. I'll let her know in the morning."

"Yes, miss." The lady curtsied and quit the room.

Lucy strode over to him with a determined set to her mouth. "Take off your jacket, Your Grace."

"Pardon?"

"I'm going to prove to you that this stuff works wonders. Don't be a prude. Take off your jacket and untie your cravat so I can gain access to your shoulder."

A prude? Him? He would have been considered by many to be a hedonist. A year ago, no one would have dared called him a prude. Challenge accepted. Hart rose to his feet slowly in front of her. After setting his cane aside, he removed his jacket with only a small wince. Keeping his eyes locked on hers. He untied the knot in his cravat. Her eyes tracked his movements as she watched him pull the length of linen slowly from around his throat. He laid both it and his jacket down on the table next to the chair. Next, he unbuttoned his vest. Lucy's gaze followed each button as he slid them loose. He spread the brocade fabric open with a grin, gratified to see her swallow hard.

"Sit down, please," she directed him in a low, soft voice.

He did as he was told and settled again in the chair. Finding himself at eye level with her gorgeous décolletage and the smooth, pale column of her throat, he closed his eyes briefly. Praying to preserve his self-control.

Lucy stepped to his side. He heard the rattle of the lid

being set aside. Then she lifted the opened jar in front of his nose. "Smell, what do you think?"

It smelled like echinacea and lemon balm. A pleasant fragrance that was, like she'd said, not at all cloying or feminine. "Smells good."

"Alright then. You just need a good dollop, then rub it between your palms to warm the oils present in the salve." She pushed aside the open collar of his shirt and was about to slip a hand underneath when he gripped her wrist.

"Are you sure you are willing to touch the scars?" he asked.

This was a mistake. She was going to be horrified by the damage.

Lucy looked down at him calmly. "Hart, I was there after the accident. I know what to expect."

She had been? "Those first few weeks are a blur of pain and opium. I didn't know who was nearby." He dropped his hand back to his lap. He didn't like that she had witnessed him at his worst. But at the same time, it was a relief to have someone truly understand how bad it had been.

Her hand slipped underneath his shirt, and she spread the salve along the top of his shoulder, rubbing it gently over the puckered skin and down the back of his shoulder blade. Her light touch felt heavenly. It didn't do anything for the ache, but he wouldn't complain about having her hands on him. It had been so long since he had allowed anyone to touch him.

Lucy stepped behind him and pushed the fabric further

off his shoulder. Then with both hands she began to knead his shoulder with deeper strokes across the muscles.

He grunted at the pain it elicited. But soon, the initial twinges smoothed out. The feel of her hands warming his skin and her fingers kneading away the tightness beneath was divine. His whole right side relaxed as he leaned into her ministrations. It was all he could do to not let out a moan of pleasure. Slowly, the shoulder began to feel looser, more pliable. Lucy moved one hand down into his sleeve to rub along his bicep and upper arm. She had to lean down to reach, and her breath tickled his ear sending a shiver of desire racing over his skin.

"How's that feel?" she murmured softly.

"Amazing."

She let out a throaty laugh, and the husky sound of her amusement bewitched him.

He tugged her around by the arm and pulled her onto his lap. "Oh, you just love to be right. Is that it?"

Her eyes were alight with humor, her lips parted in a surprised gasp. Before she could answer him. Before he could think that he shouldn't. He leaned forward and kissed her.

CHAPTER TWELVE

DEAR LORD, HE tasted like pure sin. She parted her lips for him, enjoying the passionate slide of his. He let out a low moan as their tongues tangled. His mouth was so hot she felt a flush race down her throat and across her chest. One of his hands grasped the back of her neck, keeping her in place as he explored. She should have known she was playing with fire when she touched him. Hart was no boy with shy, chaste kisses. He was a volcano of heat and fire. Lucy grasped his shoulders and kissed him back with every fiber of her being. She would not waste one moment of being in his embrace.

Hart's other hand gripped her bottom, pulling her tightly against him. She held on as he changed the angle of their kiss, sipping on her lips with a series of small kisses, then he nipped at her bottom lip. Their breath mingled. Lucy's heart raced. This was what she'd dreamed about. Wrapped in his arms, his heartbeat under her palm. No one else could make her feel this desperate or this precious. He moved his lips across her cheek to kiss her temple. She opened her eyes, staring at his silky dark hair as he sucked in a deep breath.

"Lucy, you are exquisite. I shouldn't be kissing you. I

don't deserve to even touch you. You belong to someone else."

She gulped. Why had she been so stupid? *There is no one else!*

"You are young and have a bright future." He continued as though he was trying to convince himself to let go of her. "I shouldn't be tasting what is not mine."

And then he did let go of her. His hands left where they had held her so firmly in place for his tender plunder to fall to her waist. He lifted her off his lap and set her on her feet. "I should go."

Lucy stood dumbfounded. Had she done something wrong? She opened her mouth but did not know what to say to make him stay. She had bared her heart to him once before, and he had refused to accept it. She wouldn't make the same mistake twice. Squaring her shoulders, she stepped back as he stood. Why didn't he see how they were meant to be together? Why had he kissed her if only to turn away?

Anger, hot and bright erupted in her chest. "You rogue."

"I'm sorry, Lucy."

"Sorry for what." She threw her hands into the air in frustration. "You don't have any idea why I'm upset."

Why didn't he want her? When she felt tears threaten behind her eyes, she spun on her heel and stormed from the room. Blast him to hell. She would not show him how vulnerable she felt right now. She was strong and fierce. She had to be to survive as a woman in this world. She raced up the stairs to her room and slammed the door shut with a satisfying bang. Leaning back against it, she drew in several deep breaths. She already regretted her outburst. She should have stayed calm and attempted to seduce him further with her feminine wiles. *Ha!* What feminine wiles did she have?

She made her way slowly to the bed and flopped down onto the soft counterpane. Putting her hands to her face, she let out a groan. The sear of Hart's kisses, his firm lips teasing and tasting hers, had been so much better than her fantasies. And she held many fantasies of what it would be like to be in his arms. But those had always ended in the two of them naked in bed and Hart teaching her all the wicked sensual things he must know.

Lucy ran her hands slowly over her heated cheeks and down her throat, grazing over her tight, puckered nipples. She was hot and damp between her thighs and so very frustrated. With him and his damned rationalizations, with herself and her stupid temper. She allowed herself one long dramatic sigh, then she slid off the bed and crossed the room to ring for her maid. Tomorrow was another day, and she was still curious about the Knot of Isis. She would go do some sleuthing for herself.

THE BLUE ANGEL did not look at all like Lucy had imagined. Perhaps, because it was the middle of the morning, and the sun shone brightly against the spotless windowpanes of the house, but the place looked domestic rather than sordid. She tipped her head up. The brick building's facade rose three stories tall and spanned at least a hundred feet wide. The black front door was plain; the only ornamentation was a simple brass knocker. Adding to the domestic feeling were boxes of flowers in a riot of colors that peeked through the iron bars which encased the ground-level windows.

Lucy stood on the pavement with a hand up to shield her eyes as she searched for the Knot of Isis. Next to the door, a simple brass plaque proclaimed the establishment's name. The Blue Angel. Who exactly was the Blue Angel? She lifted her gaze to the stone header above the door. *There you are.* The Knot of Isis.

Lucy jumped when the door to the Blue Angel opened. A bearded man stepped outside. He paused when he spotted her, his hand still on the doorknob. His gaze swept over her from top to bottom in a slow perusal.

Then he shut the door behind him and placed his hat on his head. "Performers go around back. See Mrs. Langley."

"Pardon?" Lucy replied.

"Dancing girls report around back."

"Oh, I'm not a performer. I am Miss Lucy Middleton. I'm here about that." She pointed up to the Knot of Isis.

The man twisted to look up to where she pointed. "About what?"

"That symbol there, above the door. It's called the Knot of Isis. It is an Egyptian symbol that means to protect against one's enemies."

"Huh, I've never noticed it before." The man turned

back to her. "Well, Miss Lucy Middleton, I am Matthew Reeves, and this is my club. Thank you for the interesting tidbit, but I must be going."

"Actually, I have a question about this place. Perhaps you could indulge me for just a moment."

Mr. Reeves smiled and stepped toward her. "I suppose I have a moment for such a beautiful lady on this fine morning."

"Lucy?" A loud exclamation rang through the air.

She and Mr. Reeves both turned. Hart was striding toward them from up the street.

He came to stop in front of her a moment later. "Lucy, what in god's name are you doing here?" Taking her arm, he pulled her to his side before turning to glare at Mr. Reeves.

But the man appeared nonplussed by Hart's scowl. He tipped his hat. "The lady and I were just having a lovely discussion about this here symbol. The Knot of…"

"Isis," Lucy supplied. "I was just about to ask Mr. Reeves if he knew any history of this building. Has your establishment been here long?"

Hart's shoulders relaxed infinitesimally, but he did not let go of her upper arm, keeping her anchored next to him.

If the quirk of Mr. Reeves's lips was any indication, he noticed this as well. "I've owned the Blue Angel for five years, but the building itself belongs to my silent partner, Mr. Seaton. In fact, he owns everything on this block and the next. Perhaps he would know more about the building's idiosyncrasies, like your symbol up there."

"Do you know where we might find Mr. Seaton?" Hart asked.

"Not really," Mr. Reeves replied.

"Oh please, Mr. Reeves. We just want to ask him a few questions. I must satisfy my curiosity about why this symbol is on this particular building."

"She is quite tenacious when she is trying to figure something out. You should see her play chess," Hart added.

Mr. Reeves looked back at her. Lucy cast him a wide-eyed and innocent look.

He sighed. "I honestly don't know where he keeps a residence, but he does stop in here regularly. I suppose I could give him your card and a message when I see him next."

Hart reached into his jacket pocket and pulled out a slim silver case, extracting from it a calling card. He passed it to Mr. Reeves. "Please ask him to contact me."

Mr. Reeves's eyebrows shot up as he read the name on the card. No doubt, he wondered what the Duke of Hartwick was doing on the east side.

But he slipped it into his pocket and gave Lucy a wide smile. "Good day, Miss Middleton." Then he strode off down the street.

"Lucy Eleanor Middleton, what do you think you are doing?" Hart glowered down at her. "This neighborhood is no place for a lady. Especially alone!"

She deliberately took a step back out of his grip. "The same thing you are doing here, I imagine. Following the clue we found out about last night." She crossed her arms in front of her chest, sending her own glare his way. "And besides, my coachman is right there." She waved across the street at Hugh, who stood feeding an apple to her carriage horse.

He tipped his cap. "You ready to go, miss?"

"Yes, I am," she called back. Then she turned to cross the street.

Hart immediately fell in step beside her. "Lucy, you should have left the investigating up to me. This is my problem." He opened the door to the coach. Then he cupped her cheek with one hand. "Please, don't put yourself at risk."

The urge to lean into his touch was immediate, so instead, she pulled back. "I was curious, just as you were. Hart, having someone trying to kill you is more than just a *problem*." She poked her finger at his chest. "And even though I am currently cross with you, I do care whether or not you die." Then before she could weaken in her resolve to stay angry with him, she stepped up into the carriage. "Good day, Your Grace."

CHAPTER THIRTEEN

A MAN STEPPED from the shadowed alley next to the Blue Angel. He drew in a long inhale from his thin cheroot as he walked into the sunshine and contemplated the tall, imposing form of the Duke of Hartwick. He watched the duke walk away down the pavement before heading in the opposite direction. It took about twenty minutes to reach the Mayfair mansion. When he entered the man's study unannounced, an older gentleman startled from where he sat in his leather upholstered chair.

"Dear God, Seaton, why must you always appear from thin air? How do you even get past the staff anyway?" the gentleman muttered.

He shrugged. "It's why I get paid so well."

"Drink?" the man gestured to the side table where a decanter of brandy sat with a pair of crystal glasses.

He shook his head. He never drank alcohol. Instead, he took a seat in the chair opposite to the gentleman. "He came to see my place today. He and a fine lady. They were interested in the symbol etched in the stone above the door. The Knot of Isis, they called it."

"Hmmm, I wonder why." The older man's gaze lowered

to his lap.

Seaton's gaze flitted over to the wall where the very same symbol carved in cherry hung beside the fireplace. "He has been visiting the others. Lavensham and Rawlings so far."

"Do you think he found the journal somewhere among his father's things?" The gentleman's brow furrowed.

"I honestly think he doesn't know much of anything. He would be plotting his revenge, not running around asking questions still. Just my opinion."

The gentleman nodded. "Well, do your job and keep him safe. There is no telling what the others will do when they feel backed into a corner."

He nodded and left the way he'd come in, melting easily into the well-dressed patrons walking around Bedford Square.

CHAPTER FOURTEEN

H ART ENTERED THE cool interior of his carriage. "Harris Street, number two," he told Thomas.

The door closed, and he leaned back against the squabs with a sigh. That woman was going to be the death of him. The kiss they'd shared last night shook him to the core. Perhaps he had always known deep down there would be no turning back if he gave into temptation and tasted her sweetness. No, not sweetness. Lucy was like a tart summer berry. The sharp flavor hit his tongue delicious and potent, with just a hint of sweet left behind after he finished.

She'd called him a rogue. And he was, for all the reasons he had told her. He was too old, too damaged, too bloody moody. But damn it, he wanted her. He'd never wanted any woman more. The urge to seduce her away from her Mr. Murdoch was strong. She wasn't some toy to steal then play with. Besides, his skills in seduction had always been based on his good looks. These days … he ran a hand down over his cheek; he wasn't a catch on any level. No, Lucy wasn't for him.

Hart glanced out the window. The carriage rolled through the neat squares and wide avenues of Mayfair. His next stop would be an ambush of sorts. The Earl of Blackpool had ignored all of his invitations to meet. It was time to pin the man down. Hart wanted to know what Blackpool knew of the time around his father's death. Someone among his father's cohorts must have known something if his father was receiving threats. The fact that Blackpool had been dodging his summons, in addition to the new information that he also had the Egyptian symbol hanging in his office, made Hart all the more suspicious.

He arrived a few minutes later. When he was greeted by the earl's staff, Hart handed over his card, and the butler disappeared up the stairs. The Blackpool's townhome was well appointed. Hart glanced up at the large crystal chandelier. It matched the crystal-laden sconces along the walls. The light grey marble floors were polished and pretty. The delicately carved cherry table to his left held a patterned blue vase full of fresh pink roses, giving the home a decidedly feminine feel, which was no surprise as the man was married with four daughters.

"This way, please, Your Grace," the butler intoned.

As Hart entered the man's study, the Earl of Blackpool rose to his feet.

"Well, it isn't often that a duke drops by unannounced to see me. Good afternoon, Your Grace."

"Blackpool." Hart nodded curtly. "I was nearby on another errand and thought since you had not responded to my invitations, I would corner you at home."

The earl had the grace to look chagrined. "Yes, sorry,

been very busy recently. Please have a seat. What can I do for you, my boy?"

Hart tried not to roll his eyes at the older man's attempt to assert his authority. "Lord Blackpool, I will get straight to the point. I hoped to speak with you candidly about the time around my father's death. I remember that you and he were close friends."

The earl's jaw visibly clenched. "Yes, Henry and I were friends since we were boys at Eton. What do you want to know?"

"Do you know of any business dealings that my father was involved in that had soured? Did he ever complain about receiving threats over a bad business deal?"

"No. I don't remember him mentioning anything about threats. But I don't suppose he would even if it was happening. Henry kept things close to the chest."

"Someone was making threats the week leading up to his death." Hart leaned forward to place his arms on his knees. "I have never accepted that their deaths were an accident of fate."

Blackpool's dark eyes turned flinty. "Son, you must accept the truth. It was a terrible incident, but crime in the city, especially in that part of town, is common."

Hart wanted to yell and rage at the platitude that his father's friends had said to him over the last fortnight. Rawlings, the Duke of Lavensham—both had looked at him with fatherly concern and told him it had just been a terrible tragedy.

In his frustration with the wall of denial his father's friends had erected, Hart almost voiced to Blackpool how Lord Galey hadn't believed it to be a robbery, that he had known who murdered them. But recalling Galey's words from that night stopped Hart from blurting it out. Galey had said that the culprits had ears everywhere. Could he trust what little he knew with the Earl of Blackpool?

Hart reached into his pocket and withdrew the small gold stamp. Moderating his tone so that Blackpool wouldn't see his frustration, he asked, "Sir, do you recognize this symbol? I found it in my father's correspondence kit. I noticed the symbol stamped on many letters that my father received from you and other friends of his."

Blackpool took the stamp. He stilled for a moment as he stared down at it. Then he passed it back to Hart with a smile—one that did not reach his eyes.

"It was the insignia for a club we had at Eton. It means to protect each other from one's enemies. Egyptian? I think. He used the stamp to mark all his letters. Henry always had a flair for the dramatic." Blackpool stared blankly across the room. "That was back when we all had a certain idealism about friendship and what the future held."

Hart pocketed the stamp. He debated whether to ask his next question. But he must find out where the earl fell in his list of suspects. "What happened between you and my father? I used to see you at gatherings all the time when I was younger. And then you and he seemed to never speak, even at social events."

The earl's lips thinned. His gaze grew sharp again, pinning Hart with its intensity. "Your father had an affair with my wife. It is hard to stay friends with someone who would betray your friendship in such a way."

The revelation pushed Hart back in his chair. No, his father was an honorable man. He would never do something like that to a friend. It must be a lie, a misunderstanding.

Blackpool let out a caustic laugh. "I can see by the shock on your face that you thought your father a perfect gentleman. Well, he shocked the hell out of me, too. I always knew he was a womanizer, but I never thought he would cross the line with one of us."

As Hart sat stunned, grappling with the phrase *womanizer* as a descriptor for his father, a discreet knock sounded at the door.

"Come in," the earl called out.

The door opened, and the butler stepped across the threshold. "Sir, Mr. Murdoch is here for your one o'clock appointment."

"Thank you. Give us a moment or two and then bring him back." Blackpool turned to Hart. "If you'll please excuse me. I have a meeting with my solicitor."

Hart rose to his feet. Wait, Lucy's Mr. Murdoch was here? "Mr. Murdoch, of Jackson and Worth?"

"Yes."

"Could I meet him?" Hart improvised. "I have heard good things about the firm."

"Are you thinking of switching?"

"Perhaps," he replied. This was his chance to size up the man in person. There was only so much Hart could infer about someone from a piece of paper.

The earl crossed the room and pushed open the door. In the corridor, a golden-haired adonis leaned with one shoulder against the wall. A toothy grin stretched across his face as he spoke with Violet Blakely, the earl's oldest daughter. The man straightened with a start when he noticed her father. Tucking his leather bag under his arm, he gave a small bow.

"Come inside, Murdoch. The Duke of Hartwick would like to meet you."

Hart watched silently while the man came into the room. Damn him for being so handsome.

LUCY RANG THE bell at Violet's house. The door swung open almost immediately, but instead of Lord Blackpool's butler, her friend stood there.

Violet grabbed Lucy's wrist and yanked her across the threshold. "I've been waiting for you."

"Sorry I'm late. I stopped to get us sticky buns from that little bakery on Derry Street." She offered her friend the small twine-wrapped box.

Violet looked over her shoulder toward the staircase. "Thank you, but there is something you should know immediately." Violet's panicked expression was worrying.

"What is it, dear?"

"Mr. Murdoch is here." Violet squeezed her hand painfully. "And the duke is here as well. They are all in my father's study. Together."

Lucy raised her hand to her heart. Panic bubbled up into her throat. "But how can that be?"

"Bad luck, I guess. The duke showed up unannounced about a half hour ago."

"How long have they been in there?" she asked.

"Maybe ten or fifteen minutes. I came to stand sentry at the door so I could make sure to tell you right away."

"We must go hide at once. Neither of them can know I am here." Lucy whispered. *Oh my Lord.* Was Hart in there grilling Mr. Murdoch about his intentions? Certainly not. Not in front of the earl. Would he?

"Thank you for meeting with me, Blackpool. Good day." Hart's deep voice echoed from the upstairs hallway.

She exchanged a panicked look with Violet. Lucy felt lightheaded as she glanced around for an escape. She might actually swoon for the first time in her life. Violet pulled her across the polished floors to the left. Yanked open the door to the coat closet and shoved her inside. Lucy stumbled back and landed against a rack that held umbrellas, making them rattle. Violet thrust the box of sticky buns into her hands and shut the door in her face.

Lucy could hear the muffled clicking of Hart's cane as he navigated the stairs down to the ground floor. She slowly cracked open the door to the closet, just enough to peer out with one eye.

Violet swung around. "Oh, Your Grace, good afternoon. I did not know you were here." Violet gripped her skirts with a white-knuckled grip.

"Didn't I see you upstairs moments ago with Mr. Murdoch?" Hart asked.

"Oh, did you? I did not know you were here." Violet repeated herself and then seemed to realize what she had done because a crazed giggle rang out.

Lucy winced. Poor Violet was not a natural at lying.

Just then, the butler came striding into the foyer. "Your hat and gloves, sir?"

"Yes, and can you tell my coachman that I am going to walk home from here? I need some fresh air."

Lucy studied Hart. His expression was tight and grim. What had he learned in his meeting with the earl? Or was it due to finding out from Mr. Murdoch that she had fabricated her fake beau? Was he upset that she had lied to him?

The butler came into view as he retrieved Hart's hat and gloves from the console table next to the closet. Lucy took a step back into the dark interior in case the man glanced toward the closet to see an eye peering back at him.

Hart donned his gloves and hat, then nodded at Violet. "Good day, Lady Blakely.

She curtsied in return. "Good day, Your Grace."

After Hart left the house, the butler turned to Violet. "Is there anything I can get you, miss?"

Violet put her hands behind her back. "Oh no, thank you, Hoby."

The butler turned and returned to whence he came from. Her friend hurried over to the closet. "The coast is clear."

Lucy emerged and lifted one hand to smooth a stray hair that had fallen into her face. "Thank you. That was quick thinking. You are a true friend, Violet."

"No thanks necessary." Violet winged out her elbow. "Shall we adjourn to the drawing room to eat sticky buns?"

"If there was ever a time for sweets, now is that time." Lucy glanced back at the door and frowned. "But Hart looked almost distraught. I think maybe I will try to catch up with him."

Violet tilted her head. "He did?"

Lucy nodded. "Better to know now if Mr. Murdoch ratted me out than to wait and fret over it for days. Can you call for my maid, please?"

"Of course, dear. But you must send me a note later, or I will simply die of curiosity."

CHAPTER FIFTEEN

H IS FATHER HAD had an affair with the wife of his close
friend. His father—a womanizer. Hart couldn't seem
to reconcile these things with the man he'd known. The man
who cautioned his sons to take care with their liaisons. To
not bring scandal to the family name. Although his father
had been stern and distant, Hart had always looked up to
him … from afar. The man had seemed larger than life, good
at everything he did—excellent horseman, hunter, even
gambler. Robert had always groused that Hart had inherited
his father's immense luck and skill with cards.

His walking stick hit against a small branch that lay
across the pavement. Hart stepped over it as he continued
down Harris Street. A light breeze raced against his skin,
cooling him from the warmth of the day. From his right,
came the loud, cheerful voices of children and he realized he
had made it to Green Park. He changed direction and
strolled through the gate, entering onto a shady path.

Of course, his father was only a man, but Hart had spent
his whole life idolizing him and older brother. Never measur-
ing up to them in his mind. He'd always been the loose
cannon, just the spare. Seeing the cracks in his father's life

made him reconsider how he felt about his own. Perhaps, he wasn't doing so badly filling the role of Duke of Hartwick. Spotting a wood bench, Hart sat down with a long sigh. He desperately wished he could speak to his brother. Had Robert known?

Damned if he wouldn't give all he had to sit here next to Robert and tell him the salacious news and commiserate in their shared shock. His brother would have been the one person who could have understood the thoughts swirling in Hart's mind. Robert had known him like no one else. Like only your sibling could. He could admit it had been lonely, he hadn't let anyone else become that close since Robert died. Except maybe Grisham. And after the attack, his sadness had been suffocating. It hadn't seemed fair to suck anyone into his own personal hell. Grisham had just married and started a new business; he needed to look forward and not worry about Hart.

A few leaves swirled in a small whirling dervish at his feet. Hart watched as a pair of tall black Hessians entered his line of view. He glanced up to find a man with a long, lean frame. The man had sharp, angular features and wore no hat. His dark hair ruffled by the breeze.

"You look as though someone has killed your puppy." The gravel in the man's deep voice surprised Hart. It reminded him so much of his brother. He blinked slowly, his thoughts of Robert interfering in reality.

"Pardon?"

"I've never seen a sadder sight than you slumped on this

bench."

Taken aback, Hart found himself answering honestly. "I just found out some shocking news." He peered up at the stranger. "Do I know you?"

"No, but I know you. You came looking for me." The man pulled out a white card from inside his jacket and held it up.

Hart recognized his calling card. "Mr. Seaton?"

The man nodded. "Yes, Rhys Seaton. What news did you hear?" Then he held up a hand. "No, let me guess, something scandalous about your dear old da?"

"How do you know that?" He rose to his feet. How would this man know that?

"Because you have just come from Blackpool's residence. And I know all sorts of secrets. It's part of what I do, sort of my currency, you could say."

Hart clenched his fists. "So, you deal in blackmail? Is that why you have approached me? To threaten to expose my family's secrets?"

Seaton threw his head back and laughed. "No, in quite the twist, I'm here to watch over you. I have been hired to protect you."

What? Protect him? "Who hired you?"

"That I cannot say. The party is aggrieved at what happened to you and wishes to protect you from further harm."

"Are you a Bow Street Runner?" Hart asked.

Seaton looked positively offended; his lip curled in disgust. "No."

Hart was confused and honestly bone-weary tired even though it was the middle of the afternoon. "What do you want, Mr. Seaton? Because I don't think I have the wherewithal for this mental chess."

Seaton shrugged. "You called for me, remember?"

Oh yes, he had asked for Seaton to contact him. What about again? Hart tried to get his thoughts together. The Knot of Isis. "Uh, yes, we were … I mean, I was interested in the history of the building you own. The one that houses the Blue Angel. I recognized the symbol above the door. The Knot of Isis."

"Is that what it's called? Hmm." Seaton tucked his hands in his pockets and rocked back on his heels. "The building came to me through family. Our family, little brother."

CHAPTER SIXTEEN

H ART SUCKED IN a ragged gasp of air. What had he
said? *Brother?*

"W-what do you mean?" he stuttered.

"I said it came to me through family. Surely, you're not
that dense. My mother was your father's mistress." His lips
thinned. "For a time."

His head reeled. "When?"

"Between you and your brother."

It was too much to believe. These things being said about
his father. He wouldn't believe it. "No, my father wasn't that
kind of man. He loved my mother; he mourned her death
deeply." He took a menacing step forward, but Seaton just
stood there with a mocking smirk on his face.

"Believe whatever you wish, little brother. It doesn't
change the facts."

"Don't call me that." Hart shoved the bastard in the
chest. "You're lying. You must be lying."

"Don't make me regret taking this job." Seaton grasped
the front of Hart's jacket. He leaned in close. "I could kill
you just as easily as breathing."

A familiar voice pierced through Hart's fog of rage.

"Get your hands off of him!"

He turned from Seaton.

Lucy was barreling toward them at full steam. She snatched up his cane from where it rested against the bench, and in a move smooth and practiced, she whipped it around so that the tip pressed against Seaton's throat. "Step back, you fiend."

Seaton's eyes widened, but he was surprisingly calm. He let go of Hart's jacket. His lips curved up into a smile. "A friend of yours?"

Hart took a step back and closed his eyes as he tried to rein in his emotions. Tried to find some balance in a world turned upside down.

"Yes. Yes, I am. No one attacks my friends." Lucy's eyes blazed with anger. "Get away from him."

Hart finally managed to find his voice. "For Christ's sake, Lucy. What are you doing here?"

"I was just taking a walk and saw this man attacking you."

"He wasn't attacking me. Well, not yet. Here, pass me back my walking stick, please."

She gave Seaton a wary once-over before lowering Hart's cane and handing it back to him. Hart looked over her shoulder and saw her maid cowering by the bushes about twenty feet away. Poor girl. How did she keep up with her mistress?

Seaton smoothed out the lapels of his black jacket. "Perhaps you don't need me after all with this hell cat at your side."

"Don't call her that." Hart growled.

He glanced around. The park was blessedly empty. The last thing they needed was to create a scene. What had he been thinking to lose his composure like that in a public place? He needed to get Lucy away from here. He would deal with Seaton later.

"Walk me home?" He asked Lucy, winging out his elbow.

Lucy put her arm through his, and he led her away from Seaton. "Who is that?" she whispered.

"Mr. Seaton."

"After you calm down," Seaton called out from behind them. "Find me if you want answers. Blood is thicker and all that."

Hart twisted around to throw out his own rejoinder, but the man was gone. Disappeared like mist.

"That was Mr. Seaton? Did he tell you about the building?" Lucy said.

Hart just shook his head. "Can we just walk?"

She nodded. They fell into an easy stride as they exited the park. The quiet of the trees bleeding away to sounds of carriages and people as they reached Pall Mall Avenue. Muscle memory had Hart making his way to the right corner of St. James Square where Hartwick House lay. He needed to be home. A gentleman would have escorted Lucy and her maid home first, but right now, he was reluctant to let go of the anchor she provided. Her familiar scent of orange blossoms and the strong grip of her hand on his arm soothed the incessant hammering of his thoughts. He would have a carriage take them home. As they entered the house, the cool, quiet interior hit his soul like a balm. *Home.* Hart drew in a deep breath.

Townson hurried over to take their things. Had the man said something? Hart couldn't focus. He felt rooted to the spot as he stared up at an ugly painting of a pack of hounds running through a bucolic scene that hung on the wall above the first landing. Lucy was right; the decor was so bland. There wasn't a single thing that indicated the house belonged to him. Everything was just as it had been when he was a lad. It was a house full of ghosts. Ghosts, which apparently, he'd known hardly at all. He scrubbed a hand down over his face. God, what a day.

"Townson, a bottle of my best brandy, to the study," he said.

"A tea tray, Townson," Lucy contradicted. "Perhaps a splash of brandy in his grace's cup." She gripped his elbow. "Come on, Hart, it's time to tell me all about your day."

He stared down at her hand. The hell if he wanted to talk about his day over tea. "Townson, have the carriage take Miss Middleton and her maid home. And bring the brandy to my study." As Hart strode down the corridor, he could hear the clicking of her shoes on the marble floor behind him.

"Hart, wait."

Ignoring her, he strode into his study. Stopping midway

across the room, he looked around. Stuffed animal heads and oil paintings depicting men on horseback following packs of hunting dogs hung along the walls. Hart preferred holidays at the sea to weeks spent hunting in the country. He spun slowly in a circle. A large wooden model of his father's yacht, Hart's yacht now, sat atop the mantle. He always got sick aboard that damn boat. Everything in this room was a reflection of his father. Why hadn't he changed anything in the last five years?

His eye caught sight of a porcelain dog that sat on top of the curio cabinet across from the desk. It was a hideous piece. The dog sat on its haunches with its paws in the air. It was dressed in a sailor uniform, a jaunty hat perched crookedly on its head. Two oversized eyes seemed to stare into his soul. His father had thought it hilarious, but Hart had always hated it. Why was it still there, staring at him day after day? He crossed, snatched up the offending object, and tossed it into the fireplace. The porcelain shattered against the cold brick interior.

"Hart!" Lucy exclaimed. "Please tell me what's wrong."

"Nothing." He turned to face her.

She was so fresh and pretty, always glowing with some inner fire. The antithesis of how he felt most days. Hart wished to reach for her, if only to be near that sense of surety and optimism she wore so naturally.

She stood with one hip resting against the side of his desk, her arms crossed across her chest. "I'm not leaving until you tell me what happened in the park with Mr. Seaton. It certainly didn't appear that nothing was wrong."

He couldn't possibly explain to her all that he had found out today. He hadn't even had time to let the shift in his reality sink in. He pinched the bridge of his nose. Why was she always pressing him? Why did she even care about a temperamental bastard like him?

He crossed to her. "I don't want to talk. I don't want to explain my foul mood. Go away, Lucy."

Her eyes went wide, but she shook her head. "No, I won't leave you to get drunk and sulk."

"Why not? Why do you care what I do?"

"Hart, of course I care about you!" She stepped closer.

Her proximity set off alarm bells in his head. His whole body tightened as he tried to keep from pulling her close.

"Why are you always pushing at me? What do you want?" he growled.

His gaze lowered to her mouth. He desperately wanted to kiss her. To lose himself in her for a few moments of peace from his churning thoughts. But she had been angry at him the last time he'd kissed her.

"I want..." Lucy stared up at him, the blue of her irises like the delicate petals of larkspur in a country field.

Pink stained her cheeks and her rosy lips parted as if to say more, but she didn't finish her thought. He couldn't tear his gaze from her mouth. She sucked her bottom lip between her teeth. That small action caused his groin to tighten in response.

Just one taste. Hart slid a hand around her nape. He took

his time lowering his lips to hers, watching for any sign of displeasure. But she stepped forward, erasing the space between them, so he captured her mouth and sank into the kiss. Her soft lips slid against his with purpose, exploring and nipping. Setting him on fire.

He'd been so wrong. There was no peace to be had in this embrace. This kiss called forth a fucking inferno of need. He groaned and wrapped his arms around her. God, she felt perfect tucked against him. With every brush of her hot tongue against his, his cock hardened in response. Her hands slid from his shoulders to tangle in his hair.

Hart picked her up under her backside and set her on top of the desk. "Is this want you want?" he murmured against her mouth. *Please say yes.*

"Yes." Her fingers tightened in his hair.

He moved his lips across her cheek as he lifted her skirts high enough so that he could press himself between her spread legs. "You shouldn't play with fire, brat, or it might consume you. It's been a long time since I had a woman in my arms."

She shook her head. "I don't want to hear about your harem, Hart." Grasping his face between her hands, she took possession of his mouth.

God, the passion inside this one small woman, perhaps it was he who would be consumed. He thrust his hips forward against her skirts. Too many clothes... He reached down to skim his fingers along her silk-covered calves and slowly pushed her skirts higher.

"Ahem, Your Grace." Townson's voice carried from the doorway.

Hart tore his lips from hers and dragged in a ragged breath. Lucy's breasts rose and fell rapidly as she also sucked in much needed air.

"The carriage for Miss Middleton is ready," Townson's voice was like a deluge of cold water pouring over his head.

"Thank you, Townson. She will be right out."

He heard the click of the door as it closed. He leaned his forehead against Lucy's. "You should go home."

"But you haven't told me—"

"You should go home." He reiterated as he tugged her skirts down.

What had he been thinking? Grabbing her around the waist, he picked her up off the edge of his desk and put her on her feet. He had not been thinking, only lusting. He was one giant mess of throbbing emotions. Lucy did not deserve to be mauled by him.

He tucked an errant lock of her hair behind her ear. "Thank you for caring. I'm sorry I'm such a miserable bastard." Then he gave her hand a tug and pulled her across the room before she could say anything else.

As he opened the door, she turned to look up at him. Her mouth opened to say something, but he placed a finger over her lips to stop her. Then he gave her a push through the threshold and firmly shut the door.

Leaning back against the solid wood, he closed his eyes. *Dear Lord*, Lucy was temptation itself. Regret wound its way through his gut. He needed to stay away from her if she was ever to have a chance at a future with a nice young gentle-man. Perhaps the paper had been right. Ruin seeks to ruin.

CHAPTER SEVENTEEN

"AND THEN HE kissed me." Lucy lay back on the blanket Adeline had provided and stared up at the stars.

"Again?" Her friend's astonished voice came from next to her.

The night air was warmer than usual for early summer, but Lucy loved it. She stretched like a cat, twisting her neck to look up at Adeline, who stood a few feet away next to her telescope. This was Adeline's retreat atop the Earl of Rawlings's residence. The small terrace jutted out from the roof about ten feet by ten-foot square and was bordered by a decorative stone parapet. They had accessed the terrace through a window in the attic. South facing, Adeline said it allowed her perfect unobstructed views of the constellations. Lucy left the scientific calculations up to Addie. She just loved gazing up at the stars.

"Yes. One minute we were arguing, and then he was kissing me senseless. It all happened so quickly."

"Did you want him to kiss you? You weren't under any duress?" Adeline came to sit next to her on the blanket. She wrapped her arms around her knees.

"No. It was a surprise, but I definitely wanted him to kiss me. He is a puzzle. I always thought—no, I knew my feelings for him were unrequited. I had convinced myself to let go of my infatuation. But these kisses have me second guessing what Hart feels for me."

Was she a fool? She had loved him from afar for so long it was hard to parse out what their new relationship was evolving into. He certainly was not the charming rogue he used to be. But his raw edges didn't make him any less appealing. She liked being the one person that could make him smile from behind all that growling and glowering.

"What was it like?" Adeline's eyes were bright with curiosity.

"Like standing too close to a bonfire. His kisses feel desperate like he can't help himself. I just don't know what to make of him these days. Perhaps he is just lonely." She frowned at the night sky. "Then his butler came into the room and interrupted."

"Didn't the butler knock first?"

Lucy shrugged one shoulder. "Most probably. If he did, we didn't hear it." She sighed. "Kissing the duke was utterly consuming. I probably wouldn't have noticed if the house had come tumbling down around us. But now I don't know what to do about him. Do I come clean about my false beau? Do I let him think I have someone else and make him jealous? Does all this make me the most horrible tart?"

"You are asking the wrong friend. Save my brother, I have no experience with the opposite sex. I am entirely invisible to men. I wouldn't know how to make one jealous if I tried."

Lucy sat up. "You are not invisible. Don't say that. You are brilliant and lovely."

Adeline rested her chin on her drawn-up knees. "I overheard my brother and father arguing over my dowry the other day. My father has lost money on some shipping venture, and he was complaining that the dowry set aside for me by my grandmother is untouchable. He said the only thing to be done was to marry me off to someone wealthy."

"That's terrible. Doesn't he wish you to have a husband that you like?"

Adeline snorted. "I don't think my father cares two wits about me. He only sees me as useful because I take care of my mother, and now, I guess, to sell me off into an advantageous marriage. At least George stood up for me."

"We will just have to find you a good husband before your father picks out one for you."

"And how will we do that? I told you I am invisible. It doesn't help that I hardly ever get to go to social functions because of Mama's health."

Lucy lay back down to think. Addie followed suit, and the two of them watched the stars for a bit. "Wait, what if we could generate some interest in you? We could start a rumor or two about you, nothing too scandalous but interesting enough that gentlemen will sit up and pay attention."

Addie's jaw dropped open. "You want to spread rumors about me?"

"Yes. Just think, if there was a rumor, for instance, that you had been seen speaking with a top-notch rake at the opera or riding with a dashing gentleman through the park. That would get people talking. Other men's interest would be piqued. Men always want women who appear to be sought after."

Addie appeared to mull the idea over. "I guess it couldn't hurt my reputation, seeing as I have no reputation to speak of. But who would we use? Wouldn't they have something to say about it?"

"We'll choose a gentleman who already splashes about in the scandal rags. That way, he will hardly notice one more rumor. Someone who your family doesn't know. We should ask Violet. She has a knack for knowing all the good gossip."

Adeline turned her head to face Lucy, her lips curved up into a tentative smile. "Well, here's to bad reputations and interesting prospects."

"Here, here!" Lucy turned her head to stare back up at the heavens. A shooting star raced across the sky. "Did you see that?"

Adeline was already scrambling to her feet. She grabbed up her notebook and charcoal pencil. Another shooting star raced across the inky night. "It's begun! I knew the meteor shower would be tonight. My calculations are never wrong."

Lucy grinned. Adeline might be shy in mixed company, but she had no trouble acknowledging her own abilities when it came to science. If only small talk at society functions could include discussions of astronomy or physics, her friend would be popular indeed.

"Do you ever imagine what you would do with your dowry if the money was actually yours to use?" she asked her friend.

Only the scratching of Addie's pencil across the page could be heard for several moments before her friend replied. "Hmm. I think I would buy a house outside of London and have a room made with a glass ceiling so I could observe the stars in the winter without freezing my fingers and toes."

Lucy chuckled. "I would open a school to teach ladies how to defend themselves against attack. Like how I taught you and Violet."

"Yes, I still remember them. Even if I have never had the opportunity to employ them." Addie sounded somewhat disappointed.

"Adeline, hopefully you will never have to. A real gentleman would never attack a lady. Unlike that snake, Fitzwilliam. I heard from Lady Weatherby that he has been out of town licking his wounds at his country estate ever since Hart refused his suit." Lucy grinned. "Good riddance. Hopefully, I will never have to see him again."

CHAPTER EIGHTEEN

HART SUPPRESSED A frustrated growl as he ascended the steps to White's. Lucy had ruined his plan for an evening of drowning his emotions in a bottle of brandy. She was right; this was no time for sulking. He had a mission, and more than ever, it was time to gather information. He hated it when Lucy was right. He hated how much he wanted to be a better version of himself so that he could gain back the esteem she once had for him.

And how much he craved the taste of her. *Fuck.* He wiped the back of a hand across his mouth. Tonight was not about his unrequited lust for a girl who was not for him. It was about finding out what business deal had led to his father's death. Comstock, or rather Lord Galey, had agreed to meet him for dinner and he hoped to gain his observations about their fathers' mutual friends.

He handed his hat to the attendant at the front desk. The young man's eyes widened in horror as his gaze flitted over Hart's face. Every muscle in Hart's body tightened in response. Would he ever get used to how others reacted to his scarred visage? Would it ever not sting like a lash against his ego every single time?

"Is Lord Galey here? I'm to join him for dinner." Hart bit out.

"Yes, Your Grace. Right this way." The attendant hurried ahead of him down the corridor.

The walls papered in a dark green damask and trimmed with dark wood always made Hart imagine the inside of a well-appointed coffin. Even the air felt staid and stuffy. To his right, the attendant opened a door to a private dining room. Hart strode inside to find Galey swirling a glass of red wine in one hand while he flirted with the wine butler. The butler laughed at something Galey said, but when the man realized Hart had entered the room, his posture straightened, and his face flushed.

"Good evening, Lord Galey," Hart said. He approached the table and sat across from his old friend.

Nonplussed, Galey sent a bright smile to the butler. "Pour my friend here a glass of this excellent wine. You have a superlative palate and always make the best recommendations."

"That will be all for now." Hart dismissed the man after his wine was poured.

He hadn't come out to watch Galey pick out his bed companion for later tonight. Besides, it just reminded him how frustrated his earlier interlude with Lucy had left him. Self-denial did not come easily to him.

The door closed with a soft click.

Galey shifted his gaze to Hart. "You probably scared him away with your scowling face."

Hart raised an eyebrow at Galey's petulant tone. "I thought you had already slept with all the employees here."

Galey grinned. "He's new."

Hart laughed. Galey was a hedonist. He swived with equal opportunity any person willing to be adventurous in bed, be it male, female, young, or more experienced. He had always been discreet with his love life, but Hart had to wonder if that was still true now that his father had passed.

"So, Your Grace, thank you for the dinner invitation." Galey raised his glass. "And what do I owe this honor?"

"What do you mean? I am dipping my toes back into society. I just wanted to catch up."

"Hmmm, I don't believe that for a moment. You liked me least of all, Grisham was always your favorite."

"Grisham was everyone's favorite."

"Not after he screwed us all by winning that bet. And then to add insult to injury, marrying the girl."

Hart chuckled. Damn, it was nice to spend time with his old friends. Even if they were all assholes.

He took a swallow of wine. "I hoped I could get your opinions on some of our father's friends. As you know, I have been looking into the time period around my father and brother's deaths. This winter I found a letter, an angry threatening one, among my father's papers. It was unsigned but had this symbol at the bottom."

Hart pulled out the stamp and handed it to Galey.

Galey turned it over in his hand. "It's their club from school."

"Yes, that's what Blackpool told me. You knew about it?"

"My father talked about their special club all the time. The bond, the friendship, blah blah." He passed the stamp back to Hart and took a swallow of his wine.

"Well, I think the bonds had grown tenuous. This letter writer was quite angry over a broken agreement. Telling my father that he must honor their agreement or else."

"Or else what?" Galey asked.

Hart shrugged. "Satisfaction? Retribution? It was all vague in that respect, but the emotion was clear. I think the reason they were found dead on the Strand was because of this broken deal. And your father's knowledge of the details leads me to believe it was one of their club."

Galey rubbed at his jaw. "My father always couched it as these men being like brothers. Do you really think one of them would kill another?"

"I don't know. I wasn't even aware the club existed. My father certainly never shared anything about his life with me. But when I met with Blackpool, I asked him straight out what had caused a rift between him and my father a decade ago, and he replied that my father had an affair with his wife. So not all the bonds of friendship were that strong."

"Well, damn."

There was a knock at the door. "Come in." Hart called out.

Two attendants rolled in a cart with two dinner plates piled high with roasted chicken, root vegetables, and gravy. Once they served, and refilled the wine glasses, they exited as quietly as they had entered.

Galey speared a piece of chicken. "I knew you had scared away the handsome one."

"Sorry." But Hart wasn't sorry in the least. He had no inclination to watch Galey try and seduce the blasted waiter. "My question to you tonight is what are your opinions about the men in the club? I know in addition to our fathers, there was Lord Blackpool, Lord Rawlings, Lord Lavensham, and Lord Griffen."

"And Lord Fleming." Galey said around a bite of food. "I feel like there was one more. That my father said there were eight. But I cannot think of who it was. Perhaps they died."

Hart stared down into his glass of wine as he mulled over what he knew about the men his father had been close with. "Blackpool admitted freely that he hated my father for what he had done. There was plenty of bitterness in his eyes, but if he were the murderer why would he admit to the bad blood between them. That alone has me crossing him off my list."

"Rawlings seems the most likely to be upset about a broken deal. That man is perennially in debt. My father used to lend him money all the time. But as far as mean bastards go, Lavensham takes the cake. Griffen also has plenty to lose. His heir is as mentally unstable as they come. I try to avoid that reprobate whenever we end up at the same establishments. Do you know he used to torture small animals for sport when we were at Eton? Kept some sick tally of it." Galey shuddered.

"I had no idea," Hart said.

He remembered Lord Griffen as a dour man. He'd never seen him smile; even when his father had everyone else laughing with his stories. But Hart had seen the two men together often, sharing a drink or riding out. Lord Griffen's family did not come to London with him often from his estate in Norfolk. Hart couldn't even remember how many offspring the man had.

"Well, its kept pretty hushed up. I know because he was in my year and lived in my dormitory. Perrin can pretend to be charming when he wants to be."

"What about Fleming?" Hart asked. "I remember him from my younger days, but I haven't seen him since my father's funeral."

"Word is he has some lung disease. I think he is ill a lot. Sort of a harmless type. nondescript, quiet."

They ate in silence for a while and Hart parsed through what Galey had told him. It matched what little Galey's father had said to Hart in the carriage that night. Powerful men, a betrayal, that was the word that the older Lord Galey had used. Hart would have to go back to the ledgers and continue his search for a business dealing that would connect to one of these men.

"Hartwick." Galey grabbed his attention. "Be careful. If someone was willing to kill a good friend in retribution and another to cover his secret, that man must be desperate or a straight-up killer. Either way, you are making yourself their next target by asking questions."

Hart rubbed a hand along his side, thinking of the gash

that was still healing there. He nodded. He would be careful, but he had no intention of backing off. Nothing would stop him from finding out the truth.

～～

AFTER DINNER, HART and Galey strolled down the hall to see what was happening in the main room. Almost immediately, Hart spotted Lord Griffen and his son at a card table at the far end of the room. "My luck is holding. I see Griffen over there playing cards. I think I will go ask him some questions."

Galey frowned. "Remember what I said. Exercise caution when revealing what you suspect. I certainly won't join you with Perrin at the table. I'll just go track down my handsome wine butler." He clapped Hart on the back and then headed for the long bar at the other end of the room.

One of the club's managers hurried over. "Your Grace, we haven't seen you in a long time. What is your pleasure tonight?"

Hart nodded at the back table where Griffen sat. "What is Lord Griffen playing back there?"

"Faro, I believe."

Perfect. "I will have a glass of ale while I play."

"Right away, Your Grace."

He made his way carefully to the table in the back. "Good evening, Lord Griffen. Mind if I join you?" Hart pulled out a chair and sat without waiting for an answer.

Lord Griffen gave a nod. "Of course, Your Grace. I wondered if you would track me down next."

"Deal me in the next round." Hart sat back as they finished their round. His glass of ale arrived, and he took a deep gulp. Refreshing and perfectly balanced, he enjoyed his drink. After the next hand was dealt, he played for a while without asking any questions. Along with Griffen and his son, there were three other men playing. Hart slowly began to win each hand, and the pile of coins in front of him grew. He held back initially to keep Griffen on the hook as he slowly pushed the bets higher. Two of the men got up in disgust after six hands. They stomped off to nurse their bad luck at the bar.

Hart knew it hadn't been bad luck. Both men had been easy to read. He'd spotted their tells within the first five minutes of play. If one understood the number of each suit that was in play versus the number already down on the table, and they paid attention to their opponent's tells, it was easy to win. He pushed up the bet to triple the last hand. The last of the three men, a young buck clearly out of his depth, showed some intelligence and folded.

Griffen turned to his son. "Why don't you take your friend and go get something to drink."

The two younger men got up and wandered away. Griffen cut the deck and shuffled. "Ask me what you want, Hartwick. I'll do my best to answer."

Hart took another sip of his beer. "I simply want to know what happened to my father and brother. I am working to piece together the events of that night."

"I did not see your father the night he was killed. I'm sorry to say I don't know what they were doing in that part of town."

"Do you know of any business deals that my father was involved in at the time of his death? Anything that he complained about? Had received threats over?"

Griffen shook his head. "No, not that he told me. Your father had more money than Midas; he was a consummate man of leisure. Rawlings was always trying to get us to invest in one thing or another, but your father was not much interested in business ventures." He flipped a card back and forth between his hands. "Their deaths were a terrible tragedy. They were at the wrong place at the wrong time."

"I never believed that their deaths were a random act of street violence." Hart had received that same prevarication from all the men he talked to. Perhaps it was time to show some of his cards. "The night Galey and I were attacked in his carriage has only reinforced this belief. He knew that their deaths were no random act."

Griffen's expression darkened. "What are you playing at, boy? What did that fool Galey fill your head with? It was simply bad luck. Your father probably fucked over the wrong woman, and she cursed the Hartwick line."

His father's friends certainly knew more of his father's weaknesses than Hart ever had. Had it been about a woman? Had Robert tried to help and gotten mixed up in some sordid scenario? A jealous husband? A mistress unhappy with being discarded? Hart studied Griffen's face. The man's angry expression had cleared. The placid look he'd worn during the game was back in place. Hart's gut was telling him the man knew something more, but Griffen had no tells which showed Hart he was lying.

Griffen set down the deck of cards on the table with a slap. "Listen, it's tough luck what happened to your family. But you are still alive. You should be focused on the future, not the past."

Hart scowled at the advice that he had heard over and over. Nobody seemed to understand he was stuck. Mired in the sins of the past. He couldn't even fathom what his future could look like right now. This was his purpose. He had to know the truth before he could find a way forward.

He rose and collected his winnings. "Thank you for speaking with me, Lord Griffen. Good night."

CHAPTER NINETEEN

H ART SWALLOWED HARD as he approached the front of the receiving line. There were too many people crammed into the Bartleby's front foyer. Under his evening jacket, a line of sweat rolled down his back. The tight-fitting style of the evening wear rubbed against the scars on his shoulders every time he moved his arm, irritating the sensitive skin. The cravat that had taken his valet more than fifteen blasted minutes to tie was strangling him. Why had he accepted the Bartleby's invitation?

Trudy's hand squeezed his forearm, and he glanced down at her. She winked saucily. They were the reason he was here. He owed Lucy an opportunity to refute the rumors that he was some damaged beast luring her into ruin. And after his lack of control the other day, he needed to prove it to Lucy as well. He looked over his shoulder where Lucy stood behind them chatting with Lord Blakely's daughter. Her eyes flitted to his, and a small smile played across her pink lips. She looked stunning tonight in a dress of icy blue silk.

The line moved, and they stepped in front of their hosts.

"Good evening, Your Grace. We are so pleased that you have chosen to attend our little soiree," said Lady Bartleby.

"Thank you so much for inviting us," he replied automatically.

"When we saw you at the theatre, and your aunt mentioned you wanted to support Miss Middleton's season, we knew our ball would be the perfect opportunity for you to be seen."

"Seen doing what?" he replied with a frown.

"Why supporting her in her season, of course. There will be many eligible gentlemen here tonight. My parties are famous for attracting the younger set." Lady Bartleby gave a wide smile. "Enjoy your evening."

A growl of displeasure rose in his chest at the thought of Lucy dancing or even talking with any *eligible* men.

"Thank you, dear." Trudy dipped her head elegantly. "I'm sure we will. You throw the best fêtes." Then she grasped his arm and tugged him away, Lucy joining them on Trudy's other side.

"No scowling, young man. Our task tonight, my dears, is to continue to refute the rumors that your interest in Lucy is anything but magnanimous. You must be perfectly behaved." She glanced pointedly at Lucy. "And Hartwick, you must mingle and speak with people. Let us dispel that nonsense about you being a monstrous recluse luring hapless maidens to their ruin."

Lucy looked across at him and raised one finely arched eyebrow. He rolled his eyes in return. Surely, one tiny tidbit in a scandal rag from more than a week ago couldn't be all that dramatic. They slowly ascended the marble staircase that led to the first-floor ballroom. Hart had to concentrate in order not to miss a step with his right foot and end up stumbling like some damn fool. The irony was that in the past, his stumbling would have been chalked up too much drink and dismissed. But now, he couldn't bear to see pity in people's eyes if he were to miss a step and bump into someone.

When they entered the ballroom, it was appalling how hot the packed room felt. His sense of being trapped was immediate as they waded into the crowd. Going to the theater had been tolerable because of the private box, but this crush made his pulse race and sweat break out across his brow.

Trudy turned to face him and Lucy. "Why don't you two dance?"

Hart grimaced. "I simply cannot." He motioned to his eye.

"Oh yes, of course. Then how about you take her on a stroll about the room? I need to go speak with some friends." She glanced to the side at three matrons who stood nearby. The ladies' fans flapped wildly as they stared in their direction. "You two go walk around, smile, and be polite. Go on." She shooed them with her hands.

Lucy looked up at him and shrugged. He offered his elbow. Lucy laid her hand lightly on his arm, and they walked away.

They strolled down the side of the long, narrow ballroom. Along one side, gilt-edged floor-to-ceiling mirrors reflected candlelight from the row of chandeliers that hung from the ornately painted ceiling. He and Lucy skirted dancers and passed guests seated on green damask settees along the edges of the room. The further along they walked, the more the tightness in his throat increased. In an effort to distract himself from the growing panic clawing at his chest, he caught Lucy's eye. "The lady you were speaking with in line, is she a friend of yours?"

"Yes, that was my good friend, Lady Violet Blakely. Why do you ask?"

"I met her the other day. I went to see her father about the symbol, the Knot of Isis, I mean. I saw her speaking with your Mr. Murdoch."

Murdoch had definitely been flirting with her friend Violet outside her father's study. Hart wondered if it would be petty of him to tell Lucy. Probably.

"You met Mr. Murdoch?" Lucy's hand rose to her throat.

"Don't look so nervous," Hart said. "He seemed perfectly nice if a bit obsequious."

"Well, he was meeting a duke and the one that watches over me. Of course, he would be."

"He didn't mention his connection to you at all. I thought it odd, but I didn't want to press him in front of Blackpool. And your friend seemed a bit scattered. Everything about the visit was strange, to say the least." He was still reeling from what he had learned about his father. Although why he should be so surprised, he didn't know. Ton marriages were infamous for their infidelity. But to betray a friend showed a lack of character in a man that Hart had always looked up to as a paragon of right and wrong.

"Perhaps she was also surprised to encounter a duke in the house. Violet is usually delightful. She is my only bright spot in this whole season. We commiserate as her parents are also parading her around to find her a match."

The tension he felt melted as he chuckled at her view of the season. "In my experience, most debutants are excited about the husband hunt."

"Is that so? And have you been hunted then?" She bumped her shoulder gently against his arm.

"Of course. I am a duke, after all. I suppose I understand your reluctance to Trudy's matchmaking since you already have a husband picked out."

"I do? Oh yes, that is exactly it. I don't need anyone else. Mr. Murdoch is the one for me."

They hit the end of the room and made a turn to reach the other side. An older couple, Lord and Lady Dalmore, nodded as they passed. "Evening, Your Grace."

"Good evening." Hart nodded politely but did not stop. He needed another turn around the room before he was ready to actually converse with anyone.

Lucy gave him a quizzical look as he whisked her past the couple.

He shrugged.

Lucy smiled and patted his arm. "Let's get some punch. It is dreadfully hot in here."

Hart nodded, relieved she wasn't going to make him

make small talk just yet. They hadn't gone but ten feet when a red-faced Lord Fitzwilliam stepped out in front of them. His fists were clenched at his sides. "You bastard."

What the hell? Hart glowered. "Language, Fitzwilliam. We are in mixed company."

"You just wanted her for yourself. You refuse my suit just so you could snatch her into your clutches."

Hart crossed his arms in front of his chest. "I refused your suit because the lady did not want your attentions nor your manhandling, you little weasel."

Lucy stood frozen next to him, her eyes wide with shock, darted back and forth between him and Fitzwilliam. Conversation in the vicinity ceased as everyone turned to hear what Fitzwilliam was yelling about.

Hart leaned close to the man. "I expressly told you to never come within fifty feet of Miss Middleton ever again. Get out of our way," he growled.

But the idiot would not stop his fool mouth. Fitzwilliam turned to Lucy. "You little tart. Flirting with me but whoring around with him."

Lucy came to life, her cheeks blazed with color. "How dare you! I would never waste my time with the likes of you. You assaulted me in the gardens at the Ponsonby's. You are nothing but a desperate fortune hunter."

Hart's first inclination to pummel the man into the ground was replaced by admiration for Lucy's fiery set down.

He smirked. "How is your chin, mate? She's got quite the right hook."

"You monster." Fitzwilliam lunged forward.

Hart raised his cane in front of himself in an automatic defensive motion, but his opponent still managed to shove him hard. He stumbled backward several steps.

"Hart!" Lucy cried out.

She stepped between the two of them with her arms outstretched, her palms facing up. But Fitzwilliam, already in attack mode, had a fist in forward motion. He made contact with Lucy's face and sent her falling backward, landing on her backside at Hart's feet. Someone in the crowd screamed.

Hart's vision went red. He reached out and grasped the stunned and sputtering Fitzwilliam by the front of his jacket. Then he clocked him out cold with one satisfying punch.

Hart fell to his knees next to Lucy. "Are you hurt? Where did he hurt you?"

She sat with one hand over her right eye. The other was glassy with tears. "He hit me. I can't believe he hit me."

"I will kill him." He glanced behind him.

Two men were attending to Fitzwilliam, who had groggily come to. The volume of conversation around them rose to a crescendo. The onlookers were a suffocating circle around them. Lucy's hand grasped his in a panicked grip. He had to get her off the floor and away from here, to somewhere he could assess her injury. Somewhere he could breathe again. Where Lucy would be safe.

He scooped her up into his arms and rose, leaving his cane on the floor. Lucy wrapped her arms around his neck and buried her face in his jacket. His shoulder screamed in protest. But he would not put her down until he had her safely away from the gawking crowd.

Hart strode across the dance floor, the dancers parting like the Red Sea.

Lord Bartleby and his wife rushed toward them. "What's happened?"

"Fitzwilliam struck her."

"No," Lady Bartleby gasped.

Trudy appeared at his elbow. "Oh dear, oh dear!" she exclaimed.

"Fitzwilliam was attacking me, and unfortunately, Miss Middleton got in between us."

"Oh dear…" Trudy's fan waved back and forth like a deranged hummingbird. "Oh dear," she muttered again.

He addressed Lord Bartleby. "We need a private room to assess her injury. And some cool water and a cloth to make a compress for her eye."

"Of course, Your Grace. Right this way."

CHAPTER TWENTY

THE BARTLEBYS LED them to an empty receiving room, where Hart gently deposited Lucy onto a chaise. Lady Bartleby moved about the room, lighting candles, bathing the room with soft light. Lucy lay flat, staring up as Hart towered over her, his harsh features etched with concern. She attempted to scoot herself up to a sitting position, but Hart laid a firm hand on her shoulder.

"Don't move," he commanded. "How much does it hurt?"

Her eye throbbed like a beating heart and hurt to open the eyelid. Lucy sank back against the cushions. "It hurts something horrible. I still can't believe that he hit me. Why do men do this to each other for sport?" The pillow behind her head was soft and forgiving as the ache in her eye spread to thrum throughout her head.

Hart chuckled. "Only you could make me laugh when I am this furious." He sat down on the edge of the chaise next to her hip. "Can you open it and tell me if you can see my finger." He held up his pointer finger in front of her face.

She ordered her eyelid to open and blinked several times as she tried to focus with that eye on Hart's finger. "It feels too swollen to open very much. But I can see with it."

"All right. Can you follow my finger without moving your head, just with your eyes?" His finger went slowly right, then back again all the way to the left.

She felt foolish lying on her back watching his finger move around above her. "It's fine. I see you. Can I sit up now?"

"Yes. Your movement of the eyeball is good. I don't think he damaged it. But I'm afraid to say that your eye is definitely starting to bruise."

"Wonderful." Lucy shut her eyes. "Now, would someone explain to me what just happened in there? I know that Fitzwilliam is delusional, but his attack was out of character even for him."

Trudy stopped her pacing. Lucy could smell her perfume as she came to a stop by the chaise where Lucy lay. She peered out of her left eye to find Trudy glowering across at Hart.

"What exactly did the man say to you?" she demanded.

"He said I refused his suit so I could snatch her into my clutches." His wry tone melted into another chuckle.

"Clearly, he reads the scandal pages too." Trudy sighed and then turned her attention to Lady Bartleby. "Eloise, thank you so much for your discretion. Could I have a moment alone with my family?"

"Of course, dear. Whatever you need," Lady Bartleby replied. A light knock at the door sent Lady Bartleby across the room to answer. "Ah, here is the compress for Miss

Middleton's eye. Thank you, Mildred." She took a bowl and cloth from the maid and passed it to Hart. "I'll leave you then. Ring if you need anything, and I expect to hear from you very soon, Trudy. You well know how many questions I will be asked." She gave Aunt Trudy a loaded glance from under her eyelashes before quitting the room.

Hart again took his seat next to her on the chaise. This time, Lucy managed to push herself up to a reclining position, leaning back against the tufted backrest. He dipped the cloth in water to soak, carefully wrang out the excess, and then placed it gently on her injured eye. "That should help, I hope."

Lucy held the cool compress against her eye and sighed. It did feel good. She glanced at Trudy with her good eye. The older woman's expression was grim. Her brow furrowed and her lips turned down into a frown.

She paced away across the plush carpet and then turned and marched back to them. Her fan jabbed the air in front of Hart's chest. "You will have to marry her."

"Pardon?" Hart's lips drew into a thin line.

"What?" Lucy's mouth fell open.

"Two men came to blows in public over Lucy's affections. She must marry one of them or be painted forever as a loose woman. If not you, then she will have to marry Fitzwilliam."

"No!" She and Hart said in tandem.

Hart rose and placed his hands on his hips. "You cannot order us to marry. A scuffle over a misunderstanding is no reason to marry."

"Scandal is always a reason to marry. It is the reason many marriages happen."

The panic on Hart's face was entirely unflattering. "I'm not fit to marry anyone right now." He glanced down at her. "And what about Lucy's choices? What about her beau?"

Good Lord. Lucy glared at Hart as best she could muster with only one eye as her lies reared their ugly head. She risked a glance over at Trudy.

"What beau?" Trudy asked.

"You should tell her now. Perhaps we can arrange for you to marry him quickly. Then you can have who you really want."

Lucy twisted her body toward Trudy, so her back would be to Hart. She tried her best to convey her panic at the tenuous situation with a small shake of her head. "He is a solicitor that works for Lord Blakely. We were waiting to tell anyone of our affection for each other until he had enough money to ask me to marry him." She told her lie, her foolish lie, once again. Then she lay back against the pillow, her headache at full volume now.

Oh dear, how could she marry a phantom beau when he didn't even know she existed? And Trudy was right; her reputation would be forever tarnished by tonight's incident. No respectable man would want to marry her. The thought suddenly bothered her. Without her dowry she would have to spend her life as a spinster governess teaching other people's children good manners.

Trudy's frown deepened. "That sounds like a plan for seduction, not for marriage. How could you fall for such a thing, young lady? Haven't I taught you better?"

Hart's heavy-lidded gaze raked over her. He ran a hand through his hair. Then his chest rose and fell with a deep intake of breath. "She's right. The only way to protect you is for us to marry. I can damn well recognize a rogue. I didn't want to tell you before, but I saw him flirting quite shamelessly with your friend. You would not be safe with this Mr. Murdoch. And I'm certainly not letting Fitzwilliam anywhere near you." He sat down next to her again and lifted her free hand. "What say you? Marry me?"

Her heart stuttered for a moment. Then it soared. But her mind panicked. *Do you really want him like this? Honor bound to marry you?* She searched the lines of his face. Under her scrutiny, one corner of his mouth tipped up in that wry half-smile that always made her heart flip flop. *Who cares? You will be the Duchess of Hartwick. You will have all the time in the world to make him love you.*

She lowered the compress to her lap. "Are you sure?" she whispered.

"I told you I would always protect you." He cupped her jaw, his thumb brushed across her cheek. "I'm just sorry that you are stuck with me now."

"Good." Trudy clapped her hands. "Take her home. Send the carriage back for me later. Let us see if I can course correct this disaster. What we need is a plausible story of how the two of you have fallen in love. Everyone loves a love match. Leave it to me, my dears."

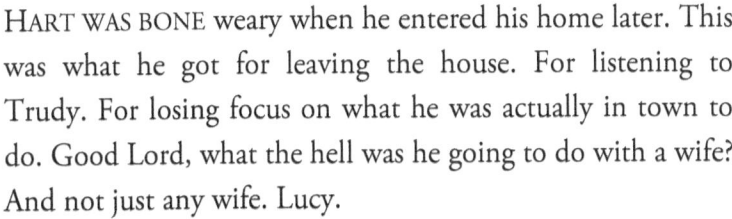

HART WAS BONE weary when he entered his home later. This was what he got for leaving the house. For listening to Trudy. For losing focus on what he was actually in town to do. Good Lord, what the hell was he going to do with a wife? And not just any wife. Lucy.

Townson took his hat and gloves. "Did you have a good evening, Your Grace?"

"It was eventful," he replied dryly. "I have news. I'm getting married."

Townson's eyebrows rose imperceptibly. He exchanged a look with an equally surprised footman as he passed Hart's effects to Timothy. "Congratulations, sir. May I ask who the lucky lady is?"

"Miss Middleton." Hart did not miss the slight quirk of a smile on the butler's face before his features settled back into their normal polite façade. "I don't know how lucky she is to be getting me as a husband. But we got into a bit of a scrape tonight, and the sensible thing to do is to marry her." He turned and headed for the stairs. At least the staff would be happy. "Bring me up a bottle of whisky," he called back over his shoulder.

After his valet helped him out of his blasted evening clothes and into the soft, silky fabric of his banyan, Hart slumped down into his favorite chair and stared into the fire in the grate. He raised the bottle of whisky to his lips. He hadn't allowed himself to indulge since the night he had been stabbed, but getting engaged to the one woman he had tried his best to avoid entangling himself with the last three years called for the mind-numbing effects of a good bottle of whisky.

The memory of his father's voice echoed in his head. "Miss Lucy Middleton is coming to stay with me. She's lost her family, and in his will, her father asked me to take care of her. You boys be respectful and kind. She has been through a terrible time. She is under our protection now."

Robert and he had exchanged a glance and a shrug. They had both been grown at twenty-four and twenty-seven and living in their own bachelor accommodations. Why did it matter if a slip of a girl shared their father's large mansion? Lucy had promptly been sent off to finishing school anyway. But it had always been Hart that his father had sent to handle the headmistress and admonish Lucy when she caused trouble. And that had been plenty.

Lucy was a spitfire, that was for sure. He chuckled. A sharp pain in his side made him wince. He pushed aside his banyan, and glancing down at the wound on his side, some blood seeped out between the stitches. Damn, he must have aggravated it tonight when he picked Lucy up off the floor. He frowned at the four-inch slash of angry red skin. Just another injury to add to his collection.

Would Lucy recoil in disgust at the raised, twisted burns and scars that marred his body? She had only seen a small portion of what covered the right side of his body when she massaged his shoulder before. Well, he didn't have to subject her to them. It wasn't necessary to take off his shirt to swive his wife. His cock agreed enthusiastically.

Thoughts of Lucy in his bed, naked beneath him, soft and eager, rose unbidden. All that silky dark hair threaded through his fingers, and her eyes luminous with desire as she begged him to make love to her. He groaned and took another swig from the bottle. He was getting ahead of the situation. Lucy was as trapped as he by their impending marriage. She had affections for another man. His gut tightened at the thought. But Murdoch's claim to her was tenuous at best. The man should have married her already if he wanted to secure her hand.

Hart would take things slowly with his new wife. First, he would give her a chance to get used to living with his surly, morose self. Let her come to his bed when she was ready. When she had let go of her feelings for that rogue Murdoch. Hart could be a bloody gentleman. Even if he wanted her with every fiber of his being.

He would focus his attention on his search for the answers to his father's death. He set the bottle down with a clank against the wooden table. Closing his eyes, he let out a long sigh. This marriage was an inconvenience, that was what it was. He didn't need a wife. What he needed was to find the killer and exact some well-deserved revenge.

CHAPTER TWENTY-ONE

TWO DAYS LATER, Hart walked over to Trudy's town-home, the special license he had procured from the archbishop in his front pocket. The butler ushered him into the foyer and Hart gave over his hat and gloves. He glanced up to find Trudy descending the stairs her expression tight with annoyance, she frowned down at him.

"You're early."

"Am I? I thought your note said eleven."

"Oh dear, yes. I'm sorry didn't I inform you? I was sure I had," she muttered. "The minister couldn't make it until one." Trudy descended the last couple of stairs and came over to look him over from head to toe. "You look very handsome in your morning suit."

Hart rolled his eyes. "Very handsome, my foot."

Trudy harrumphed. "But you needn't look as though you are about to be executed. When our guests arrive, perhaps you can look as though you are happy to be getting married and less like this was all hastily arranged to avoid scandal."

Having Lucy for a wife was going to be messy. She was not going to be happy just spending his money and leaving him alone. She was going to be around. Challenging his moods, making him go for walks, prodding him to eat his damn breakfast. He didn't need messy. Didn't want to feel the way he did about her. "But it *was* hastily arranged to avoid scandal."

"That may be, darling, but is it so terrible that you are gaining a witty, beautiful wife?"

He cleared his throat of the lump of guilt that suddenly lodged there. "No, of course not. It's just—" Hart cocked his head as a loud grunt echoed from across the foyer. It was followed by more noises of exertion and then a loud clatter. "What's that?"

Trudy sighed as she looked over his shoulder at the closed door to the music room. Which was odd, as the last time he'd looked into the room, it had been mostly empty.

His aunt raised a hand and gestured toward the door. "You might as well find out now. Perhaps you can convince her to come out and get ready for her wedding day."

"Find out what?" he asked cautiously.

"You'll see. Go on in."

Hart crossed the foyer and hesitated for a moment outside the music room with his hand on the doorknob. A rhythmic sound like the dull thud of something being struck filtered out. Carefully, he opened the door. Nothing could have surprised him more when he saw Lucy, her back to him, holding a wooden staff, both hands gripping it about six inches from each end. She repeatedly struck a large hanging bag. Her motions were graceful as she hit the bag in a pattern of precise movements.

She wore a skirt over a sleeveless shift, and he spotted the matching jacket flung over a nearby chaise. The muscles in her shoulders and arms, sinewy and lean, captured his attention as she continued to maneuver the wooden staff. He licked his lips, his throat suddenly parched at the way her muscles shifted under all that creamy skin.

Suddenly conscious that anyone in the hallway could see into the room, he quickly stepped inside and shut the door with a snap.

Lucy whirled around, her feet planted wide, and the staff pointed directly at him. Her hair was loosely knotted at her nape, and several strands from the front floated down around her flushed cheeks. The energy that poured from her hit him like a hard punch in the gut. God, she was so beautiful.

"Hart! What are you doing in here?" Her breath came out fast and shallow.

He raised a sardonic eyebrow. "That was going to be my question."

The red stain on her cheeks deepened. She looked down at her staff. Lowering it to the ground, she held it loosely in one hand as the other hand moved to her hip. "Yes, well, who let you in here anyway? I didn't hear a knock."

"I guess Trudy thought I should know that my future wife could be a danger to my person."

Lucy huffed and tucked a piece of her hair behind one ear. The bruising around her right eye was a dark bluish green. He had seen worse in the mirror in his younger days when he spent time boxing at Gentleman Jim's. But to see Lucy's porcelain complexion marred gave fire to his anger toward Fitzwilliam all over again. He was going to ruin that man. Hart tried to keep his tone light for Lucy's sake.

"I had no idea you were so fierce. I mean with something other than that sharp tongue. This explains how you handled my cane so gracefully when you threatened Seaton. Is this part of the defensive tactics you mentioned?"

"When I was young, there was an incident while my father was away. Some local thugs thought my mother was the perfect target; she was assaulted." Her eyes clouded with sadness. "Afterward, my father insisted on teaching both my mother and me some defensive skills. Basic fighting skills. How to escape a hold." Her eyes drifted down to the front of his pants. "Vulnerable places to strike at someone bigger than you. Learning to fight with the staff was something I picked up in Italy two summers ago."

"That was the tutor I paid for? I thought a trip to the continent was for culture and self-improvement."

"It was self-improving." She grinned. "I saw some men fighting in the square as a demonstration during a festival and became entranced. Now I use it to expend anger and alter my mood when I am having a bad day. Plus, it is just plain fun."

She stood tall and powerful with that staff in her hand like some ancient goddess. Hart couldn't stop his gaze from traveling over the length of her from her strong shoulders down to the tantalizing view of her decolletage through the summer weight white shift and all the way down to the sturdy brown half boots she wore on her feet.

She glanced down and seemed to realize how little she was wearing. With a small squeak, Lucy turned and strode over to the chaise to grab her jacket.

Hart followed her, coming to a stop just behind her. Lucy froze and gripped the garment to her chest.

He bent low next to her ear. "I was just admiring the beautiful lines of your muscles. I have never seen a woman exude such strength."

A small shiver accompanied a long exhale from Lucy. He desperately wanted to kiss the hollow right below her ear. To feel her shiver again against his lips. But he meant to take things slowly, and at this moment, his blood was running far too hot. He stepped back so she could slip her arms into the jacket. Once she buttoned up the front, Lucy turned to face him, her blue eyes luminous with some emotion that he could not read. Was it desire? A man could hope.

"Trudy says I need to convince you to come out and get ready for our nuptials. Are you having second thoughts?" He clasped his hands behind his back.

She shook her head. "No. Are you having second thoughts?"

"No, I would never go back on my word. But perhaps we should speak about our expectations."

"Our expectations?"

"Yes, will you join me?" He sat down on the chaise and patted the seat beside him. "Perhaps without the big stick?"

"It's a quarterstaff." She gripped the staff with white knuckles and didn't move to put it away.

"The quarterstaff. Will you need a space at my house for your … um exercise?"

Lucy's grip on the staff loosened. "That would be nice." She walked across the room and opened a door in the wall that turned out to be a closet for instruments. After setting her staff inside, she returned to stand in front of him with her eyes filled with questions.

Hart reached out and tugged her hand, pulling her gently to sit next to him.

He ran his fingers over the top of her knuckles as he tried to gather his thoughts. "I know that neither of us was expecting this marriage to happen. And I am still not convinced it is in your best interests to be married to me. I am moody and still fight with my demons. I'm truly not fit to take care of anyone." He would try his best to be a good husband, for her sake. "So, you must promise to tell me what you need, what you want from me. Can you do that?"

Lucy nodded as she bit her bottom lip, worrying it with her teeth.

"Lucy, I know that your affections are engaged elsewhere. I understand this must be difficult, but you are going to be my wife now. I won't have my duchess be involved with another. You belong to me, do you understand?"

Her lips parted in surprise. Hart took a deep breath in. He hadn't meant to come off so possessive. But the thought of her in any other man's arms made him want to howl like a wolf.

He gripped her hand. "Have you spoken to Mr. Murdoch?"

She shook her head. "I did write to him to tell him I couldn't marry him. I haven't received any sort of response."

Hart nodded. Perhaps the man wouldn't become a problem after all. Something loosened in his chest as he stared at Lucy. She looked so uncertain, at odds with the fierceness she exuded a few moments ago with that staff in her hands. But he needed to make sure she understood what she was getting into.

"Lucy, I won't be the charming, handsome husband you probably imagined you would marry, but I will always keep you safe. And you needn't worry about the marriage bed tonight. I want you to take the time you need to feel comfortable in your role as my wife. Whenever you are ready to come to my bed, I will be waiting." He let his desire for her show in his gaze. "I just ask that you come freely. Not because of any duty. Do you understand?"

"I guess so." She bit down on her lower lip. "You don't want me to share your bed tonight?"

"No, I mean yes, I want you more than you can imagine. But I want you to have time to get used to me … I mean to being married to me." He was mucking this up. "What I'm trying to say is the choice of when and where to consummate our union is entirely up to you."

Lucy nodded.

Hart plowed onto his next point. "I don't know where

you wish to reside. It matters not to me in the long run, but for now, I need to stay in London. I am a man with a mission to find a murderer. I must continue my investigation."

"I can help you. We can figure it out together." She gripped his hand. "Later, I think I would prefer to live at Belstoke. At least most of the time. Trudy loves town, but I am tired of the constant merry-go-round of social events in London."

He squeezed it back. "Then we are in perfect agreement."

Her gaze ensnared him as she looked up at him with those expressive cerulean eyes. What was she thinking so hard about? He could practically see the gears in her head turning. Her gaze flitted down to his mouth, and then she bit her lower lip again. Dear Lord, if she continued to worry that ripe berry of a lip, he would certainly lose hold of his tenuous control and devour that tart mouth.

He cleared his throat. "So, what is it that has you angry today?"

"Pardon?"

"You said you used your staff when you were in a bad mood? What has you beating that poor bag to death?"

She grimaced. "It's the blasted *Piccadilly Press* once again." She rose and crossed to a small side table by the window. She returned and handed him a folded newsprint. With one finger, she pointed. "That's why."

Hart looked down. The drawing portrayed the scene at the Bartleby ball. In a grotesque caricature, Lucy sat splay-legged on the floor between him and Fitzwilliam, crying big fat tears with her hair disheveled and stockinged legs showing. He, of course, was drawn to look like a villain, scarred and snarling. And Fitzwilliam, dressed foppish in the extreme, had his fists up and one arm winding up to throw a punch. The caption read "A Monstrous Night at the Ball." Hart crumpled the paper in his fist. "What the hell does this ridiculous paper have against us?"

"I think it's simply that it makes entertaining fodder to print." Lucy's bottom lip trembled. "I did not cry. That's not at all what happened."

Most women would be upset at being portrayed in such a disgraceful way, but Lucy was upset that they had shown her crying. "Scandalous, everyone knows fierce warriors don't cry. They beat people with big sticks," he teased.

Lucy was not amused. She glared down at him with arms crossed across her chest. Then a tear escaped and rolled down her cheek. The single tear tore a hole in his chest.

Hart rose to his feet and brushed the tear away. "Unacceptable. No one makes my future duchess cry or portrays her as such." For the first time in a long time, he wasn't thinking about his own pain. Lucy was upset, and his need to champion her overwhelmed him. He grabbed her hand. "Gather your things; we are going to march down to the newspaper so I can give them a piece of my mind." He headed for the door with Lucy in tow.

"What right now?" she sputtered.

"Yes." He would tear that newspaperman to shreds.

"Hart! There is the small matter that we are getting married in a few hours."

He stopped and blinked hard several times, trying to clear away the red haze of anger that had flared when he saw her tears.

Now, she looked up at him with amusement instead of sadness.

"You are quite right." He took a deep breath and raised her hand to his lips. "We'll save the set down for another day. Now go put on a pretty dress and get ready for our wedding."

Lucy made a sour face. "I guess it's best there will only be a handful of guests. I will make quite the spectacle with this black eye."

"Don't worry, you will be in good company standing next to me. We will make a spectacle together." He winked. "The monstrous Duke of Hartwick and his pugilist bride."

CHAPTER TWENTY-TWO

L UCY STOOD WAITING outside the drawing room, flanked by Adeline and Violet. Based on the volume of conversation coming from the other side of the door, she doubted there was only a *handful* of people. "How many people did Trudy invite?" she asked Violet.

Her friend shrugged. "My best guess is there are about twenty or so guests."

She hoped Hart was all right in there. Forced to make small talk with people for the last hour, he probably was grumpy as a bear. "How do I look?" She nervously brushed a hand down her pale blue skirt.

"You look beautiful," Adeline assured her. "Nothing to worry about, just marrying a duke today. Happens all the time." Addie giggled at her own joke.

Lucy's nerves were frayed. Ever since her talk with Hart, she could focus on nothing except what he said about their wedding night. He was being so kind, but she must tell him that there never had been an engagement to Mr. Murdoch. She didn't want Hart to think she pined for anyone but him. Even if the idea of their wedding night scared her to death.

She knew absolutely nothing about what happens between husband and wife. She had been too young when her mother died to have had any more than a cursory conversation about becoming a woman when she had started her courses. Beyond a few stolen kisses, the mysterious act of love was just a hazy concept that everyone seemed to have an opinion about. Matrons warned that it was something to avoid before marriage and after marriage, something to be endured.

But why then did so many women risk their reputations for trysts in dark gardens or elicit affairs with a rake? It couldn't be so unpleasant, right? Besides, Hart was an expert at pleasure. For years, she had watched women throwing themselves in his path. And his kisses had been sinful and delicious, making her want more, making her wonder what more pleasures could be had.

Lucy leaned in and gave her friend a hug. Then she turned and embraced Violet as well. "Dear Lord, what have I gotten myself into?"

Violet gave her a knowing look. "This is everything you have been longing for since you were sixteen. Don't worry. Are you sure you don't want me to cover that bruise with some powder?"

Lucy shook her head. If Hart could walk with courage each day, showing his scars to the world, she could certainly join him without shame over one small bruise. Besides, she quite liked his idea of them making a spectacle. She had spent far too much time in her life keeping herself in check, hiding the bits of herself that were too outlandish, too bold for society. She was going to be the Duchess of Hartwick; she could be a spectacle if she chose.

The door opened, and Trudy came through the threshold. "Are you ready, dear?

Lucy nodded. Violet and Adeline walked ahead of her down a makeshift aisle. Chairs had been set up on each side and were filled with guests. As she walked with Trudy to the front of the room, she kept her eyes fixed on Hart.

He stood tall and ramrod straight next to the minister. He had forgone his cane, although she spotted it nearby, leaning against a windowsill. He looked every inch the handsome aristocrat with his dark hair tucked behind his ears and his bland social mask firmly in place. But she could see his hot gaze track her as she made her way toward him, transforming the nerves in her stomach into a warm pool of desire. This man would be hers in just a few short minutes.

The ceremony itself was a blur. She said yes at the appropriate times and smiled brightly at each well-wisher afterward. Hart's warm grip kept her hand in his for the entire afternoon. Wine was served, and someone played a lively song on the pianoforte. Guests danced and mingled. Only after everyone had the opportunity to ask them about their courtship, make exclamations about her eye and what a devil Fitzwilliam was, and comment how glad they were that Hart was recovered and back in society, did they all finally leave.

"Success, my darlings!" Trudy clapped her hands together. "Now, the two of you may go home. Everything is packed in the carriage. Thomas Kent is waiting outside."

"Everything is packed?" Lucy dropped Hart's hand. She felt a bit panicked at the reality that her life here with Trudy was ending so abruptly.

"Well, everything you will need for the next few days. I will send the rest over soon." She winked at Lucy. "You both did a wonderful job handling the guests today. Even I believed you two were a happy couple."

Lucy glanced at Hart and found that he was staring at her contemplatively. "I am happy to have Lucy as my wife." His lips quirked up at one side. "Who else will badger me into taking care of myself?"

"No one, that's who," Lucy replied tartly. She relaxed at his gentle teasing. Inhaling a deep breath through her nose, she turned to embrace Trudy. "Thank you for all you have done for me. You took me in as part of your family, and I will always be grateful for all the advice and wisdom you have imparted over the years. And be grateful for all the adventures we have shared."

Trudy patted her back. "Me, too. You have kept me young, my dear. Now, don't get sentimental on me. You are not going so far."

Lucy pulled back and slipped her hand back into Hart's. He led them outside.

Thomas opened the carriage door. "Many felicitations on your nuptials, Lady Hartwick."

At hearing the moniker, Lucy paused for a moment before giving the man a smile. "Thank you, Mr. Kent."

Hart followed her inside and sat across from her with a smirk on his face.

"What?" she asked.

"It's just strange. Lady Hartwick. It reminds me of my mother."

Lucy stuck out her tongue at him.

Hart laughed and the carriage set into motion. He switched sides to slide next to her on the bench seat, slipping his arm around her waist. He placed a kiss to her temple. "What shall we do first when we get home, Lady Hartwick?"

"Eat." As if on cue, her stomach growled in the most unladylike fashion. "I'm famished."

Hart scooted her closer, tucking her against his side. "Your wish is my command, Your Grace."

CHAPTER TWENTY-THREE

WHEN THEY ARRIVED at Hart's house in St James Square, the entire household staff was lined up in the front hall to greet her.

Mr. Townson greeted her with a rare smile. "Felicitations on your marriage, Your Grace. We are pleased to have you return to Hartwick House as its new mistress." He gave a low bow.

"Thank you, Mr. Townson."

Next was the housekeeper, Mrs. Hunt. "It's lovely to have you with us again, my dear. Please let me know if there is anything you need. Helen is already busy unpacking your things in the duchess's suite."

Helen was here already? Of course, she was. While Lucy had been handling wedding guests, Trudy had made sure that her transition to Hart's household would be seamless. Knowing that her lady's maid was here already smoothed some of her nerves.

"Thank you, Mrs. Hunt."

Hart put a hand on her lower back. "Let me introduce you to everyone. Some you may know already as many of the staff have been with the family for years."

She walked down the line of staff members greeting each one with a smile, Hart's hand warm and firm at her back as he guided her down the line. Hart introduced her with surprising ease. He knew the name of every person on his staff, all the way down to the kitchen scullery maids. When they got to the end Townson clapped his hands and the staff dispersed.

She glanced up at Hart. "Well, how did I do?"

He smiled. "Excellent first impression, Your Grace. I'm just glad none of the maids ran away in horror at having to face me. I haven't seen half those girls since the accident. I know they work here but they must do their best to avoid me."

"Actually, sir," Townson interrupted. "I told the staff to be discreet and stay out of your way. I wished to give you time to adjust to being back in town."

"That is his polite way of saying he wanted to see if I would still be drunk and wandering the halls scaring the maids with my unkempt appearance." Hart's wry half smile was in place but behind it she could see regret in his eyes.

Townson for his part remained silent and stoic. Always the utmost professional.

Lucy clapped her hands together. "Well, there will be none of that when I am here. I will keep my husband far too busy to be roaming the halls at night."

Hart made a choked sound from next to her. She turned to see what the problem was and caught him covering a grin with one fist as he coughed. Strange.

"Mr. Townson, could we have some refreshment set out? I'm famished. I spent too much time this afternoon talking and not enough time eating. And I know I did not see His Grace eat a single thing either. Perhaps just in the breakfast room?" She turned back to Hart. "I don't think I am up for spending our first meal together as husband and wife at that large imposing dining table."

"I have a better idea," Hart said. "Why don't you let Mrs. Hunt show you to your room to freshen up. And when you come down, I will have everything arranged."

"What are you arranging? Where will we eat?"

Hart gave her a little nudge toward the stairs. "Just change into something comfortable for an evening in."

Lucy couldn't imagine what he had in mind, but she was grateful to go to her room for a few moments of peace. And to change from her silk gown with its five layers of petticoats and stiff-boned corset. The layers of undergarments had made the skirts look lovely and full, and the corset had given her small breasts a well needed lift to fill out the bodice. But as Helen helped her take off each layer, Lucy also began to shed the nerves she had carried with her all day.

She donned her more comfortable short stays over a fresh chemise, and then Helen held out her favorite cotton summer dress, the empire waist style comfortable and cool and the lilac color flattering to her complexion. She stared into the looking glass and felt like herself again. She needed to remember that even though the man downstairs was the Duke of Hartwick, he was also just Hart. There was no reason to be nervous.

She made her way back downstairs and found Hart standing at the bottom, waiting for her. He had removed his jacket and rolled up the sleeves of his shirt to reveal his forearms. One covered lightly in dark hair, and the other covered in smooth pink scars. Pleased that he felt comfortable enough to show her some of the scars he usually kept concealed, she gave him a bright smile as she descended the last few stairs.

He held out a hand. When she crossed to him, he tucked her arm through his elbow.

"Where are we going to eat? We are still going to eat?" she asked.

"Yes. You have often made sure I ate, and now it is my turn to feed you. This way." He led them to the back of the house and out through French doors to the back garden. The sun low in the sky cast golden light over the lawn and pierced through the leaves of the great aspen tree, leaving patterns of dappled light on the grass underneath. Past the stone terrace, in front of the Koi pond, a blanket was laid out in the grass. A large wicker basket sat in the center.

"How about an evening picnic? It's beautiful weather, and we have been cooped up inside all day."

"I've never heard of having a picnic in the evening."

"Welcome to my world; haven't you heard?" Hart lowered his voice conspiratorially. "Dukes can do whatever they choose."

She grinned and hopped off the terrace to make her way

to the blanket. Settling herself as gracefully as possible, Lucy spread out her skirts. "It is lovely out here."

Hart grabbed two lit lanterns from a table and came to join her. He set the lanterns at the far edge of the blanket. "These are for when the sun sets. Now let's see what my cook has packed for us."

He reached into the basket and brought out a small bouquet of daisies. He handed them to her with a flourish. "For you, Lady Hartwick."

Their yellow centers were so cheerful and sunny that Lucy couldn't help but smile as she petted the delicate petals with one finger. "How did you know what my favorite flowers were?"

"I know everything about you."

"Ha! You've never paid an ounce of attention to me except when your father made you come fix things at the school."

"You were a lot of trouble back then. But I admired your spirit. You didn't let that finishing school mold you into some insipid debutant. And I do so know all about you." He held up one finger. "You like daisies. You have them planted all throughout the garden at the house in Portman Square." He raised another finger. "You never wear the color yellow. You dislike fish of all kinds."

Lucy scrunched her nose and nodded her agreement.

"You never back down from an argument. You like to beat on bags of sand with a big staff, although that is a new discovery."

Lucy laughed out loud at the last one. "I only fight the sandbag because it's socially unacceptable to pick fights with people on the street. I could teach you some techniques, and then we could spar together. It might even be a good way to loosen up your shoulder."

"I'm not sure my ego could take being taken to task by such a small woman."

She laughed again because she absolutely could beat him in a match. He noticed more than she ever thought about her. "I concede, I am surprised at the things you've noticed."

Hart leaned forward. "Lucy, you are a beautiful woman. There are a myriad of things for a man to notice."

Lucy's breath caught. *Kiss me.* But Hart pulled back and dug into the basket again.

"Try this." He held out a small bite of cheese. "It's an Italian variety, made from goat's milk. My chef says it is creamy and a bit tangy."

Lucy reached out and took the bite. Indeed, the cheese melted in her mouth. "Delicious." She glanced at him through her lashes as he continued to pull food out from the basket and arrange it on the blanket. "Hart, will you tell me what happened between you and that Seaton fellow?"

Hart plucked a large strawberry from a bowl and offered it to her. "I was told these are perfectly ripe and sweet."

"Hart," she warned as she took the berry from him. "I won't be distracted by food."

"Are you sure? Mr. Bell makes divine bread. Try a piece with a bit of that cheese."

She sent him a stern look. "Hart, please tell me what happened. Maybe I can help."

"Like you helped by threatening him with the end of my cane pressed to his neck?" Hart held up his hands when she huffed. "Alright, I will tell you. But I guess I should start earlier that day. All of it pertains to my father. I went to the Earl of Blackpool's home. He had been ignoring my invitations to meet, so I stopped by unannounced in the hope of catching him at home." Hart plucked a berry and popped it into his mouth. After a moment, he continued. "I saw the Knot of Isis on his wall and asked him about it. He said they had a club at Eton, just as you guessed. My father had chosen the symbol to represent it, for protection against their enemies."

Lucy nodded and tore off a piece of crusty bread from a loaf that had been wrapped in a colorful gingham cloth.

"I asked him what had happened to their friendship, my father and his. They used to be close, but years ago, they ceased socializing." Hart looked out toward the tall garden wall at the back of the property. "Blackpool said my father had an affair with his wife. That he'd always known my father was a womanizer but that he never thought he would cross that line with a friend." He blew out a long breath.

"Oh my," Lucy said, at a loss for the appropriate response. She watched Hart carefully to judge his reaction.

He turned stormy eyes to her. "I know it's naïve to think that ton marriages aren't rife with infidelity." He ran a hand through his hair. "But I suppose I had held my father to a high standard. I guess I always thought he was so upright. He taught me everything I know about being a gentleman."

"I understand that. I have always held my father up as the ideal husband and father. Of course, a son would look up to his father. And your father was wonderful. I knew him to be kind and magnanimous to a frightened young girl just because of a promise to a friend. So, he wasn't perfect, but that doesn't change the good parts of who he was."

"There's more." Hart grimaced. "Let's have some of this champagne." He pulled a bottle from the basket and two glasses. Then he uncorked it with a pop and poured the sparkling wine for them.

Lucy sipped her wine and waited for the more.

Hart took a long swallow, draining half the glass. "I was walking a bit, thinking about what I had just learned, when out of nowhere, Seaton appeared. He knew where I had been. He had been following me, I guess. He said that he'd been hired to watch over me. That the person who hired him felt guilty about what happened to me and that they wanted to prevent me from coming to further harm."

"Who?" she asked.

"He wouldn't say. Seaton is a cryptic bast … man. But during the course of our conversation, he said something else. He tauntingly called me little brother. He claims to be my half-brother. That his mother was my father's mistress."

She gasped. She couldn't help it. A half-brother?

Hart's lips lifted in a wry half smile at her gasp. "That's how I felt as well. What you saw was my denial in the form of anger. I don't think he would have hurt me despite his threats, but I have no doubt that he is deadly. I don't know exactly what he does, but somehow, I think protection is not his normal job assignment."

"Dear Lord. Do you think he is some sort of criminal?"

Hart shrugged and finished his glass of wine in one long gulp.

"I guess it's better to have him protecting you than the opposite." Lucy shook her head. This was a lot of scandal to absorb. How had his father kept it all a secret? She frowned. Perhaps it wasn't. Perhaps many knew. Did it even matter if a duke had affairs or illegitimate children? "Do you think it is well known that your father had sired illegitimate children?"

"I honestly don't think so. I feel as though I would have known or heard the rumors if that was his reputation. My guess is that he was discreet and preferred to keep a more spotless reputation. Perhaps to protect my mother. I think he did love her or at least respected her enough to not flaunt his affairs."

Lucy bit down to rip off another piece of bread. Did Hart feel the same about marriage? Would he take a mistress once he had his heir? Their marriage was just one of convenience, a way to protect her from scandal. It wasn't as though he loved her. But the thought of him finding pleasure in the arms of another woman made her stomach churn.

"Lucy, your expression is pained. What's the matter?"

She shook her head. "Nothing." She would not admit

how upset she was at the prospect of him taking a mistress.

She was in no position to make demands on his affection. But he had said she belonged to him, and didn't that mean he belonged to her as well? She would not share. Lucy hurled the last of her bread at him.

"What was that for?" Hart brushed the crumbs off the front of his jacket. Moving quickly, he placed his arms on the ground on either side of her, crowding her back until she lay down staring up at him. "I never can figure out what you are thinking when that clever brain of yours starts churning. Tell me what's the matter," he demanded.

There was nowhere to hide from his direct gaze. Overwhelmed, she turned her head to the side.

Don't ruin everything. He doesn't want to hear about your jealousy over fantasy women.

Hart leaned in to rub his nose along the side of her neck. His warm breath tickled her ear. "Are you worried about what sort of husband I will make? Lucy, look at me."

She reluctantly turned her head back to meet his gaze. "I understand that powerful men often take mistresses. But…"

"You wouldn't like that?"

She huffed. "Of course not! No woman wants to feel that she is not enough."

Hart froze, staring down at her. "Lucy, I would never want to make you feel that you were not enough. I know too well what that feels like. I promise, no affairs." His features softened to a half smile. "I always intended to be a faithful husband. My biggest concern is whether you will be satisfied with this wreck of a man in front of you. Because once I make you mine, I won't let you go to another."

His sweet, possessive words settled into her heart. She nodded because she didn't have the words to reply. Reaching up, she caressed his cheek, tracing his scars lightly with her fingertips. She would love him so well that he would have no choice but to love her back. Right now, though, she might expire from the heat burning in his eyes. He'd told her to tell him what she needed. "Hart."

"Yes?"

"I need you to kiss me."

He leaned forward until his lips were millimeters from hers. "A kiss, hmm? My pleasure." He kissed one corner of her mouth feather lite. Then brushed another light kiss across her lips before sinking against her and languidly exploring her mouth, his tongue dipping inside to taste before he pulled back to suck her bottom lip. Unlike the other kisses they had shared, this kiss was long and sultry, leaving her wanting more.

But then Hart sat up and pulled her up to sitting as well. He tore off a piece of bread and spread some of the goat cheese across it. "Eat. I promised you food, and I shan't be distracted."

"But kissing is so much more fun." She bit down on her bottom lip and grinned.

Hart groaned and leaned forward to place a swift kiss against her lips. "You are addictive. But I promised you time and space. Eat."

Lucy dutifully took a bite of bread. Noting to herself that his eyes heated every time they strayed to her mouth. She tucked the information away for later.

THIS WAS NOT what she had dreamed her wedding night to be like. Tucked into bed, alone. Lucy stared up at the canopy. The yellow-gold fringe along the edge of the pale pink velvet was the most hideous thing she had ever seen. She blew out a long breath. This morning Hart's sweet words that they would wait until she was ready seemed so chivalrous. Now she craved his presence. More kisses, more heated looks, more ... well ... more.

After dinner, Hart had led her up to their suite. He had given the room a cursory glance and asked her if it was satisfactory. When she nodded, he had strode across to open a door and proceeded to show her the dressing room and adjoining sitting room.

Then back through to the bedroom they had trooped, where he had opened another door to reveal the water closet, which had a large claw foot tub at its center. He pointed to the other side of the room. "That leads to my bedroom. If you need anything at all, let me know." He had stood there for a long moment, almost as though he wanted to say something else. But then he turned and disappeared into his suite.

Lucy had stared at the carved wooden door. What now?

Was she to get ready for bed? She'd called for her maid. Helen helped her change into a beautifully embroidered nightgown in a gossamer fabric that was quite transparent. When she raised her eyebrows at her reflection, Helen had giggled, actually giggled, and then said that the duke would be so pleased. She'd brushed out Lucy's hair and tucked her into bed before leaving for the night. And that was where Lucy had lain for the last hour.

Hart was not going to come to her. She sat up in bed with a huff, pushing the sheets off. He had made it plain he planned to wait for her to make the decision as to when they would consummate their marriage. But she had not expected it to be this hard to gather her courage. Just get out of bed and go to him. *Perhaps he is waiting for you, desperate, wanting you.* She swung her legs over the edge of the bed. Crossed through the water closet to the door to his room, but then she paused. *Should she knock?* It was polite to knock.

She knocked. No response. *Was he asleep?* She knocked louder. Still nothing. If he was asleep, would he mind if she crawled in next to him? She glanced back over her shoulder toward her bedroom. Anything was better than sleeping in that cavernous bed by herself.

Lucy turned the knob and slowly opened the door. The room was dark save for the moonlight that shone through an open window onto an obviously empty bed. Lucy crossed her arms over her chest. So much for her fantasy that he would be in bed desperately waiting for her to come to him.

Where was her husband? She glanced around the room.

Just as large as hers, his was decorated in dark blues and greens. A single leather chair sat in front of the fireplace. Beyond that, she could make out the shadowed shape of an armoire and a wash basin beside it. A breeze blew into the room, fluttering gauzy curtains. Lucy turned and went back to her room. She marched across to the dressing table and snatched up a silky robe from the chair. She tied the belt tightly, slipped out of the room, and headed for the stairs.

At the top, she paused. Should she be walking through the house in her nightclothes? This was her house now; she could explore it looking for her errant husband if she chose. Resolved, she padded down the stairs. The footman assigned to the front door startled when he spotted her. Which one was he? Herman? Herbert?

"May I help you with anything, Your Grace?"

Lucy pulled herself up as tall as she could. Trying not to blush at being seen in her robe and bare feet. "Yes, Herbert. I'm in search of my husband."

"Yes, ma'am. I saw him go into his study about an hour ago. Down the corridor, third door on your left."

"Thank you." She hurried towards Hart's study and, without knocking, slipped inside. She leaned back against the door and briefly shut her eyes.

"Lucy?" Hart's deep voice called out.

CHAPTER TWENTY-FOUR

HART TURNED AT the snick of the door shutting. Across the room, Lucy leaned against the door, her eyes shut. What was she doing down here? He set his drink down on the windowsill.

"Lucy?"

Her eyes popped open, and she straightened. She wore a white satin robe. Her russet hair fell over her shoulders in long waves. God, a man could get lost in all that silky hair. His fingers twitched.

"I was looking for you. You weren't in your room."

"You went to my room?" His voice felt hoarse. She had come to his bedroom. In her nightgown. To find him. His brain slowed as all the blood raced farther south.

He had escaped downstairs shortly after leaving her in her room. Being separated by only an unlocked door had been torture, and he had immediately regretted his big speech this morning. His cock didn't give a rat's ass whether she still had feelings for Murdoch. She had agreed to be his wife, and it turned out he was one possessive bastard. He'd sat on the edge of the bed for less than ten minutes before deciding to come downstairs and brood over his choices.

He had been sure it would take time for her to come to him. More time for him to flirt and to kiss and to seduce. More time for her to get used to his ugly scars. But here she was, searching him out like an angel, all dressed in virginal white.

She floated toward him. "You said you'd be waiting."

The catch in her voice had him moving to her. He searched her face for clues to how she was feeling. "I didn't think you would come so soon."

"I didn't like being alone in that big bed with the ugly canopy." Her eyes were luminous in the lamplight as they gazed up at him.

"Ugly?" he couldn't help but smile.

Lucy nodded. "But mostly lonely."

"That's no way to spend your wedding night," he murmured. Entranced by her fingers as they played across his chest. He took her hand and brought it to his lips. "Are you sure you are ready?"

Lucy pulled her hand away and stepped back. "Why is it you're still reluctant? Do you still see me as the girl you are responsible for?" She turned her back to him. "I know that your offer of protection is the reason for our marriage. But am I so hideous that you cannot bear to bed me?"

God, she was so adorable and so very wrong.

Hart wrapped his arms around her from behind. "I have not thought of you as a girl in many years. Why do you think I sent you with Trudy to travel on the continent?"

"You did not want to be bothered with me."

"No, because it was my responsibility to protect you, and all I wanted to do was defile you." He leaned down to nuzzle her ear. "You bother me plenty."

She relaxed against him. "I do?"

"Yes, and I know that this marriage was not your first choice. That you had other plans with your beau. I just don't want to rush you. You are definitely not the hideous one in this marriage."

"You are not hideous!" She twisted around in his arms. Then she shut her eyes and sighed deeply. "There was never an understanding with Mr. Murdoch."

"So, he was just seducing you without promising marriage? Rogue! I'll kill him myself."

"No, I mean I made it all up. Mr. Murdoch doesn't even know I exist."

Hart stared down at her flushed cheeks. *What?*

"You looked at me with so much pity that day. Poor Lucy, no prospects except money-grubbing fortune hunters. So, I made up a beau. And when you asked for his name, the first name that popped into my head was Murdoch. Violet is always telling me what a handsome flirt he is when he comes to see her father." Lucy shrugged.

No Mr. Murdoch. No lovers at all. He grasped handfuls of her robe and tugged her close. "There is no one else that you wish to be with?"

Her hands rose and cupped his face. "Oh, Hart, there's never been anyone but you."

He saw the truth of it in her eyes. That truth scared him.

Just like it had a year ago. But he would not turn her away again. He did not know why she would pledge her heart to a damaged rogue like him, but she was his wife. *Mine.* He bent and captured her lips.

Lucy slid her arms around his neck and sank into the kiss. Her lips opened for him on a sigh, and he dipped his tongue in to play with hers. Her kiss incited a fire low in his belly, the burn of arousal like a shot of fine Irish whisky. Hart was suddenly desperate for every inch of her. He slipped his hands into her hair, running through the waterfall of glossy strands. It was just as soft as he imagined. "Lucy, will you show me what you are wearing under this robe?" He murmured against her mouth.

She nodded. Stepping back, she tugged loose the belt. The robe parted. She slipped one shoulder off, exposing pale creamy skin, then she shrugged off the other. Underneath she wore a nightgown in a gossamer white to match. It fell to her knees and showcased the lovely length of her legs. The outline of her small pert breasts was visible through the thin fabric, and her tightly pebbled nipples jutted out, tempting him to pull one into his mouth. His gaze wandered down the soft curves of her hips and to the thatch of dark hair at the apex of her thighs. Hart licked his lips.

"Helen said you would like it. There is not much of it to speak of."

Hart grabbed her around the waist. "Oh, I like it. You are like a gossamer angel. I can't believe you are mine." He slowly walked her backward toward the tufted sofa in front of the fireplace. Dipping his head, he kissed her again. Nipping at her bottom lip, he then soothed it with his tongue. "This plump bottom lip drives me mad with desire. When you worry it with your teeth, when you lick at the corner, all I can think about is nibbling on it." He sucked that berry pink lip between his teeth for a second time before slanting his head and devouring her mouth once more. The taste of her was intoxicating.

She let out a squeak as her bottom hit the back of the sofa. Hart picked her up and wrapped her legs around his waist. Having her pussy notched against his erection was divine torture.

Lucy tore her lips from his with a gasp. Her eyes widened. "What is that?"

Hart froze. "Lucy, did Trudy talk with you about what to expect on your wedding night?"

Lucy shook her head.

"Your mother?"

Lucy shook her head.

Good Lord. He moved them around to the other side of the sofa and sat down. Lucy still straddled him, but he set her back a few inches onto his thighs, already missing the sweet heat of her sex. She stared down at the bulge in his trousers, and he sucked in a deep breath. He'd never bedded anyone so innocent. How did one explain the mechanics? Or was showing better than telling?

"I'm sorry." Her cheeks stained pink. "I was just surprised."

"Don't be sorry, sweetness." He cupped her cheek. "I let myself get carried away, forgetting that you are a virgin. I assumed that you had some knowledge of what happens between a man and a woman."

"The only thing I've overheard was that a woman must lie there quietly and bear the attentions of her husband. Is that what I am supposed to do? Because your kisses don't make me feel like I can lie there and be still." She rolled her hips restlessly.

Hart groaned and leaned forward to kiss her. "Is that what they are telling young women? Christ. What you heard is wrong. I hope that my kisses and my touch enflame you and bring you pleasure. You should never have to endure anything." He grasped her chin gently. "If there is anything I do that does not feel good, you tell me. Do you hear me?"

She nodded. Her gaze again flitted down to his erection.

"This is my desire for you." He slowly began to unbutton his falls. "When a man becomes excited his cock lengthens and hardens."

He peeled back the flap of fabric and grasped his cock, drawing it out. He gave it a slow stroke as she watched.

"Is it sensitive?"

"Uh-mmm," he managed as he stroked it again. Her curious gaze was killing him. He'd never been this hard in his life. Taking his cock out had definitely been a mistake.

Then she reached out and stroked one finger over the head, changing his mind. It had been a bloody brilliant idea.

"It's so smooth," she murmured.

He let go of his shaft and let her explore. Her fingers were gentle as she petted him. Perhaps he would lose his mind before she had satisfied her curiosity, but he'd happily sacrifice his sanity if he could continue to have her hands on him. Then her fingers wrapped around his cock. She pumped her hand once with the kind of grip he craved, causing him to jerk his hips in response. Christ, he was going to come in her hand and ruin her first experience. He pulled her hand from around him, bringing her fingers up to kiss them.

"Sweetness, your first time should be about your pleasure. Let me show you. Can I touch you?"

Lucy's eyes tracked his hands as he quickly tucked himself back into his trousers. Then he slid his hands up her thighs, rubbing small circles on the soft skin along the inside. The small gasp that escaped her lips was more desire than alarm but he stopped at the hem of her nightgown, where it had been rucked up, just barely covering her sex.

Her rosy nipples were right at his eye level, the tips puckered and begging to be sucked. Hart leaned forward to lave one with his tongue right through the thin fabric covering it. Her soft moan encouraged him to take it into his mouth and give the tight bud a long suck. Her breasts were lush, her nipple stiff as he flicked his tongue against it. Then he switched to the other nipple and gave it the same attention.

He glanced up to gauge her reaction and found her watching him with eyes full of need. Her fingers were tangled in his hair, and her hips undulated again. "Hart, please show me what else. I feel as though I'm on a precipice." Her fingers flexed, tugging at his hair in the most delicious way.

"I know what you need, sweetness." He slowly moved his hands up higher to her center, brushing his thumbs over the curls of her mons while he watched her face for any signs of discomfort. "Have you ever touched yourself here, Lucy?"

She shook her head.

"Not in the bath or at night when you lay in bed?"

"No, should I have?" Lucy gasped as he ran one finger down her seam and circled lightly over her opening. She was already wet, and he spread the moisture back and forth gently as she circled her hips. "That feels good." She moved her hands to grasp his forearms, her nails biting into his skin.

"Yes, sweet, move those hips. That's a good girl." He found her clit with his thumb. When he pressed it firmly, she shouted his name. "That's the spot, isn't it?" He rubbed tight circles relentlessly over her clit.

"Yes, yes, that feel so good."

Only then did he slide a finger into the wet silky heat of her pussy. Pumping it in and out slowly into the silky heat as she soaked his hand. He inserted another finger and sought out the spot that he knew would make her scream his name.

Lucy lunged forward and captured his mouth in a fierce kiss that stole his breath. She panted against his mouth, her tongue tangling with his, her teeth scraping across his bottom lip. The unguarded passion in her eyes had his hunger for her snapping against the leash of his self-control.

Her hips never stopped circling, chasing her pleasure, and he imagined them pumping up and down on his cock.

Gripping the back of her neck, he kissed her back as his other hand worked her tight pussy. Taking her higher and higher until, with a gasp, she pulled off his mouth. Her eyes closed, and her head fell back on a long moan. He rubbed his fingers in the same spot again and again. "That's it sweet, come for me," he demanded. His need to see her come apart in his arms wild and desperate. In the next moment, she seized up, her inner muscles pulsating around his fingers, as she screamed his name.

Magnificent in her crisis, Lucy gave herself over to the pleasure with pure abandon. Watching her come apart sent him over the edge. His cock pulsed and bucked as he came in his trousers for the first time since he was a randy boy of fourteen. He brought her lips to his for a long kiss. Then he laid his forehead against hers and tried to regain control of his racing heart. Christ, this woman was going to bring him to knees.

"That was amazing," Lucy whispered after a few minutes.

He nodded, incapable of putting into words how he felt. Amazing, yes. Destroyed might be the better descriptor.

"That was love making? Maybe the other men are doing it wrong."

Hart let out a hoarse chuckle. "That was just part of it. Let's call that lesson one."

Lucy's eyes widened. "When is lesson two?"

He shifted them so that he lay down along the sofa with

her on top of him, her head tucked into his good shoulder. He brushed her hair away from her face, indulging his fantasy and combing his finger through the long, satin locks. "Maybe in a little bit. A man needs a few moments to recover."

"Oh," she said with a small sleepy yawn. With her eyes falling closed, she snuggled against him.

Hart wrapped his arm tightly around her. The intimacy of holding her this close hit him hard in the center of his chest. The loneliness of the past year had been of his own making. A self-protective shell he had created. But Lucy had not paid any attention to his walls. She had marched right back into his life without permission and turned the whole thing on its head. She was a gift he certainly didn't deserve.

He kissed the top of her head. "Rest. We will get to lesson two soon enough."

CHAPTER TWENTY-FIVE

L UCY BLINKED HER eyes against the sunlight that streamed into the room. Dark stubble across a strong jawline was the first thing she saw as she came awake. Wrapped in his arms, Hart's big body kept her warm even though she still wore only her filmy nightgown. Had they slept down here in his study all night? A lazy smile stretched across her face as she played her fingers over his chest. She lay atop her husband, *her husband*, who had made her see stars last night with his lovemaking.

Last night had been amazing. Eye-opening and Hart had said it was just lesson one. After the way he made her orgasm with his mouth on her breasts and his hand between her legs, she had a fairly good idea where his thick manhood was meant to go. The thought of being filled by him made her wiggle her hips in anticipation.

The man beneath her grunted. His hand at her back slid lower to her bottom and squeezed. "What a delicious way to wake up. Do it again."

Lucy wiggled her hips, and this time, she felt his hard shaft pressing against her hip. Hmmm, was he always like this?

"Only when I'm around you, sweetness," Hart murmured.

Had she asked her question out loud? She lifted her head to look down at him. He still hadn't opened his eyes, but a smile played across his lips. His hair was a wild mess.

She brushed some of it off his brow, playing with the end of one strand. "Good morning, husband."

His eyes opened the grey mist of them alluring and languid. He squeezed her bottom again. "Good morning, wife."

From outside the room, a furious female voice made its way through the door. "My mistress is missing; of course, this is my business."

A male voice replied, "I saw them enter here last night, and no one has come out since. I tell you, they are still in there."

"Why would they sleep in his study when they have a sumptuous suite upstairs?"

Townson's authoritative voice cut through. "No one disturbs His Grace when he is in his study."

"Here, here," Hart muttered.

Lucy scrunched her nose. "I think we have caused some concern with the staff."

"You were so lovely sleeping on me. I didn't see why I should disturb you. I guess I fell asleep as well." He sat up, taking her with him and landing her in his lap, straddling him. Gripping her hips, he guided her in a slow roll over his erection.

"Oh!" The sensation was exquisite.

"Let's go upstairs," he murmured.

She reluctantly climbed off him and donned her discarded robe. Hart stood as well and buttoned the last few buttons left undone on his falls but left his shirt untucked to cover the bulge in his trousers. He looked so deliciously disheveled in his stocking feet with his vest hanging open. She rose onto her toes and kissed him.

Hart immediately pulled her close. His lips sliding against her in a slow kiss that left her panting for more. "Upstairs," he growled against her mouth.

Then he took her hand and, spinning her on her heels, he led them across the room. When they opened the door, the three servants visibly startled.

Hart didn't even pause his stride. "We require breakfast sent up to my room and a hot bath prepared for my wife."

Lucy sent Helen a small wave and contrite look as Hart tugged her down the corridor and up the main stairs. He didn't stop until they reached the door to the duchess suite. Then he scooped her up over his good shoulder and strode into the room.

"Hart," she squeaked. "Why are you manhandling me?"

He tossed her onto the center of the bed. "Time for lesson two."

She laughed as she bounced on the bed. "Aren't we having breakfast?" She watched him cross to the door and turn the lock. Then he stalked back to her like a lion prowling toward his prey ... and how she wanted him to pounce. His eyes tracked over her as he returned to the bed. Reaching out, he pulled the ties that closed her robe, and with a satisfied grunt, he spread the two sides apart, pushing them off her shoulders.

Lucy grabbed hold of his vest to pull him onto the bed. But he shook his head. Instead, he hooked his hands under her knees, tugging her closer to the edge of the bed. The move forced her onto her back.

"I want to see all of you." His hands roamed up the length of her legs, slowly pushing the hem of her nightgown up over her thighs, her stomach. When he had almost exposed her breasts, she raised her arms. With a hum of approval, Hart dragged the garment over her head. One of his hands pinned her wrists above her head as the other skimmed down the length of her body, causing her to shiver with anticipation.

Far from self-conscious, Hart made her feel beautiful. Desire turned his eyes molten silver as his gaze roamed over her body. The unadulterated look of craving on his face utterly ruined her.

Lucy squeezed her thighs together as her sex grew wet under his perusal. "What about you?" she panted. "Don't you need to take off your clothes?"

Again, he shook his head. "Trust me, I don't need to be unclothed to do what I am craving." He let go of her wrists and leaned over her to take one of her breasts into his mouth.

The slow pull on her nipple created a quiver of need she felt all the way down at her core. She gripped his hair to keep him in place as he licked and kissed her breast. Lord, this man's mouth seemed to know exactly how to tease out her pleasure. He continued to flutter kisses down across her stomach, stopping to dip his tongue in her navel, making her jolt at the tickling sensation. Hart raised his head to pin her with his searing gaze. Her crazed giggle died in her throat as he slowly lowered to his knees beside the bed.

He kissed the inside of her thigh, his eyes never leaving hers. With each kiss, she sighed at the soft whisper of his lips against her skin. Then his fingers brushed over the curls at her center. She gasped as his warm breath followed the path. He stared with reverent focus at her sex for a moment. Was he going to touch her like he had last night? She writhed under his gaze. But then his head dipped down, and he licked her, his tongue delving between her folds. Lucy bucked her hips, chasing the sensation his tongue left behind. Hart seemed to know exactly what she needed because he leaned in and repeated the motion with vigor; over and over, he licked her sex.

She couldn't hold back the mewling sounds of pleasure his ministrations caused. It felt so good. His tongue laved at the small bundle of nerves hidden between her folds, leaving her mindless with the pleasure it wrought. She pulsed her hips up against his mouth, *don't stop, don't stop.*

"Oh, I won't sweetness, not until you come all over my tongue."

Had she said that out loud? Again, Hart managed to scramble her thoughts to the point where she wasn't sure which were internal and which she was letting fall from her lips.

She raked her nails over his scalp. "Please, please," she panted.

Mindless with the pleasure he wrought right at the center of her as it built to a crescendo. Just like last night, she thought she couldn't endure another moment of this building pressure. Then the dam broke. She screamed his name as the wave of pleasure crashed through her.

Hart nuzzled her as she came down from her crisis, placing open-mouth kisses along the inside of her thigh. But unlike last night, there was a certain crackling tension radiating from him. He stood and stripped off his trousers and stockings. His shirt fell low over his hips, but it could not hide his erection, which jutted out from the dark hair at its base.

With one hand, he gripped his shaft, long and thick; he squeezed the base for a moment. "Lucy, I need … I need…"

She reached out for him. He climbed onto the bed. Braced over her with his left arm, he sucked in a deep breath. "Lucy, I don't want to hurt you. But I've been told the first time can be uncomfortable for the lady."

"I don't mind. I need you, too. Fill me up."

He groaned, a low rumble in his chest. "You don't know the things you do to me with that mouth." Then he leaned down and kissed her.

His mouth was so hot and hungry that she almost didn't notice the head of his manhood pressing into her. He pulsed in and out in short thrusts that had her spreading her legs farther apart to accommodate him. She was so slick from her arousal that even though his intrusion felt overwhelming, it didn't hurt. Then Hart's self-control seemed to break. He thrust inside her like a piston. They both moaned low as his hips met hers. Wrapping an arm around her waist, he drove into her again and again. Her back arched as he pulled her close, and he bent to suck one of her nipples into his mouth.

The indescribable sensations began to build again. Lucy gripped his shoulders. She felt out of control, totally at his mercy. Hart leaned back, and his hand snuck between their bodies. His thumb pressed in firm circles over that magic spot as he thrust inside her.

"You feel incredible. God, Lucy, I want to feel your pussy convulse around me. Come for me, sweetness."

Lucy felt his erection throb inside her. She came apart just as he asked, shouting his name. Hart thrust one more time with a hoarse shout of his own, and then she felt his manhood pulse over and over. Shudders of delicious pleasure rendered her boneless in his arms. Her arms slipped from around him, and he laid her gently on the covers. His fingers brushed her cheek. She lazily opened her eyes to find his face inches from hers. He gazed down at her reverently.

She managed to raise her hand to cup his cheek. "Lesson two was my favorite so far. What does lesson three involve?"

Hart chuckled and kissed her before rolling over to lay on his back next to her. He threaded his fingers through hers. The two of them stared up at the canopy as their breathing slowly returned to normal.

"This really is a hideous color," he said a few moments later.

"I think it's meant to be pale pink, maybe?"

"It almost looks flesh colored. What is the trim, puce?"

Lucy couldn't hold back a snort of laughter. "Now I really will not be able to sleep in here by myself thinking of the canopy as skin colored." She gave an exaggerated shiver.

Hart turned onto his side. Reaching out, he tickled her, making her howl in surprise. "Stop at once! I cannot abide being tickled. I will scream, and the staff will think you are torturing me."

"I think they all heard you screaming already, sweet." His eyebrows waggled up and down as his hand hovered just inches over her stomach.

"No?! Do you think so?" Mortified at the thought, she reached for a pillow and brought it over her face. "I'm never leaving this room again."

Hart wrapped an arm around her waist and pulled her against him. He kissed her behind her ear. "Not all the servants. Just the servants who brought up the water for your bath and maybe the maid who brought up breakfast." He nibbled on her earlobe. "Besides, I like it when you scream my name. When you beg me for more."

She lifted the pillow from her face and turned to face him. "You do?"

He nodded. "I always want to know that I am bringing you pleasure. How are you feeling? Did I hurt you?"

Lucy took stock of her body. She felt a little sore between her legs now that her body was beginning to cool from the intensity of their lovemaking.

She shook her head. "You didn't hurt me. Everything we did felt good. I may be a bit sore…"

Hart sat up. "Let's get you into a hot bath before the water cools. That should help your lady bits." He crossed to the door to the adjoining dressing room and disappeared through it to the bathing room. "It's all set up. Come on in," he called out.

Lucy walked through to find him swirling his hands in the water of the large claw foot tub. Hart helped her step into the bathtub, which was filled about halfway to the top. She sank slowly down into the warm water with a sigh. This was pure decadence. A knock sounded at the door.

"Yes?" Hart walked over to the door that led to his rooms.

"Two more buckets of hot water, sir."

"Just put them down by the door. Then leave us be." Hart replied. After a moment, he opened the door and pulled in the hot water one by one to pour into the bath.

"That feels wonderful. Won't you come in and join me? There is plenty of room." She swirled the hot water around her, hoping she looked inviting.

Hart bent to press a kiss to her lips. "I'll just go see what they brought up for breakfast."

Disappointed, Lucy frowned. She knew why Hart refused to remove his shirt in front of her. What she didn't know was how to encourage him to trust that she wasn't going to be repulsed by his scars. There was nothing that could change how she felt about him. That could change how much she desired him. She traced her fingers back and forth across the lip of the bathtub as she contemplated how she could lure him back into the room.

Letting out a long sigh, she laid her head back against the porcelain edge of the bath. He had been so patient with her naivety last night. Showing her how good sexual relations could feel. All the while holding back on his own needs as she now understood that he had. She should be just as patient with his insecurities.

Lucy finished washing quickly, not wanting the water to get cold before Hart had a chance to wash as well. A stack of fluffy towels sat on a chair next to the bathtub. She dried herself and then wrapped the towel around her, tucking the ends together at her breasts. When she entered Hart's room, she found him standing by the window looking out. He had layered a dark blue banyan over his shirt, and she mourned how it covered his muscled thighs.

"The water is still warm for you," she said.

Hart turned around. "I thought you would soak for a while. You didn't have to get out yet."

She crossed to him and laid her hands on his chest. "Go on and wash. I'm going to get dressed. Then we can have breakfast."

"Dressed?" His brows knitted together in disapproval. He stripped off his banyan and draped it around her shoulders. "That's plenty of clothing for breakfast. I'm not done with you yet."

"You're not?" Her breath hitched.

His response was a kiss that had her going weak in the knees. Then Hart crossed toward the bathing room. The hem of his shirt barely skimmed halfway down his buttocks, allowing her a tantalizing view of the taut globes as he walked away.

CHAPTER TWENTY-SIX

LUCY OPENED THE door to Hart's study and peeked in to see if he was inside. His dark head of hair was bent over a ledger as he sat at his desk. It popped up as she slid into the room.

"Hello, sweetness." A smile tugged at his lips.

His endearment caused a spread of syrupy warmth through her chest. "Hello, husband. I thought you might be in here." She walked over and rounded the desk. He swiveled in his chair and raised his hands to her waist. Lucy threaded her fingers through his hair, pushing it back from where it fell over his eyes. It still felt like a fantasy that she could touch him whenever she wanted. This gorgeous beast of a man.

He would roll his eyes at her if she said that out loud. Hart still would not accept that she saw him as handsome. His vanity had received a huge blow. What Hart didn't understand was that it was the way held himself with confident assuredness, the humor he conveyed with the quirk of his sensual lips, and the way his sultry eyes promised all kinds of wicked pleasures that made him so attractive. The physical scars he bore did not change how she saw him.

"What are you reading?" she asked.

"This is the ledger for the year leading up to my father and Robert's deaths. I am cross referencing any deals my father invested money in with the six remaining members of their club from school."

"Find any correlations?" she asked.

"No, my father didn't diversify much. The duchy owns sizable estates and his income, our income, comes largely from them. He had given money to some charities, and to some friends, most notably the Earl of Rawlings. The records are meticulous kept."

"Perhaps it was a verbal agreement? Something promised but not recorded?"

"Possible. It's damn frustrating. I am chasing something elusive. It is as though everyone knows more about my father than I did."

"Hart, I know you wish to know the truth about what happened to them but my question for you is, what will you do with this knowledge? Is it really revenge that you seek?"

His stormy gaze stared into hers. "I don't plan to take an eye for an eye if that's what you are asking. I won't become a murderer. But even powerful men have weaknesses. I will ruin the life of the person who killed my family. Just as they ruined mine."

She cupped his cheeks and placed a kiss to his lips hoping to ease some of his turmoil. The loneliness that came with losing everyone he loved was something she recognized. As was the need to make sense of tragedy. "I understand why you need to figure out who the villain is, but I worry for your safety."

Hart shrugged as though his safety was hardly important. His jaw clenched. "It is a matter of honor to avenge their deaths. It is increasingly looking like the man responsible is one of my father's closest confidants. This man will slither out of the consequences if I bring my accusations to the magistrate. No, it will be more effective to strike them where it will hurt most. Their finances and their reputation."

"How do you mean?"

"Like with Fitzwilliam, I purchased all his outstanding markers. He now owes me an enormous sum."

Lucy gaped. "You did?"

He nodded. "I will make him squirm for a while. Then call in the debts. We will see what he must sacrifice to pay off the sum."

Was it wrong that she was inordinately pleased by Hart's version of justice? She couldn't hold back her smile. "I find that terribly romantic."

To her delight Hart's cheeks flushed.

She leaned and brushed a kiss across his lips. "Well, I don't want to disturb your work further. I'll just sit over on the sofa with my book."

Lucy snuggled into the corner of the tufted sofa. Her book was right where she had left yesterday, and she grabbed it and began to read. But today the story could not hold her attention for long. The sofa reminded her of their wedding night and all the wonderful nights that had recently followed. She glanced up at Hart and found him looking across at her. He quickly lowered his eyes to the ledger in front of him and, with a small sigh, Lucy began to read again. Not ten minutes later she heard a muttered curse.

Hart stood and rounded his desk. He slid onto the sofa next to her and leaned in to bury his face in her neck, making her laugh as he nibbled down her neck.

She wrapped her arms around his shoulders. "Am I being a distraction? Shall I leave?"

His growl vibrated against her skin. "No, it's not your fault you are much more appealing than those dusty ledgers." He lifted his head a sent her a boyish grin. "Besides, my eye is aching already."

Lucy combed her fingers through his hair again and Hart's eyes closed as a hum of pleasure rumbled out. It hadn't escaped her attention how starved for touch he was. Perhaps starved for some fun as well. "Why don't we go do something? We haven't left the house in what? Six days? You need some fresh air and sunshine."

"What am I? A houseplant?" Hart chuckled.

"No, I think a classic rose. Pretty but prickly."

He huffed, but he cupped her face, brushing a thumb across her cheekbone. "You would be a sunny daffodil. The first sign of spring, harbinger of new beginnings."

For all his gruffness, Hart could be surprisingly sweet. "Come on, you, let's go stretch our legs and you can treat me to an ice from Gunter's."

It was indeed a beautiful day outside. Lucy tipped her

parasol back and let the sun warm her face for a moment. She reveled in the simple pleasure of walking down the street with her husband. She was married to Alexander Barclay, the Duke of Hartwick. She was Hart's wife. Her smile felt ever present these days. They stepped into Gunter's and the gaze of every patron seemed to swing their way. Hart tugged his hat lower on his brow. She squeezed his hand and led him to a small table for two.

"What flavor is your favorite?" she asked as waiter handed them two menus.

"I have no idea. I've never been in here."

Lucy lowered her menu. "What? Never?"

His lips twitched in amusement. "Gunter's didn't exactly fit with my reputation. This is a place to woo innocents."

She rolled eyes before raising her menu to pick a flavor. "I like to choose something new each time. I will choose lavender today."

Hart ordered lemon for himself. He glanced around. "It's not a bad place, a bit crowed for my taste. I will admit to wondering what all the fuss was about."

"I have been here three or four times, mostly with friends and once with a suitor."

"Who?" Hart demanded.

"No one who matters," Lucy replied, secretly glad at hearing the gravel in his tone. How nice to be the object of jealousy. "I thought since we are out, perhaps we should stroll to some of the shops and find something new for your study. Something to put into the room that would make it feel more yours."

"Shopping? I guess so."

"Nothing too taxing. I know of this curiosity shop that has all sorts of interesting things."

"Well, I do owe you a birthday present."

Their ices arrived. Lucy scooped up a bite. She scrunched her nose, yuck. She tried another bite and then set her spoon down. It tasted like soap. How disappointing.

Hart slid his lemon ice across the table switching it for hers.

Lucy smiled up at him and then dug into the delicious lemon ice.

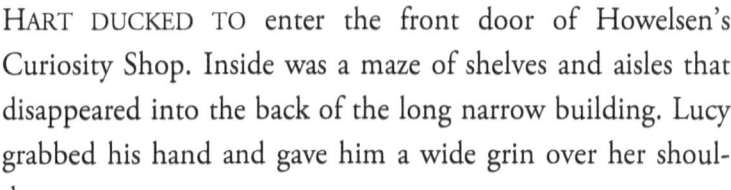

HART DUCKED TO enter the front door of Howelsen's Curiosity Shop. Inside was a maze of shelves and aisles that disappeared into the back of the long narrow building. Lucy grabbed his hand and gave him a wide grin over her shoulder.

"There are two floors. This one has most of the furniture, but the second floor is full of knickknacks. Come on, let's explore!"

Her enthusiasm was infectious, and he followed her down an aisle to their right. There was all manner of objects crammed together in every nook and cranny of the store. A long sofa covered in deep purple velvet held a collection of porcelain dolls that stared at him with glass eyes as they walked past. Hart smacked his head against something as they turned to go down the next aisle. Glancing up he saw a balsawood dragon hung from the low ceiling. It breathed bright red paper fire as it swung to-and-fro.

After exploring the ground floor, Lucy led the way up an iron circular staircase. Hart put a hand on her waist to keep her steady as they climbed. Or perhaps it was to keep him steady. The twisty stairs made his head swim by the time they reached the next floor. More light flooded this level thanks to large sky lights. They spotted a rack full of masquerade masks at the same time and exchanged grins. Lucy browsed one side of the rack as he perused the other. A matte gold mask painted with intricate black vines and sporting an exaggerated long nose caught his eye. It covered his whole face as he held it up and turned to show Lucy.

"Miss, may I have your next dance?"

She turned to face him. "That sounds *purrr-fect*." The mask she had on sported silver whiskers and a pink nose.

He chuckled. "Wait, I have the perfect partner for you." He turned back to the shelf and traded the gold mask for a grey one painted with the furry face of a wolf with snarling lips and sharp white teeth. He turned and grabbed Lucy around the waist to pull her up against him. "Beware, of the wolves, little pussy."

Lucy howled with laughter. "Oh no! Don't eat me!"

Hart pushed the mask up onto his head then leaned in to capture her earlobe between his teeth. "I thought you liked it when I nibbled on you."

More giggles erupted before she pushed him away. "Behave." Lucy untied her mask and put it back on the rack. "Let's look over here."

Hart put his mask back as well. He strolled down the room after his wife, watching her run her fingers over items she found interesting. She paused in front of a painting, tilting her head to one side as she studied it. Curious to see what had caught her eye, he came up behind her. The painting was of a flurry of butterflies in flight. It hung on a wall with a dozen other paintings.

One just a couple of paintings further down caught his attention, and he moved to get a better look. The painting depicted the seaside. Gentle waves lapped at the shore. Birds in flight dotted the horizon, and woman in a white dress stood staring out at the ocean, her parasol a splash of pink against the blue sky. Or perhaps she watched the two small boys in short pants as they crouched to play in the sand. Hart could almost feel the ocean breeze flutter the lace on her dress. He absently rubbed a hand over his heart. The peaceful scene reminded him so much of his childhood outings to the sea when his mother was still alive.

"I like the butterflies. You may purchase it for me as my birthday present." Lucy came next to him. She slid her hand in his. "This one is nice, too."

He squeezed her hand. "We'll take both of them."

CHAPTER TWENTY-SEVEN

THE NEXT FORTNIGHT was an idyllic blur. She and Hart spent all their time together, lounging in the gardens as she read out loud to him, going for rides in the park, and eating intimate dinners in the cozy breakfast room, which was fast becoming her favorite room in the house. Hart spent as much time nibbling on her as he did actual food. He would set her on the table, pushing her skirts up and up. Then he spread her legs, kissing up their length to feast on her sex until she was moaning his name.

Lucy sighed and squeezed her thighs together under the table as she thought about last night's feasting. She glanced across the table at Hart, who watched her with his stormy eyes. That look, she'd learned meant he was thinking about the same thing. He seemed to always know when she was aroused. Perhaps it was his particular talent, or perhaps she had always underestimated how much he noticed about her. Today, though, they couldn't get distracted. They had promised to attend the garden party of Lord and Lady Hollins, who were good friends of Trudy's.

"Don't look at me like that," she said. "We have to leave soon. It takes almost an hour to get to the Hollins's home."

"Then don't sigh and bite your bottom lip like that. You know it drives me mad with lust," he replied. "Why are we going to social functions? I thought we were supposed to be on our honeymoon."

"Trudy said that since we are still in town, we only get a short reprieve. If we were traveling, we could take longer." She took a bite of eggs; she was famished.

Hart frowned. "I wish I could disappear with you to Belstoke immediately, but I must still pursue the few leads we have discovered about my family."

She nodded. "Today may be an opportunity to observe some of your father's friends. According to Trudy, everyone will be there. It is the Hollins's twenty-fifth anniversary, and their annual party is well attended."

Hart nodded and speared a sausage with his fork, taking a bite. His appetite had returned. She was gratified to see him eating so well at every meal. The hollowness around his eyes and cheeks that she had noticed weeks ago when he first arrived in town was gone. She liked to think she had a part in his recovery.

It was clear he had not been taking care of himself for the past year. And not just from his eating habits. His shoulder often pained him, not that he would admit it. Stubborn ass. She planned to convince him to let her massage it again. If she could ever get him unclothed all the way. Even at night, while they slept in his big bed, he always had a nightshirt on to cover him. She'd had glimpses of the terrible burns that started on his right hip and which she knew stretched all the way up to his shoulder and to the back of his neck. She sighed again. *Patience is a virtue.*

"Perhaps the threatening letter was not from a man at all," she said. "Based on what we've learned about your father's private life, it could be from a woman. A mistress that he discarded? Perhaps it turned into a crime of passion."

"But what of the symbol at the bottom?"

"True. And how would it involve your brother? Unless Robert decided to accompany him to meet her and work out some deal. Perhaps they planned to pay her off to leave your father alone." She picked up a ripe tomato slice. "But that does not explain the symbol stamped on the letter." Biting into the slice, she chewed thoughtfully. "No, it has to be one of his cronies. Sometimes, my imagination runs away with me."

"I love your imagination." Hart winked. Then he took a sip of tea. "I have been thinking that it was all about some business deal, but maybe you're right. His murder could have been an act of passion. Blackpool all but admitted how much he hated my father for what he had done. But I doubt if he were the murderer, he would have told me his motive."

Lucy nodded in agreement. "I'll keep an ear out for gossip. Have you spoken with Trudy?"

"Yes, I asked her about the stamp and told her my suspicions. But she didn't remember anything about that time period. She seemed to believe the official story."

"At her age, she has seen many family and friends pass on. She would have had to make peace with their deaths."

Hart tugged at his hair, shoving his fingers through it viciously. "I cannot make peace with their deaths until I know the truth."

Lucy rose and came around the table to slide onto his lap. She smoothed his hair where he had tousled it. "I know. We will solve the mystery. I promise."

His arms came around her waist. He placed a kiss to the hollow where her neck met her shoulder. She felt his long inhale.

"This dress is far too low cut. How will I be able to focus on anything but your pert breasts today."

Lucy giggled as he made snuffling noises against her neck, placing open-mouth kisses as he went. She leaned her head back to give him better access.

A knock sounded at the door.

"Go away," Hart called out. It was his habitual response to anything that interrupted them.

But she pushed at his shoulders. "Hart, we cannot get distracted."

His mouth returned to her neck. "I promise I won't muss you," he mumbled as his tongue licked behind her ear.

"Come in," she called as she pushed again at her husband. "Behave."

"Never." But Hart straightened, although his arms still banded around her waist, keeping her on his lap.

Mr. Townson came into the room, his gaze firmly directed at a spot above their heads. "Your carriage is ready."

"Thank you, Townson," Hart said as he ground his hard

length up against her bottom.

The butler disappeared, closing the door behind him.

She twisted to face Hart. "I see you are determined to be a naughty boy."

Hart grinned at her admonishment.

She reached down to unbutton the falls on his trousers. "I think I will just have to take you in hand and see what we can do about this hard cock." She had learned so many new words for various body parts, but cock was her favorite.

Every time she said it, her husband groaned in approval. He loved when she told him explicitly what she wanted to do to him or what she wanted him to do to her. The power of having him literally in hand was heady and becoming addictive. His eyes fell shut as she grasped his cock.

She grinned down at him. "I guess we can be a few minutes late."

CHAPTER TWENTY-EIGHT

HART STOOD NEXT to Lucy, his hand on her lower back as she spoke with a small group of people around them. The sun beat down on them, making him sweat and increasing his displeasure. It wasn't that the conversation was all that boring but rather that he found himself supremely annoyed that he had to share Lucy with anyone at all. His new wife had proven to be as much of a distraction as he had feared. His obsession with every detail of her consumed him. The way she moved across a room, the many moods reflected in her expressive eyes, every inch of her lithe body, and the myriad of thoughts that tumbled randomly out of that beautiful, filthy mouth. Her clever brain was sharp and intuitive. Keeping up with her in conversation was a challenge he enjoyed every day.

This morning's conversation reminded him that he hadn't thought about his mission to find his family's murderer in more than a week. Guilt lodged in his chest. He needed to get his focus back to where it belonged. Lucy glanced up at him with a smile, which melted some of that guilt. She had promised to help. Surely, it was okay to take a small reprieve from his task. His thirst for revenge had pulled him from the mire of melancholy he had fallen into after the accident, giving him a purpose. And it still was his purpose, but maybe it didn't have to be the only thing in his life that was important.

The couple that Lucy had been conversing with wandered away. She turned to him. "Are you all right? You seem a million miles away."

Hart nodded. "Yes, sorry." He scanned the people crowded on the stone terrace where they stood.

The cream of society was all here to celebrate the Hollins's anniversary. The crowd of elegantly dressed people made him uncomfortable but less so than he had felt at the Bartleby's ball. Perhaps it was the outdoor setting. Large gardens extended out from the terrace. Landscaped in the formal French style, small boxwoods arranged in neat squares outlined cheerful flower gardens. White pea gravel paths intersected the bushes and led down to a long pool with colorful fish swimming amidst green lily pads. Guests dotted the lawns and paths everywhere he looked.

"You weren't wrong about the party being well attended. It is very crowded out here, isn't it?"

"It is a grand house. Although, it doesn't have the same gothic atmosphere as Belstoke, which I prefer." She shaded her eyes as she looked up at the house's brick façade. "The ivy climbing the walls does give it some charm."

Despite her wide-brimmed hat, which shaded her face, Hart saw a droplet of sweat slide down from her temple. And then he noticed that the hair at her nape was damp as well.

"Are you too hot?"

She opened her fan and flicked it back and forth. "It has become quite warm, hasn't it?"

"Let's sneak inside. Maybe it will be cooler in the shade." He guided her through the throng of guests across the terrace toward the house. They managed to make it the whole way without more than a few polite nods in passing. The back doors were propped open, and they escaped into a shadowed hallway.

"Where to?" he asked.

"Let's explore," Lucy whispered conspiratorially. She took hold of his hand and Hart followed her down the corridor. They passed by a stone staircase that descended belowstairs. The noise of voices and the clatter of pans led him to believe it went to the kitchens. Further along, the hallway opened to the center of the house. A carpeted grand staircase climbed up to the first floor. Lucy gave his hand a tug and continued down to the right.

This corridor was lined with windows that looked out the front of the house. In between each window, statues sat atop identical white pillars. They stopped in front of one that was a bust of their host, Lord Hollins.

Lucy scrunched her nose in distaste. "Why would you want a likeness of just your head? It's a bit gruesome, in my opinion."

"His lady is the next one down." Hart pointed.

They walked down and peered at Lady Hollins's head. The casting was eerily accurate, and it felt as though Lady

Hollins was glaring disapprovingly at them for wandering through her home. "Maybe it is to deter bad behavior among the servants," he said. "She certainly is scaring me."

"Come, let's see what's in here." Lucy turned and opened a door behind them. "Oh, it's the ballroom!"

Hart followed her inside. The ballroom stretched in a long rectangle, about three hundred feet at least. Three sets of double doors would open to the corridor they had just come from. Along the opposite wall, tall mirrors hung every few feet down its length, giving the illusion of the room being wider than it actually was. Above those mirrors, small square windows lined the upper half of the wall, letting in some natural light. The room was gilded from top to bottom. Mirrors, molding, and chandeliers all done in gold tones.

Lucy raced out into the middle of the patterned wood floor. Spreading her arms wide, she twirled in circles. She laughed as she came to a stop. "I've always wanted to do that in the middle of the dance floor, but there is always the pesky problem of the other guests."

Hart smiled at her enthusiasm, and not for the first time, he wondered how she lived with so much joy inside her. It never seemed to dim. He walked to her, reaching out, needing to see if some of that joy would transfer to him if he held her tight.

She continued to smile up at him, when he wrapped his arm around her. "Hart," she fluttered those lush eyelashes at him.

"Yes?"

"Would you dance with me?"

He stiffened. "I can't dance anymore."

"I know that usually you are afraid to bump into anyone. But there is not a soul here but the two of us. You do remember how to waltz, don't you?"

Of course, he remembered how to dance. He glanced around the empty room. Could he still lead a woman gracefully across the floor without stumbling? His gaze returned to his wife's hopeful expression.

Lucy reached up and pulled the pin from her hat, removing it. She held out her hand. Her blue eyes sparkled irresistibly with mischief. "Dance with me, Hart?"

Since when had he ever turned down an opportunity to seduce a beautiful woman while dancing? He'd be damned if he let his blasted eye stop him now. He handed her his walking stick. She took both it and her hat to a chair on the edge of the room and set them down. When she returned, he was ready for her. He scooped her up against him tightly, one hand splayed at her back, and the other clasped her hand out in the ready position. He bent to nuzzle the spot behind her ear that always made her shiver. "Since there are no society matrons watching, I shall hold you indecently close, like they do in the French court."

"Lovely," she murmured. "Now, for some music." She began to hum.

Hart's instincts kicked in, and he led them around the floor. One, two, three ... one, two, three. After accomplishing the first couple of turns without stumbling, he began to relax. He would never be able to do this on a crowded dance floor while people danced around them and through his blind spot, but Lucy was right. There was nothing wrong with his dancing skills. He twirled them in wide circles, enjoying the freedom of movement the empty room afforded. Holding her in his arms was a pleasure. She let out a small sigh and laid her head against his shoulder. Another thing they would never be able to do in public.

"I always had fantasies about you waltzing me around a glittering ballroom."

"You did?"

"Of course. You were the most sophisticated gentleman I knew. Well, except for your brother, perhaps. When I was sixteen, the two of you were like golden gods to my eyes."

He chuckled. "That was the old me. I used to think I was quite the catch."

Lucy lifted her head. "I think you were. You always had plenty of women to dance with, especially after you became the duke. I didn't stand a chance against your harem."

"I didn't have as many women as you seem to think." Hart frowned; that wasn't entirely true. He had had his share of affairs. Didn't every young man? Perhaps he'd been too casual in his attitude toward women. But when there were always ladies willing to vie for your attention, it was hard to say no. It made him uncomfortable to think maybe he was more like his father than he would like to admit.

Glancing down at Lucy, this woman who had become so

dear so quickly, he felt the need to reiterate, "That was the old me." He pulled them to a stop. "You are the only woman that I want to dance with now," he admitted.

"Good, because I don't like to share." She planted a possessive kiss on his lips.

And as he sank into her kiss, he found that he quite liked being possessed by this one lady. "Me either," he said against her lips. "If we were at a ball surrounded by people on the dance floor, I would spirit you away to a dark corner and try to convince you to let me pleasure you until you were breathless and begging for more."

"I would let you. I have become addicted to your charms, husband."

Good. He pulled her hard against him with every intention of charming his way right under her skirts. A glance around the room showed a decided lack of furniture, save for a few chairs left along the wall. He briefly considered one, but the lack of privacy if someone else were to wander in was not acceptable. He gripped her hand and walked over to gather their things. "Let's get out of here." He shoved her hat into her hands.

"Are we going back to the party?"

"Hell, no. I'm going in search of a dark corner."

He pulled her from the ballroom back out to the corridor. One of these rooms must be empty. Halfway down the corridor, past the ballroom, they heard male voices coming from a room at the end of the hallway. The door to that room was cracked open a couple of inches. Hart paused to listen when he recognized Lord Blackpool's voice.

"Gentlemen, let's all calm down."

"I cannot." Another voice, which Hart couldn't quite put his finger on, rang out. "That girl out there is living what should have been my daughter's life."

"Your bad decisions coming back to haunt you, eh?" A different, deeper voice chuckled.

"If you hadn't killed the boy, maybe I could have convinced him to honor the agreement!"

"Are you insane? After you killed his father?"

"It was a matter of honor." The voice was filled with righteous indignation.

Another voice he didn't recognize cut through the others. "Enough about the girl. We are here to discuss the journal. We need to know if he found it. What he knows. Each one of us is at risk."

"Hartwick was a crafty bastard. He wouldn't have left it lying around. I sent my man to look for it at both homes. And he came back empty-handed. I still think the boy doesn't know anything."

They were talking about his father. This was his chance to find out who killed his father. He started toward the room, but Lucy's hand grasped his arm. "No," she whispered furiously. "We don't know who is in there. You can't just walk into the lion's den unprepared."

He stared down at her hand clinging to him and tried to think logically. What risk would she be in if he went charging into a room? The men in there were all likely peers. The best he could do would be to challenge his father's murderer to a duel. He flexed his right hand into a fist. He would be as good as dead with this blasted bad shooting arm. He raised his gaze to meet Lucy's frantic one. He would not leave her unprotected. Revenge was best served cold.

She pulled him across the corridor. Opening the first door, she yanked him inside. They pushed the door almost all the way closed, leaving a crack to peer into the hall. "First, we need to find out who is in that room." She kept her voice low.

"I recognized Blackpool's voice. I just met with him, so it's fresh in my mind. But I can't place the other voices," he whispered back as he tried hard to listen to the voices down the hallway.

"I tell you, he knows something." Fear threaded through the man's voice. "He wouldn't be asking so many questions after all this time if Galey hadn't betrayed us."

"But does he have the journal? I say we tie up loose ends."

"I forbid it, James. How many more of us are you willing to sacrifice? We have always protected each other, and we can continue to do so without taking such drastic measures."

The slam of a door hitting the wall reverberated down the hall. Hart froze as he watched carefully out the crack. The Duke of Lavensham stalked past. After another moment, the Earl of Blackpool and the Duke of Fleming followed. Lastly, the Earl of Rawlings and Viscount Griffen, heads together, walked past their conversation low and impossible to decipher.

Hart waited several long moments before carefully shutting the door the rest of the way. He leaned back against the wall and stared across the room. His father's murderer had been one of those men, one of his father's closest friends.

"Everyone in that room seemed to know exactly what happened to your father and brother. They have been hiding the truth."

"For five years." He closed his eyes. "Galey said that they were powerful. He broke ranks to try to tell me what happened."

When he opened his eyes, Lucy was pacing in front of him. "But we still don't know which voices belonged to whom. Which of these men is the killer."

"Two men, you mean. The first man reproached a second man for killing the boy. I assume he meant Robert," Hart replied. Christ, why had they killed Robert?

"Yes, and what did he mean about his daughter? None of it makes sense."

Hart tugged on her hand; her pacing increased his own anxiety. What secrets did these men keep at such a high cost of killing one of their own? Hauling her close, he wrapped her in his arms.

Panic began to claw at his chest. "I'm worried I have pulled you into something that is far larger than I thought. Perhaps I should send you to Belstoke. You would be safer there."

She pulled back to look up at him. "And who will protect you? No, absolutely not."

"But—" he began.

"No. Hart, your life has been endangered twice now. They are clearly worried you know some of the secrets they are keeping, so they will try again. I will not let you deal with this alone. You need me."

He squeezed her tight. "I need to keep you safe. Why are you so fierce, sweetness? Let me take care of you."

"I have lost every single one of the people that I loved in this world. I will not lose you, too." Her eyes began to shine with tears again.

He could not stand to see the pain shimmering in them. He battled against his instincts to hide her away. To keep her from harm. A bead of sweat rolled down his back as his panic intensified. They needed to leave this house. They needed to go home.

"All right. But we will have a discussion about adding some extra protection when you go out."

"For you as well." Lucy raised an imperious eyebrow.

He sighed. "For me as well. For now, let's get back to the party and say our farewells. I want to go home and tuck you into bed." *And never let you leave it.* He sucked in a deep breath and prepared himself to walk back into the crowded party. He would master this tightness in his chest for her. He would get Lucy home safe.

CHAPTER TWENTY-NINE

L UCY PADDED DOWNSTAIRS around eleven that night. The light from her single candle flickered and pushed against the shadows. Once she had reached the main level, the ever-present Herbert straightened from his watch near the front door.

"He's in the library tonight, Your Grace."

"Thank you. I'll go get him so you can get to bed."

When they returned that afternoon, she and Hart had met with Townson and discussed safety concerns for the house. This had included having a couple of men on guard outside at night and also which footman would be assigned as her new bodyguard of sorts. When she had argued that she could protect herself, Hart had insisted, saying it was for his own peace of mind. How was she to argue with him when his eyes had silently pleaded? Hart had not been himself since the afternoon. He seemed to withdraw into his own thoughts, telling her after they ate dinner that he would be up later. Well, this was late enough for her.

When she entered the library, it appeared Herbert had been mistaken; Hart was not in the room. Several candelabras had been placed around, and they illuminated the mess that had been made of the shelves. In the gaps where books had been unshelved, others lay on their sides or were shoved in backward so the spines faced the wall. There were books stacked haphazardly on the library table. The writing desk under the window had received the same ransacking. Lucy spun in a slow circle. Had a thief broken into the house?

Then she saw the painting, the one she had always admired, of the field of sunflowers leaning against the wall. Next to it, Hart sat on the floor, his legs bent and his forearms resting on his knees. "It isn't here," he said.

Above him, a safe built into the wall was open; its door swung ajar above Hart's head.

"What is not here?" she asked.

"The journal. Today, one of the men said they were all meeting to find out if I had found my father's journal. I looked in the safe. It took me a while to even remember where he kept the key. Then I searched through the shelves. It would be just like him to hide it in plain sight."

His voice sounded hollow. He stared down at his hands.

Lucy walked over to crouch in front of him. "Hart, how long have you been sitting here?"

"What time is it?" His gaze lifted.

"Almost midnight."

"A couple of hours, I suppose."

Lucy moved next to him and lowered herself to the floor. "I know that today it was hard to be so close to the men who killed your family. But those men are all powerful peers. I'm not saying they are above the law, but unless we have proof of their involvement in what happened, it doesn't make sense to confront them. You made the right decision to exercise caution."

Hart was silent next to her for several minutes. When he spoke, his voice was low. "I feel as though I didn't know him at all. Robert was always his confidant; I was just the spare son. But even though ... I never expected all these secrets that he kept."

"Do we ever truly know our parents? Why wouldn't they shield us from the worst of themselves? They are humans who make mistakes. My father tried to shield me from what happened to my mother. She never fully recovered from the assault. He came home for a time after the news reached him. The longest the navy would allow him. I think he felt guilty that he had been so far away when she needed him. That's when he taught me to fight. He said I should always fight even if the other person was bigger or stronger. That I should never give up."

Hart intertwined his fingers with hers. "I don't think I ever asked you what happened to your parents."

Lucy swallowed around the memories lodged in her throat. "We lived near the sea, in a cove where the water sprayed up against the rocks at high tide. When I was young, my mother said that it was where the mermaids played. But the truth was that my mother felt connected to my father when she looked out to the ocean. She said that she could picture his ship sailing on the far-off waves. In the end, the sea took them both. One day, a year after the assault, she lost her internal struggle, and she jumped off the cliff into the water. My father and I were out rambling and saw her disappear over the edge. He raced over and dove in to save her. But the tide was too rough, and they both perished against the rocks."

His hand flexed, squeezing hers. "Christ, Lucy. How horrible."

She rested her head on his shoulder. "It was. But it also was a long time ago. I have learned to think of them both as the best versions of themselves. I choose to remember them that way."

"Ever since the accident last year, I have these terrible moments of anxiety. They creep up from behind me like a specter in the night. The fear that I experienced that night is too big to keep hidden inside. Just when I think I have mastered it, it rears its ugly head when I least expect. Perhaps, that is how your mother felt. Maybe it overwhelmed her that day."

Lucy nodded. It made sense. At fourteen, she hadn't been able to comprehend the depth of her mother's pain. She had only understood that her mother had left her. And taken her father as well. The fear she felt that day, long buried, rose and squeezed her lungs making it hard to breathe. She couldn't bear to lose another person she loved.

She twisted to face Hart. "Do you feel that way often?"

"Not as much as I did at first. I haven't had a nightmare about that night in months." He leaned in and pressed his lips to hers. "The last few weeks lying next to you in bed has afforded me the best sleep of my life."

"Then let's go to bed." She rose to her feet and tugged at his hands.

Hart stood up stiffly. He lifted his arms above his head and groaned as he stretched. "I'm too old to sit on the floor for so long."

Lucy laughed, and some of the tension she felt drained. "Come on, old man. I'm going to get the salve and massage your shoulder. I bet you haven't used it at all since I gave it to you."

Hart shrugged. But he followed her, and together, they blew out the candles from around the room. Then with her single taper, she led him out into the corridor. Herbert looked relieved as they passed by. Now that the master of the house was going to bed, so could he. When they reached their suite Hart pulled loose the ties of her dressing gown and pushed it off her shoulders, letting it pool on the floor. He pulled her flush against him, peppering her neck with light kisses.

"Oh no, you go sit there." She pointed to a rectangular footstool that sat at the end of the bed. "Pull it out here. It will put you low enough so that I can really work the salve into the muscles." She crossed to the dresser where the jar of salve that she had gifted him sat unused, just as she thought.

When she returned, she found him sitting obediently on the footstool, which he had pulled out to the center of the rug. His lazy smile made him look like a dangerous jungle cat lounging on a toadstool.

She giggled. "Do you need a bigger chair to sit on?"

"No, I'm fine." He unbuttoned his vest and pulled it off his shoulders. Next was the cravat pulled lazily from around his neck.

Lucy approached him and ran her fingers through his dark hair. She tugged until his gaze rose to meet hers. "It would be better if you removed your shirt as well. Then I could really see what I was doing."

He stiffened, and she could see the denial in his eyes. She tugged again at his hair. "I do not care about your scars, Hart. I care about you, the man you are inside. Nothing on the outside can change that. Can you trust me?" She held her breath.

❧

HART STARED UP into Lucy's eyes and felt the truth in her words. Her fingers threaded through his hair, holding him in place, and her grip tightened as she asked her question. Lucy was the first woman he'd ever been with who cared not a whit about his title, his reputation, or his money. What she asked for was much harder to give. She wanted him to bare himself. She wanted the whole of him, not just the shiny, pretty bits.

He had never considered himself a coward, so he reached down and tugged his shirt from his waistband. Slowly, without breaking eye contact, he pulled the shirt over his torso and then up over his head. He braced for her gasp.

But it never came. Lucy stood before him, her eyes still locked on his face. She reached out and traced his cheek with the back of her fingers. Then her gaze drifted down, and her fingers followed their path. Over his red, mottled skin and puckered scars. Her fingertips fluttered down his neck, curved across his shoulder, and then down his chest.

"Oh, Hart." She sighed. "I can't imagine the pain that you endured."

He sucked in a ragged breath as her palms smoothed over his chest. Her touch unlocking a part of him he thought he had firmly suppressed. The part of him that needed. Needed to be touched, needed to be seen. She leaned down and kissed him, her lips sliding against his slowly. But he didn't want gentle kisses; he wanted to let loose the deluge of emotions her touch unlocked.

Grasping the back of her neck, he changed the angle of their kiss and, with a deep moan, took control. She responded immediately to his passion-fueled desperation. Her tongue tangled with his as he plundered her mouth. Lucy climbed into his lap and ground herself against his hardening cock.

He ached to feel her bare skin against his. Taking handfuls of her nightgown, he ripped it off over her head. Exposing all that smooth skin drove him wild. He dragged her fully against him, exulting in the soft press of her breasts against his bare chest.

He stroked his hands up and down her back. "Lucy, I can't get enough of you. You are more addictive than any vice I've found in London."

"Don't deny yourself. I'm yours."

Christ, this woman would kill him with her words, with what she offered. He rose, taking both of them over to the bed. Laying her down, he ran a hand down the center of her body, enjoying the gentle swells and dips. Then, he undressed, toeing off his shoes and dropping his trousers.

"Spread those pretty thighs for me." His gaze latched onto the dark curls that hid the glistening pink of her pussy as she opened for him. "Good girl," he murmured as he slid his hands up her thighs and bent to bury his nose between her legs. He tongued her opening, enjoying the taste of her arousal. Then continued to lick up to that perfect pearl of a clit.

"Oh god, Hart!"

He grinned at her shout. Lucy didn't know how to be quiet when she was aroused, and he loved it. She moaned and screamed his name. She had a mouth that would put a sailor to shame when she instructed him on what felt good. After her first blush of embarrassment the morning after their wedding, she hadn't held back any of her pleasure. Right now, he lapped it up, feeding on her passionate abandon.

"Hart." She grasped at his hair.

He raised his head to look up at her. "Yes?"

"Come here and fuck me properly. I want to feel your hard cock inside me."

"Yes, ma'am." He grinned and climbed onto the bed and

over her body.

She pulled her knees up and thrust her hips up to meet his slow slide into her. They both moaned. Being inside her tight sex was like coming home. Lucy's hands frantically roamed over his chest and upward to trace over his shoulders and then down his back as if it were her last chance to touch him.

He captured one of them against his heart. "Lucy, having your hands roam my body feels amazing. You have opened a floodgate. I want to make love to you for hours. I wish to drown in your tender touch."

She sighed and met his thrusts, taking him deep. They made love slowly. The intimacy of her touch saturated every fiber of his being as she stroked his damaged skin with soft fingertips, learning the grooves and the smooth, shiny stretches. He leaned over to take one of her breasts in his mouth and flicked the pebbled tip with his tongue. A strangled cry of pleasure escaped her lips, and with that plea, the time for going slow was gone.

He pumped into her, angling for the spot inside that made her writhe. His mouth moved to her throat, and he scraped his teeth down the pale column. Wanting to mark her. *Mine.* He bit down. Lucy climaxed with a shout. With another deep thrust, he followed her over the edge. Filling her up with his seed. Marking her again as his.

Rolling over, he took her with him. She lay sprawled on him, her head on his chest. Then he felt the hot caress of her breath as she began to pepper his chest with light kisses.

Closing his eyes, he allowed himself, with each brush of her lips, to believe that Lucy was telling the truth when she said that his scars did not change how she saw him. To believe that somehow this precious woman cared not about what he looked like on the outside. What a damn gift she was.

Hart ran his fingers slowly through her hair. He would protect her at all costs. Even if it meant sending her away to Belstoke with an army of guards until he could figure out how to deal with his father's so-called friends. He needed to locate that journal. If it truly contained secrets he could use to destroy the others, then it could be the key to keeping all that was his safe.

CHAPTER THIRTY

LUCY INCREASED THE pressure of her kneading, and Hart groaned, but in a good way that meant she had loosened the muscle she massaged. The soft morning light filtered through the sheer curtains. She had finally gotten around to working the salve into his right shoulder and arm muscles.

Hart leaned his head back against her stomach and looked up at her. "I plan to go to the bank this morning and check the safe box we have there. Perhaps the journal is in it."

"What do you keep at the safe at the bank as opposed to the safe here at the house?"

"Mostly money and family jewelry. But you never know. It certainly would be a secure place to hide the journal." He reached up and took her hand from his shoulder. His thumb ran over her ring finger. "This unadorned finger is a travesty. I will rectify that today as well."

"You don't have to get me a ring," she replied half-heartedly because, really, the idea of wearing Hart's ring made her heart sing.

"Nonsense. As my duchess, the jewels are yours now. Do you want to come with me and pick something out yourself?"

She reached down to wrap her arms around his neck. "No, you choose. This will be your first test as a husband." Grinning, she gave him a peck on the cheek. Then she returned to massaging his shoulder. "Give me a few more minutes with this, and then we can eat breakfast."

"Naked?"

Lucy smacked the back of his head lightly. "You are such a hedonist."

"I've been called worse."

After she finished his massage, they sat in their robes at the small round table in her sitting room and had breakfast. The morning's newspapers lay on the tray. Lucy picked up the *Piccadilly Press* while Hart took the *Times*. After perusing the headlines, she turned to page three for the scandal sheet. She was still peeved about that unflattering caricature. The first section of tidbits was largely a recap of events she had not attended last week. Then she saw their names.

The newly married Duke and Duchess of Hartwick briefly attended the Hollins's twenty-fifth anniversary party on Thursday. They deigned to speak with a few guests before disappearing for most of the party. I dare to say that the duchess is setting a bad example for all the young ladies out this season; mire yourself in scandal, and perhaps you too may be scooped up into marriage by a duke. Although, we all know his desperation to have an heir most likely inspired his proposal. For who would marry such a beast?

Lucy knew her mouth hung open in astonishment, but she could not stop sputtering. The nerve of the man! Any woman would be lucky to marry Hart. He was wonderful, kind, a bit moody, but so caring for those he considered in his domain. She slapped the paper down on the table. "They can go to hell," she muttered.

"What is it this time?" Hart's amused voice cut through her indignation.

Lucy slid the paper across the table. She watched Hart's expression darken as he read the piece. He looked up from the paper, his grey eyes flinty with anger. "This time, we are going down to this scandal rag. If he ever mentions your name again, I am going to tear the man to pieces."

Hart looked positively murderous. Lord, she loved this man. She clapped her hands together in glee. She had a few things to say to the newspaper editor herself.

LUCY FELT FAR less confident standing in front of the door to the newspaper. The townhouse itself was narrow, squashed between two others as part of a long row down the street. The place looked entirely unassuming, but above the door, a shingle proclaimed it was indeed the Piccadilly Press. Lucy scanned the residential street. Perhaps this was a poor idea. What if they angered the editor, and he printed more lies about them?

A feeling of outrage bubbled up in her chest at what had been said in today's edition. She squared her shoulders. This man had maligned Hart at every turn. It was unfair and cruel to use Hart's scars to entertain their readers. It stepped past the bounds of common decency. She stepped forward and knocked.

A few moments later, the door opened, and a small boy peeked out. "Hullo, who may I ask is calling?"

Lucy stared down at the child in shock. The boy was a miniature version of Hart. The grey eyes fringed with dark lashes, the black hair, high cheekbones, and even though softer in the boy's features, the square chin that all the Hartwick males had. Lucy glanced over at Hart, who also stared at the boy.

"Robert, I told you never to answer the door without a grownup." A female voice came from inside. The door opened fully, and a woman stepped forward with a smile. She looked up at Hart and gasped. Her smile disappeared, and she reached for the boy and shoved him behind her.

Lucy grasped Hart's arm, forcing him to look at her. She raised her eyebrows in question.

Hart glanced at the woman and then back at her. "I have never seen this woman before in my life. I swear."

CHAPTER THIRTY-ONE

H ART STARED DOWN at the boy, who couldn't be anything but a Hartwick. The child resembled his brother right down to the slightly upturned tilt of his nose. And there was no mistaking those unusual grey eyes that Hart shared with his father and brother.

He cleared his throat. "Ma'am, whose child is this?" he demanded.

"My child." She narrowed her eyes. "What are you doing here, Your Grace?"

"We are here to see the editor of the *Piccadilly Press*," Lucy said.

"Well, you've found her."

"Her?" he replied dumbly.

He stared at the child who peeked around his mother's skirts. His heart clenched. Family. A piece of his brother alive and right in front of him. "Ma'am, I must know. Is this boy a Hartwick?"

The woman glanced past them up and down the street, then sighed. "You best come in. I don't need my neighbors seeing a duke at my doorstep." She stepped back and ushered them in. Still keeping the boy next to her with his hand grasped in hers, she said, "Follow me."

Lucy looked up at him and silently mouthed, "*Good Lord.*"

He fully shared in her shocked statement. They followed the woman as she led them into the large front room. At one end of the room, two large desks sat facing each other across a deep red oriental rug. The surfaces of both desks were covered in newsprint, paper, and what looked to be small wooden tiles.

"Please have a seat." The woman motioned them to follow her to the other end of the room, where a settee and chairs were arranged in a cozy seating area. Hart carefully stepped around an army of toy soldiers engaged in battle on the rug.

"I apologize for the mess, but we weren't expecting company."

After removing a tin cannon from the couch cushion, Lucy sat down gingerly next to Hart on the settee. "So, you are E. Harper?"

"Yes, my father was Edward Harper, the owner of the Piccadilly Press. He passed away three years ago. I am Elizabeth. After I took over operations, I kept the moniker. It is purposefully vague as anonymity for a woman in this business is important."

Hart didn't give a whit whether the editor was a man or a woman. All he wanted to know about was the boy who sat at his mother's feet playing with his soldiers. He must be at least five years old. Had his brother known about the child?

"How old is he?" Hart asked softly.

Miss Harper ran a hand over her son's hair. "He will be five this September." She looked Hart squarely in the eye. "Robert is named after his father."

Hart expelled a long breath. "Did he know?"

Miss Harper shook her head. "I found out I was pregnant after they were killed."

Lucy reached for his hand and squeezed it tightly. "Miss Harper, would you be willing to tell us what happened between you and Robert? The duke has been trying to discover the truth behind their deaths."

Miss Harper's mouth was pressed into a thin line. She looked like she was waging an internal battle.

Hart leaned forward, resting his arms on his knees. "Please, Miss Harper, I beg you. I need to know what happened to them. If you know anything at all that can help me understand. Someone has tried very hard to stop me from knowing the truth." He raised a hand to his face.

She gave a tight nod, then leaned down. "Robert, go see Mrs. Todd in the kitchen and tell her I said you could have a biscuit or two and a glass of milk."

"Yay!" The boy jumped to his feet and scampered out of the room.

Miss Harper clasped her hands in her lap. Hart waited for her to gather her thoughts. Her brow furrowed over her deep brown eyes for a moment before she looked up at them.

"I met your brother at a ball quite by accident. We literally bumped into each other coming around a corner. I know you must be thinking, what is the daughter of a newspaper-man doing at a high society function? My maternal grandmother is the Marchioness of Rollinsford. They disowned my mother when she married beneath her station for love. But after my mother died, my grandmother had a change of heart and wanted to help me to find an advantageous marriage. She sponsored a season for me when I was nineteen."

"That was kind of her," Lucy said.

Miss Harper's lip turned up into a wry smile. "Yes, well, she promptly dumped me out of her life when I became pregnant out of wedlock. I've learned the hard way that the ton are fickle with their affections. But I digress. Robert quite literally swept me off my feet. Our romance was a whirlwind, a precious few weeks. He took me sailing one afternoon and asked me to marry him.

"When he spoke to your father about marrying me, he was told that an agreement between your father and one of his friends had been made years ago to betroth Robert and the man's daughter. This man's daughter was much younger than Robert, not even fourteen, I believe, so they had been waiting for her to come of age before making the match.

"Robert was incensed that he had never been told about a deal that would impact his future so immensely. He told your father how much he loved me and how he simply wouldn't accept another. In the end, your father agreed to support Robert. But when your father broke the news to the other man, his friend felt betrayed. He demanded satisfaction."

Hart sat back against the cushions. Jesus, how could he not have known about this? "I spent that spring in Edinburgh visiting a friend at his estate. Planned to stay the whole summer." His visit had been cut short by the news of his family's death. He'd spent a week racing home on horseback when he had gotten the news of their deaths. "He never wrote me about any of this."

"He spoke about you often." Miss Harper offered him a small smile. "Said you were an incorrigible flirt, an excellent card player, and a good friend to all those you cared about."

His throat clogged with emotion. Lucy squeezed his hand tightly. She had never let go of it during this whole conversation.

He squeezed hers back, grateful for her silent support. "I found a threatening letter in my father's papers ranting about a broken deal. Now I see it wasn't a business deal."

"Wasn't it? A merger between wealthy families is always about business." Miss Harper's voice was laced with bitterness.

"What happened next?" he asked.

"Robert came to see me the night before the duel. He was to act as your father's second. He was worried but said your father assured him that it was just for show, that they would shoot into the air like gentlemen and consider the matter done. Your father was confident that his friend didn't really want to hurt him but that it was just a matter of honor." She let out a shaky breath.

"I didn't hear from Robert the next day, and I began to worry. Then, the following morning, my father came into my room. He had heard through one of his sources that the duke and his son had been found dead in a hack down on the Strand. Both had gunshot wounds in the chest. The magistrate was saying it had been a robbery gone wrong. I knew that couldn't be true. Something must have gone terribly wrong at the duel. My father agreed that it sounded like the truth was being covered up."

Hart stood and strode over to the window. His head reeled at the information she shared. He had never accepted that it had been a robbery. There were too many unanswered questions. Why had they been down there at night in a hired hack? And where had the coachman been? Many rumors abounded in the weeks after the news of their deaths had spread. Rumors that said his father had been discreetly extracting his brother from a brothel in that part of town. Some said that they had been involved in unsavory business dealings. Hart had dismissed all of the ridiculous assertions.

Lucy came to stand next to him. "Are you alright?"

He stared blankly out the window onto the quiet street. Was he alright? A certain sense of relief came with the truth. But it didn't diminish the anger he felt. Nothing would assuage that until he knew who to punish. He still had questions.

He turned back to Miss Harper. "Why was Robert killed? He was just the second."

"I don't know the answer to that," she replied. "My

whole future died that day with your brother. I thought I would never recover from the loss. But then I discovered I was pregnant, and it gave me something to live for, a piece of Robert to cherish." Her voice broke. He watched her draw in a deep breath. "I didn't know what had led to his death. But I knew it had to have been something to do with this duel. I needed to keep my baby safe, so I kept the identity of the father to myself. My father was the only one who knew of my relationship with Robert."

"I have one more question. Who was my father dueling with?"

Miss Harper looked up at him with wide, solemn eyes. "The Viscount Griffen."

CHAPTER THIRTY-TWO

L UCY SAT DOWN abruptly on the settee; they finally had an answer. The Viscount Griffen. She glanced over at Hart. "It must have been he who commented bitterly about me living his daughter's life."

Hart stood still as a statue with his jaw clenched. Then he nodded. "Right. When I met with him, my instincts told me he was hiding something." He ran a hand over his face. "He sat calmly across the table and lectured me about focusing on the future when every word out of his mouth was a lie."

"Covering his tracks from the very beginning. And he had help based on the conversation we overheard yesterday."

"What conversation yesterday?" Miss Harper asked.

She glanced at Hart. *Should we trust her?* She asked him silently.

Hart moved to retake his spot next to her. "Miss Harper, thank you for sharing your heartbreak. You don't know how much it means to me to know the truth. I wish I had known sooner; I would have taken care of you."

Miss Harper tilted her head, another wry half smile on her face. "Would you have? Would you have even believed me if I had come to you?"

"I like to think I would have. I believe you now. And I would like to help you with my nephew's care."

Miss Harper stiffened, her back going ramrod straight. "We are doing just fine on our own. We don't need your money."

"But surely—"

Lucy gripped Hart's arm before he could make it worse.

She tried to turn the conversation back on topic. "Miss Harper, we aren't just looking for answers to the how of their deaths but also to who helped cover it up. Someone has attempted to kill Hart before he finds the truth."

"Is that what happened to you?" Miss Harper asked.

Hart nodded. "Last year, Lord Galey sent me a message asking me to meet him. He said the guilt of knowing what had happened to my father was eating at him. I joined him in his carriage to speak privately, but before he could say much, a small handheld bomb was thrown into the carriage." Hart paused, his brow furrowed.

"What is it?" Lucy murmured.

"Galey said they were very powerful, they had ears everywhere, they had found us. Not him, they."

"It has to be the club. The Knot of Isis. Don't you think?"

"The club?" Miss Harper asked.

"Yes, Hart's father used to be part of a club in his school days, and they used the Knot of Isis as a symbol for their group. It means—"

"To protect against one's enemies." Miss Harper nodded.

Lucy grinned. Smart lady. "Yes. Hart's father still used a stamp with the symbol on it in his correspondence with these old friends. The stamp was also on a threatening letter he received warning him to not back out of some deal. We've figured out who a few of the members are. Yesterday, we overheard through a partially open door, a group of men talking about Hart's father at the Hollins's party. We couldn't place the voices, but we do know who exited that room." She turned to Hart. "But how to know which ones were involved in the duel and the subsequent whitewashing of the incident?" Her brain tumbled over all the information they had learned. "And how did Robert end up in the middle and dead?" She continued to muse.

Hart and Miss Harper stared at her aghast.

Lucy cringed. "Oh dear. I'm sorry I did not mean to sound blasé about Robert's death. I should have kept my thoughts to myself."

"No, that's not why I'm staring. I love how your clever mind works," Hart said. "I was thinking that the men in that room yesterday all knew what happened and so we can safely assume they are all members. The betrothal must have been the broken deal."

"I feel as though you two are speaking in code. I hate not knowing all the information," Miss Harper grumbled.

Lucy exchanged another look with Hart. The editor of a scandal rag hardly seemed a good person to confide in what they had figured out thus far. They had probably told her too much as it was. Hart wore a matching skeptical expression.

She speared Miss Harper with a piercing look. "You have hardly been kind to us in your paper. Why would we trust you not to spill the information we have gathered all over London?"

The lady sighed. She looked at Hart. "I suppose ... that the vitriol came from a place of bitterness. You are still alive where he is dead." She grimaced as she turned her gaze to Lucy. "And you are living the life that would have been mine. It makes me a bit ashamed to say out loud that I feel the same way as the despicable Lord Griffen. I thought I had made peace with my life." She shook her head. "I have made peace. I have a wonderful little boy and a business that supports us. It is enough."

Lucy didn't know what to say. She was still angry at what had been said in the paper at Hart's expense, but she also could understand Miss Harper's bitterness. The woman had suffered an enormous loss. She squeezed Hart's hand. He sat with his brows lowered, his expression heartbreakingly sad.

"I have wished many times over the last five years that he was still alive. I would have willingly taken his place to have that be a reality." Hart turned his gaze to her and lifted Lucy's fingers to his lips. "Not anymore though. Now, thanks to my wife, I can finally see the bright possibilities my future can hold."

Lucy leaned forward and kissed him tenderly. This man, with his surprisingly sweet moments, was going to make her cry again. And she did not like to cry. Lucy made herself turn back to the editor.

Miss Harper glanced back and forth between the two of them. "Listen, I have a large network of informants that could be of use in this matter. Finding out what happened to Robert is just as important to me as it is to you. You can trust me. I swear."

Hart nodded. "After Griffen said, 'That girl is living the life my daughter should have had,' another man taunted him for his bad decisions."

"But it was the other man who Griffen accused of 'killing the boy.' It seems both deaths weren't Lord Griffen's doing," Lucy said.

Miss Harper's lips pressed into a tight, thin line. "The sheer gall of these lords. They just do whatever they want with no consequences. Protect each other at all costs. It's disgusting."

"These were my father's trusted confidants, and they killed him. Some brotherhood." Hart spat out. "There will be consequences. I promise you that, Miss Harper."

Miss Harper nodded. "I believe you, Lord Hartwick. Give me the names of all the men in that room. And I will gather every piece of dirt I can on them. Maybe something useful will come to light."

Lucy rose to her feet. "Thank you, Miss Harper. We truly appreciate your help. And if there is anything we can do to help you, let us know."

Hart stood as well. "Yes, I won't let you or my brother's

son flounder in any way. Whatever you need. You are both now under the protection of the Duke of Hartwick."

Miss Harper's mouth fell open. Lucy chuckled at the lady's shocked expression.

She leaned down to buss her cheek and whispered, "It's a wonderful place to be."

CHAPTER THIRTY-THREE

THE ATMOSPHERE INSIDE the carriage was tense at best. Across from her, Hart was deep in thought. Lucy didn't blame him. The truth behind his father and brother's death was shocking. And the child ... in another life, the boy would have been heir to the dukedom. She stared out the window as they headed back into Mayfair. These men had been friends since adolescence. And still they had killed each other. Men and their stupid honor.

"Hart, what will you do now that you know?" she asked.

Hart's gaze sharpened as he focused on her. "I don't know. My first instinct is to confront Griffen. Yell and rage. But to what end? It was a duel, a matter of honor. It was his right to take his shot."

"But they were friends, long-time friends if we believe he was part of their group at school."

"Yes." Hart's eyes turned steely. "My father trusted him enough that he thought they would raise their pistols. That his friend wouldn't kill him. And what of Robert? How did he end up dead? Griffen accused another man in that room of killing Robert, but who?"

"I can't figure out that part. There would be no reason to

kill his second. Unless something is not as it seems or something went very wrong," she mused.

"I need to figure out who was at the duel, who of his trusted circle would let the tragedy happen, and then help keep it a secret. Then I can decide properly what retribution must be dispensed."

The violence in his eyes concerned her, but his anger was well deserved. She was angry too. Hart's family had become hers as well for the time she lived at Belstoke. Their deaths had been her heartache, too.

"I know Miss Harper will be digging into the lives of the club members, but I think it is imperative we find—"

"The journal." Hart grinned. "I was thinking the same."

Lucy grinned back, but then another thought crossed her mind. Goodness, what would Trudy think of all they had discovered? Should they even tell her? Perhaps it was better to keep all these scandalous rumors to themselves. But little Robert, how would they explain him?

Hart took her hand and pulled her over to sit next to him. Using his teeth, he pulled off his glove. Then he brushed his thumb over her lip. "What are you worrying about?"

"Are you going to tell Trudy all this? What about the child?"

"I think we should wait to tell Trudy until we know the whole story. I'm not sure how she will feel about Miss Harper and little Robert. She is part of the old set where one didn't acknowledge mistresses and illegitimate children."

"But Robert planned to marry her; she wasn't his mistress."

"I know, and to me, family is family. I have so little left I cannot afford to be a snob."

WHEN HART ARRIVED home, he immediately called for Mr. Townson. The day had not turned out at all the way he'd thought. His stomach churned with unresolved rage at the events he had learned. He would find and punish every one of the men who had been party to his father and brother's deaths. Dying on a field of honor was one thing, but his brother had been murdered. Shot by someone to hide what? What secrets did these men hold?

Hart rubbed hard at his head, the headache brewing between his eyes increasing in volume. First, he needed to find out who else knew about the duel. Starting with the servants. A knock sounded at the door.

Hart rose from his chair. "Come in."

"You called for me, sir." Townson entered the room and shut the door behind him.

Hart leaned his arm on the fireplace mantel. "Townson, I would like to ask you a few questions about the day that my father died."

Townson straightened his shoulders. His bushy brows drew together. "Certainly, sir. I will do my best to remember every detail."

Not wanting to give away what he had learned today, he purposefully kept his question open-ended. "Do you remember my father's schedule that day?"

"He left the house early in the morning on horseback, and he did not return. He missed several appointments he had that day. I found it to be very out of character for him. Of course, later, we found out about his demise."

"And my brother, did you see him that morning?"

"No, sir, your brother had his own lodgings. I was not apprised of his schedule."

"And my father didn't say where he was going? Didn't bring anything with him?"

"No, sir. Wait, I do remember he had a leather satchel with him. But I am sorry, I do not know what the contents were."

Apparently, his father had told no one of the duel. Which made sense; duels were illegal. But this was also frustrating because if no one knew of it, the possibility of convincing the authorities now, five years later, that it even happened at all was slim.

Hart ran a hand down over his face. "Thank you, Townson. I have been investigating the circumstances surrounding their deaths."

Townson nodded. "Sir, I don't want to overstep, but I have never believed the rumors that the duke's death was part of a robbery."

Interesting. "What makes you say that?"

"For one, your father would never take a rented hack an-

RUMORS, RUIN AND THE DUKE

ywhere. Even if he had private business to attend, he would have taken one of his own conveyances or simply rode his horse, just as he had that morning. What happened to his horse? He wouldn't have left behind such an expensive piece of horseflesh to travel through London in a *hack*." Townson sniffed.

"I feel the same way, Townson. And I suspect that whatever happened that day is connected to the attack on Lord Galey and I last year."

Again, Townson nodded.

Hart studied his butler's face as the realization hit him. "You kept everyone away this past year, not to spare my feelings, but because you didn't know who we could trust."

"It was a bit of both, my lord," Townson replied.

"I have never properly thanked you for the care you took of me and this entire household over the last year. Thank you for keeping things afloat while I wallowed. I am in your debt."

Townson cleared his throat. "Not at all, my lord. It is my honor to serve the Dukes of Hartwick." He bowed and hurried from the room.

Hart's lips turned up into a smile at the man's retreating back. He had probably embarrassed the old guy, but the thank you needed to be said, should have been expressed earlier. Unfortunately, the conversation hadn't revealed any new information. Once again, he was at a dead end.

Hart knew what he had to do. He really did not want to speak with his half-brother. But the smug bastard did seem to know more about his family than anyone else. He quickly penned a note requesting a meeting and addressed it to the Blue Angel, hoping that Seaton would receive it. As he stepped out of the room, his wife came down the corridor wearing a loose-fitting tunic over a pair of pantaloons. Her mind focused on whatever was making her frown, she stalked past his study without seeing him.

Quick as a wink, he snagged her elbow. "Where are you going, wife?"

Lucy blinked up at him, her eyes cleared, and she smiled. "Oh, I was going to work with my staff for a bit. I haven't even touched it since our wedding day."

Seeing her shapely legs encased in the tight-fitting trousers was making him semi-hard already. He slid a hand around to squeeze her behind and pull her against him.

She giggled. "You like my outfit?"

His hand flexed again on her soft backside. "Yes, where did you even find a pair of pantaloons that would fit you?"

"Helen assessed some of the old livery made for the footman and found a pair in my size. Do you want to spar with me? I could teach you a few of the movements."

"No, thank you. You go think things through in your way, and I will go think things through in my way." He smiled and ran a finger down the slope of her nose.

"And what is your way to think things through?"

"Sit with a glass of wine and stare out the window at the falling rain."

"You mean isolate yourself and brood," she quipped.

"I think I made it sound rather more romantic." He patted her backside one more time. He couldn't wait to peel her out of those later. "Go on. Have fun with your big stick."

She stuck her tongue out at him and then disappeared down the hall. Hart gave over his note to a footman and returned to his study. The afternoon had indeed turned rainy. He twisted his desk chair around so he could look out at the back garden as a steady summer rain made all the plants glisten.

Barely twenty minutes had passed when there was a knock at the door. "Come in," he called out.

Townson entered. "A Mr. Seaton to see you, sir."

"Show him down."

"No need." Seaton strolled in from behind Townson.

The butler's eyebrows lowered, but he stepped back through the threshold and shut the door.

Hart stood and came around his desk. "That was fast. I just gave the note over to a footman. He couldn't have made it to the Blue Angel already."

"He didn't. I was nearby, and I intercepted the boy. I told you my job is to stay near and keep you safe."

Well, that was unsettling. Hart waved to the two chairs by the fireplace. "Please sit. Wine? Brandy?"

Seaton shook his head. "I don't drink alcohol." He crossed to sit, arranging his long, rangy body casually in the chair, one ankle crossed over the other knee.

Hart grabbed his wine glass and sat opposite him. "Where were you the night I got stabbed?"

Seaton actually winced. "I was on the roof havin' a smoke. I didn't think the back entrance to a toff club would be so dangerous. My mistake."

Hart studied the man across from him. That day in the park, he hadn't really looked at the man. Emotions had been too high. But now he could see Seaton had the same grey eyes as him and the square jaw that ran in the family. That was where the resemblance ended though. Seaton was fair, his golden blond hair cropped short, his skin almost as pale as Lucy's, and his features were softer than the sharp lines of the Hartwick men. He had a long, thin scar that ran down his left cheek and pulled up at the corner of his lip, making him look like he was permanently snarling.

"I have questions," Hart said.

"I figured you would."

"What do you know about the duel?"

"I wasn't there. But I have a certain reputation for taking care of problems. And I was called to move their bodies and make it look like an accident. I didn't know who it was that had been killed until me and my man arrived at the park. Usually, it wouldn't matter who the dead toff was."

Christ. "Did you know he was your father then?"

"Yes, I always knew. Never expected anything from him. But he came through in the end."

"What do you mean?"

"After their deaths. The man who hired me for the cleanup hired me again to look for some journal that our father had." A small smile played at the corner of Seaton's lips. "The one they are all still sweating about. When I was looking through our father's papers in here, I came across his will. He left me the property down in Holburn. Two whole blocks that was what used to be the land where the old manse was positioned on, back when it was all sheep and shit. The Blue Angel was part of the old house. That symbol on the arch above the door a family motto of sorts, I guess." Seaton shrugged. "Seemed wrong to turn over our father's secrets when he'd thought of me after all. I didn't bother looking further. Just told them I didn't find it."

Hart couldn't help but see the irony. His father's secret son, keeping his other secrets safe. "Wait, did you know that Griffen was the one who killed my father?"

"Nah, like I said, I wasn't there 'til after. Doesn't surprise me. I do know it was a different gun that shot our brother."

"How?"

"Gunshot wounds were different sizes. The second one was made with a smaller pistol. Smaller hole. The dueling pistols leave a gruesome hole."

Hart grimaced. He had no doubt the man knew what he was talking about. "Do you know about the child?"

Seaton shook his head.

Hart continued. "The duel was about the breach of promise over a betrothal. Robert was supposed to marry Griffen's daughter. But he met another woman and fell in love. When my father supported his decision to marry her instead, Griffen demanded satisfaction. We discovered this today when we went to the paper. The editor of the *Piccadil-*

ly Press is Elizabeth Harper and was Robert's intended. She realized she was pregnant with Robert's son after he died. The boy is now five years old."

"More family," Seaton murmured.

The door swung open, and Lucy barreled into the room, red-faced from exertion and with her staff still in hand. "Hart, I know you won't like the idea, but I think that we really need to contact Mr. Seat—" She froze in her tracks as she spotted his guest.

Hart stood and crossed the carpet to capture her hand. "Great minds think alike." He kissed her fingers.

Behind him, Seaton also rose. He ambled over. "Good afternoon, Lady Hartwick. I did not know that duchesses wore trousers at home." He tilted his head and studied her staff. "Although I know nothing about what duchesses do, so perhaps it is very duchess-like to wear trousers and carry around a quarterstaff."

Hart laughed outright at his wife's terrifying, dark expression.

"I'd be pleased to show you first-hand how it works, Mr. Seaton."

"I would like that very much." Lightning quick, Seaton struck out with his hand in a downward blow, which Lucy deflected easily in an almost automatic flick of her wrist. Seaton kicked out next, and again, his attack was met by her staff.

Hart stumbled back. "Hey, what the hell do you think you are doing?"

"Don't worry, I won't hurt her," Seaton replied.

Lucy grunted and landed a glancing blow to Seaton's shoulder as the man, lithe as a cat, moved left. "I can't promise you the same thing."

Seaton advanced, lunging forward to shove at her shoulder with one hand and sweep his leg out to topple her. Lucy jumped back before he could touch her, and this time, when she retaliated, she landed a blow to his thigh with a resounding smack.

Seaton grabbed hold of the end of the staff and tugged them around in a circle. If he hoped to unbalance her, he had miscalculated because Lucy changed her grip and thrust the staff forward, so the end of it drove into Seaton's stomach.

He grunted and held his hand up in surrender. "I concede, Your Grace."

Lucy beamed. "That was so much fun." She held out a hand to Seaton.

Seaton slowly straightened and shook her outstretched hand. "I have been wondering about the way you handled that cane since the park. It's not often someone surprises me or gets that close to me with a weapon."

Hart moved to pull Lucy to his side. "Was that really necessary, you two?" he said scowling at each of them. Their scuffle had taken a year off his life and had been over in less than three minutes.

"I can't convince Hart to spar with me. Thank you, Mr. Seaton, it was quite exhilarating," Lucy said.

"Anytime," Seaton replied.

"No," Hart barked. Then he turned to Lucy and kissed her cheek just in case she thought he was cross at her. "You were magnificent, sweet." Seeing his fierce warrior in action had more than surprise and worry racing through his veins. The look between them heated. Lucy bit down on her lower lip immediately making him go hard. Making him want to devour those lips.

"I'll just be going," Seaton said.

Hart nodded but didn't tear his gaze from Lucy's. "Don't worry about watching me tonight. I plan on staying in."

Seaton chuckled, his voice like gravel. "Good day to you, brother."

CHAPTER THIRTY-FOUR

LUCY LEANED IN to kiss Violet's cheek. "Goodbye. Thanks for meeting with me today."

"I have been dying to see you, but my mother said that I must allow you time to honeymoon with your new husband. I am so pleased and relieved to see you glowing with happiness." Violet squeezed her hands.

Lucy held tight to her friend's hands. Knowing what she did now about Violet's father made her worry. But surely the earl wouldn't ever put his own children at risk? She would keep a close eye on both her friends just in case. The Knot of Isis brotherhood was a dangerous group. And she did not want to see either of her friends caught up in the sins of their fathers.

A cart full of flowers rolled by them down the busy street. In the middle of a Friday afternoon, Covent Gardens bustled with activity. The market was the biggest in the city. and people from all levels of society came to shop the stalls, and Lucy had plenty of shopping to accomplish today. Violet waved goodbye and then stepped up into her carriage to head home.

Lucy turned to her maid. "Helen, do you have our list?

There are so many items to find I can hardly wait to get started."

Yes, ma'am." Helen pulled the list from her pocket. "Come on, Herbert."

Herbert had been taken off the night watch and been given the job of watching over her. Lucy smiled to herself. Helen seemed to enjoy bossing the man around, and Lucy thought that her maid secretly had a tendre for the burly footman.

Today, Lucy's goal was to buy some fabrics to use as inspiration as she thought about which rooms to redecorate first. Certainly, her bedroom canopy was first on the list and perhaps some new curtains and decoration for Hart's study. She was also on the lookout for bath salts that would suit her tastes. Seeing the flower cart rumble by also made her want a few bouquets of fresh flowers to brighten up the front hall. She started walking toward the market stalls down the street.

An hour later, Lucy ran her fingers over a bolt of icy blue velvet that would be perfect for her bed canopy and curtains. "We will take four."

"Yes, ma'am. Would you like that delivered?"

She glanced over at Herbert. "Do you think you can carry them. I'm almost done, I promise."

Herbert nodded.

"Excellent." Lucy passed her basket laden with treats she had purchased at the roasted nuts vendor to Helen, who already had a large basket filled with linens then stepped forward to pay the vendor.

"Lady Hartwick, what a treat to bump into you on this lovely day." A voice came from directly behind Lucy.

She turned around to find the Viscount Griffen's son behind her with a charming smile on his face. "Good day to you, Lord Perrin," she replied tightly.

"Shopping I see. Are you decorating your new home?"

"Yes, in fact I am just beginning to make plans. It has been a long time since Hartwick House has had a duchess in residence. Things are quite outdated."

"I must show you something then. I've just passed a stall with all sorts of beautiful clocks. I myself was eyeing a beautiful pocket watch. But the mantle clocks were exquisite." He grabbed her elbow. "It was just the next aisle over."

"No, thank you, Lord Perrin. I must get home with all my purchases."

His grip tightened on her arm. "I insist. It will only take a moment of your time. I truly think you will be delighted by these clocks."

Lord Perrin's expression was open and friendly. Even if the twinkle in his eye was almost mischievous. Just because his father was a fiend didn't mean that the son was anything but friendly. She certainly didn't want to be rude, but she had no interest in clocks.

He tugged her toward him and pulled her arm through his winged-out elbow. "It's just down this way."

Lucy twisted her head to look back at her servants. Helen was piling the bolts of cloth into Herbert's arms. Her maid said something that made the footman smile as he gazed down at her adoringly. Lord Perrin tugged Lucy along into the crowd. Before she could even protest further, they made a sharp turn to the right between two stalls.

"Lord Perrin, you must cease. I have no interest in looking at clocks." She dug her heels into the ground bringing them to a stop. Honestly what was happening? Lucy looked around and found herself in the mouth of an alley behind a large stall hung with flanks of meat. "You are a rogue, sir." She turned on her heel and started back to the street, but a strong arm circled her waist from behind.

"You are correct, my lady." His voice murmured next to her ear.

A large hand covered her nose and mouth. Panic rose fast and she kicked back with her booted foot hearing a low grunt from her attacker. But his other hand moved to squeeze her throat, his thumb pressing painfully under her chin. Her vision began to go fuzzy and then the world around her went black.

CHAPTER THIRTY-FIVE

HART LOOKED DOWN at his watch fob. It was four o'clock, and he'd seen neither hide nor hair of his wife all afternoon. Not that they had to spend all their time together ... but also, he would happily spend all his time with her. Christ, what a lovesick fool he had become. Since when had one woman consumed his thoughts so fully, so endlessly. He ran a hand over his face. Lovesick was exactly it. He had fallen in love with his wife.

Hart stared straight ahead, a smile spreading across his face until the stretch of it began to ache. He slapped his hands on his desk and stood up. He should go to the bank vault and pick out a proper ring for her. There had to be something among the Hartwick jewels that exemplified how big his feelings were for Lucy. Something with a sapphire to match her eyes.

The door to his study swung open without a knock first. Townson stood on the threshold his expression grim, brows furrowed together like one long hairy caterpillar.

"Please excuse the interruption, sir. But these two have distressing news to impart about Lady Hartwick." He stepped into the room.

Behind him Herbert and Helen stood clutching hands. Helen's face was red and mottled with tears.

Hart's stomach lurched. "Where is she?"

"We was shopping at the Covent Garden market this afternoon after she'd had lunch with Lady Blakely." Herbert began, his cockney accent thick with worry. "We was just collecting the fabric she selected, and then I turned around and she was gone."

Helen met Hart's gaze. "She was right next to us one minute. And then she was gone."

"We spent the last two hours searching the entire market for her. We thought maybe she ended up coming home…" Herbert hung his head.

Nausea rolled in his gut. Hart sucked in a deep breath. "What happened right before you noticed her missing. I need to know every detail. Did she speak with anyone?"

"Yes," Helen said. "Yes, a gentleman approached, and I saw her converse with him,"

Hart stepped forward. "Do you know who it was?"

Helen screwed up her face as she thought about it. "She called him Lord Perrin. He said he saw some clocks she might like? I think he said clocks. We were gathering up the things we bought. I never thought she wasn't waiting for us." Helen voice hitched with emotion. "I'm so sorry, Your Grace."

Hart's blood froze. Lord Perrin was Griffen's son. Lucy would know better than to go anywhere with him. Unless she was forced somehow. Fury cold and hard raced through his veins. Griffen would pay with his life if he hurt one hair on her head.

"If she is harmed the both of you are sacked. You had one damn job, to keep an eye on her!" Panic had a vice grip around his heart. He pushed past the servants and stormed down the corridor to the front hall. He needed help and there was only one person who could figure out where she was. Hart opened the front door and raced down the front stoop to the drive.

"Seaton," he shouted up into the ether. "Seaton!"

Across the street Seaton melted out from the shadows of a large oak in the park. He walked casually up to the front gate. "You bellowed?" he said with a smirk.

"Do you know where she is?" he demanded.

"I'm paid to follow you, not her," Seaton replied.

Hart stalked toward his half-brother. "She's gone. Disappeared from the Covent Garden market this afternoon. Last person she spoke with was Griffen's son, Lord Perrin."

His breath came out hard and fast as his thoughts started to spiral. Everyone he loved had been taken from him. Griffen wouldn't have been able to use her to get to him if he had just followed his first instinct and kept her at arm's length. Now she was in danger because of him. Grabbing the iron gate, he flung it open and Seaton walked through eyeing Hart with serious grey eyes.

Hart paced away his hands clenched into fists at his side. The hell if he would lose Lucy too. He would burn down the whole city to find her. He swung around. "*Fuck.* This is all my fault. She is in danger because of me."

Seaton let out a sharp whistle. Hart followed Seaton's gaze up to the roof line. Less than two minutes passed and a young man maybe sixteen shimmied down the drain pipe landing on his feet with more grace than any adolescent usually possessed. Hart couldn't help but gape.

The boy reported to Seaton who said, "Gabe, race on down to the garden and talk with the lads who was working it today. We are looking for Lady Hartwick. See if any of them saw her this afternoon. Then report back to me."

"Yes, sir." The boy ran off down the street.

Seaton turned back to Hart. "What? I can't sit around and keep an eye on you personally every minute. I have my team on the job."

Hart didn't care who was on his roof or which scruffy street urchin followed him around the city as long as they could use them to find Lucy. Some of the panic that mixed with the rage in chest loosened as he watched the boy disappear.

"She is in danger because Griffen and his cronies are bastards who wish to keep their secrets. You have nothing to do with the sins of our father." His gaze was flat and devoid of emotion.

In contrast, Hart's emotions felt out of control. Despair and the desire to rip apart anyone who harmed Lucy warred with his ability to think logically. He sighed. "I just wanted to know the truth. I wanted to be able to punish those who destroyed my family. Who ruined my life."

"I understand that more than you know, brother. But aren't you being overly dramatic? What happened to you was terrible but you are still the duke, still in possession of all your money and lands."

Hart ran a hand down over his face. "Those things don't matter, she does." He would do whatever it took to have Lucy back in his arms. God, he never told her how much she had come to mean to him. How much he loved her. She had given him her heart, and the whole time he had been too scared to love her back because of exactly this, he ruined everything he touched.

"Tell me this, would you have even seen how special she is before? Or would she have just been another notch on your bedpost?"

Hart sucked in a sharp breath. Seaton's words stung as only the truth could.

"You think what happened to you ruined your life. But perhaps it simply gave you the opportunity for a different life from the ashes of your old one. Stop looking at what you lost and start seeing what you have gained."

Hart straightened his shoulders. Seaton was right. This was no time to fucking wallow. They had to find her. He looked across at Seaton. "Will you help me find her? Please?"

Seaton stared at him for a long moment. Then he nodded. "But don't mistake me for the good guy. I have no fucking reason to be a hero."

"Then why are you agreeing to help?"

"I like your lady."

Well then. If he hadn't felt so panicked, he might have laughed at how Lucy managed to win over everyone she met, even this coarse dangerous man. The slapping of footsteps echoed from his left and another boy, much younger than the one that had come off his roof, raced down the street toward them.

Hart turned to Seaton. "One of yours?"

Seaton shook his head. He put a hand out to stop the boy. "What's your business today in St. James Square?"

The boy was out of breath. He leaned forward with his hands on his knees. "I have a note for the Duke of Hartwick. Do you know which house is his?"

Hart stood. "I am the Duke of Hartwick."

The boy's eyes went wide as saucers. He held out a shaking hand with a sealed letter between his fingers.

Hart strode over and snatched it up. He tore through the plain wax seal and read the neat script.

I have your wife. Bring the journal to Vauxhall Gardens tonight at ten o'clock and we will make the exchange like gentlemen.

Hart stared down at the words *make the exchange like gentlemen.* Like fucking gentlemen who used women as ransom? He handed the note to Seaton.

Seaton snorted in disgust. He fished out a coin from his pocket and held it up in front of the boy's nose. "Where did you get this note from?"

The boy's eyes locked on the gold coin. "A nob approached me on Westminster Bridge."

Seaton flipped the coin to the lad, and the boy ran off. Turning to Hart, he shook his head. "They are stupid. Haven't hired anyone to do the dirty work this time. Didn't take her far; my bet is they're keeping her on the river."

Hart scrubbed his hand through his hair. "But I don't have the journal. I've looked through all of my father's things, the safe. He must have kept it at Belstoke."

"Doesn't matter. I'll find out where they have her before tonight. Give me a few hours. Then we'll go ambush them in their hidey hole." Then Seaton walked away without another word.

Hart stood on the drive, watching his best chance to find Lucy stroll away like he was enjoying an afternoon off from work. What was he supposed to do until ten o'clock this evening? What if they were hurting her? She would certainly fight. *Damn it, Lucy, be smart. Don't aggravate your captors.* He flipped up the cover on his watch fob, four-thirty. The bank was still open. He would go there and see if the journal was kept in the Hartwick safe. Trusting Seaton was not easy, and it couldn't hurt to have the journal to trade if it came down to that.

"Townson," he called out as he took the front stairs two at a time. "Get my carriage ready immediately."

CHAPTER THIRTY-SIX

L UCY WIGGLED AGAINST the ropes that tied her wrists behind her back. Blast! Where the hell was she? It was too dark for her to see past her nose. She sat in a ladderback chair, her arms bound around the smooth wooden back. Underneath her, the floor swayed and bobbed gently. She must be on a boat. Panic bubbled up into her chest.

She called out, "Help! Someone help me!" She screamed at full volume despite her parched throat and aching head.

"Jesus, woman. Stop caterwauling!" Heavy footsteps clomped down from above, and with them, a lantern illuminated the space.

Lucy's blinked as her eyes adjusted. The room she was in came into focus. She was indeed belowdecks of a boat. Not a large space but furnished. The chair she was tied to had a counterpart on the other side of a polished wood table. Beyond that was a long bench along one wall fitted with cushions for seating. And the ladder where the man come down was wide with a railing attached for balance. He raised the lantern. Lord Perrin.

"What would you expect me to do after being kidnapped?" she snapped.

"Be quiet like a good girl. Your husband will come for you. The note has been delivered." He moved through the hold, a small leather bag in one hand.

"Lord Perrin, please let me out of these bindings," Lucy inserted a hitch in her voice. "They are cutting into my wrists terribly."

"Yes, yes, in a minute." He waved a hand distractedly as he turned in a circle, assessing the room. She watched as he walked over to a small barrel and squatted to pull it across the floor. After setting it next to a thick wood pole in the center of the room, he opened his bag and pulled from it a length of rope. No, it was far too thin to be a rope. He snaked it under the lid of the barrel and then unwound it so that it lay along the edge of the room all the way to the bottom of the stairs. Oh Lord, it was a length of fuse.

Lucy began to struggle again, panic roiling in her stomach. "Get me out of here!" She yelled at him.

Lord Perrin did not appear phased by her screaming.

He turned and put a finger to his lips. "Shush. This is not for you. My father will be down shortly to collect you. It's almost time." Then he along with his light climbed the short ladder, disappearing into the dark night above.

Lucy stilled and sucked in several deep breaths. He said a note had been delivered. A ransom note? What was she to be ransomed for? Regardless, she wasn't going to sit here like a good girl while Hart risked himself with these bastards. Instead of fighting her bindings, she used her fingers to explore the knot between her wrists. If she stretched her fingertips just a little further left … yes, there it was, the end of the tie.

Lucy pushed her shoulder blades back as far as they could go to gain the extra half-inch of leverage. She pulled the frayed rope edge, and it slid free of the knot, which honestly wasn't much of a knot. Two more tugs and the bindings were slipping to the ground. Nobody would win a prize for tying those knots today, but Lucy couldn't be more relieved that Griffen and his son were poor sailors.

She lifted her skirts with one hand and gripped the railing with the other and ascended slowly. Climbing just far enough to peek her head out the hatch. The cool night air hit her face as she looked up at the sky, clearing her head. Two low but angry male voices came from her right.

"Father, you do realize that you cannot just hand her over. Hartwick will go straight to the magistrate. You are the insane one if you think he won't want retribution. Once we have the journal, I will take care of them both."

Lucy sucked in a sharp breath, immediately regretting it when she heard footsteps coming her way. A large hand grasped her arm and hauled her up the last couple of steps. "Why is it you won't follow directions, Your Grace? Although I will give you credit for your gumption."

She glared at him. "If you think I won't fight you every moment until you release me, you are sadly mistaken." She thrust the heel of her hand up at his chin.

But Perrin was quick, and he grabbed her wrist before she could make contact. Gripping it painfully, his pale eyes bored into her. There was unholy glee in them that made a shiver of fear run down her spine.

He shook her like a rag doll. "Perhaps I will play with you first. I do like it when they fight."

"Gabriel. Control yourself. Remember that control is the key." Lord Griffen's voice calm and authoritative, rumbled. "Bring her to me."

Perrin dragged her down the deck to his father. Letting go of her wrist, he shoved her toward the older gentleman before stalking off into the shadows at the other end of the ship.

"I'm sorry about that, Lady Hartwick. I will ask that you cooperate. We will be heading to meet with your husband in less than an hour. Have a seat, and all will be well."

Liar. Lucy didn't say it out loud. Lord Griffen didn't seem to want to harm her. She could use that to her advantage. She glanced around to try and gain some indication of where they were. There were boats berthed on each side of them. Sleek schooners, definitely pleasure sailing ships. She walked over to the railing where a built-in bench could seat two passengers. Beyond the dark, quiet dock, she could see lights through the trees and the faint strains of music. "Where are we?"

"Vauxhall. Just around the bend are the stairs. We will go meet your husband inside, and once he gives me the journal, you can go home."

Lucy swung around to confront him. "Do you think we will just let it go that you kidnapped me? That my husband will not demand satisfaction?"

He sighed. "I hope it won't come to that. We shall see how reasonable your husband can be."

Lucy laughed outright at that. This man was delusional. "What makes you think he wants anything but revenge for you murdering his father?"

Lord Griffen took a menacing step forward. "That was a matter of honor," he scoffed.

"Then why cover it up by making it look like a robbery gone wrong?" Her anger pushed her to her feet. "And what about Robert? Why was he shot? Is it a matter of honor to shoot the second?"

"You don't understand. What would a woman know about matters of honor?" He grabbed her arm and shook her.

"I understand that it would make you kill your friend." Lucy stomped down onto his foot. Then she punched as hard as she could into his stomach.

But despite his yowl of pain, it did not make him release his grip on her like she hoped. Instead, he raised his hand. "You bitch." He struck her hard on the side of her head, making her see stars.

"Lucy!" Hart's shout echoed through the night.

He was here. Relief flowed through her. Her cheek throbbed where Griffen had struck her. But for once, she knew she didn't have to fight back. Hart would take care of Griffen and his horrible son. He wouldn't let any more harm come to her. She let her body go lax and slid gracefully to the deck.

CHAPTER THIRTY-SEVEN

HART RACED DOWN the dock. His focus fully on getting to Lucy before Griffen killed her. She crumpled to the deck. He was still too fucking far away. His lungs burned. Seaton's heavy footfalls came from next to him as they ran toward the schooner. When they reached the boat, he could see her lying on the deck, her arms up in front of her as though she was trying to protect herself from the next blow. Hart lost his mind. He lowered his shoulders, and with a primal yell, he launched himself up the gangplank and tackled Griffen. They flew through the air and landed against the gunwale. Griffen's head made a loud crack as it struck the thick wooden railing.

They both tumbled down to the floor in a heap.

Hart got off the unconscious earl and scrambled over to Lucy. "How badly are you hurt?" He gently cupped her face.

Her eyes looked glassy, but she flung her arms around his neck with a cry.

"Oh, Hart!" Her voice cracked on a sob.

He gathered her close. "I'm so glad you are alive. Did they hurt you? Tell me where, and I will take a piece of flesh from them for each bruise."

Seaton ran past them. Hart raised his gaze from Lucy to see why. A tall, shadowed figure emerged from a hatch on the deck and raced over to the port side railing, launching himself over. Seaton did the same. Jumping over the railing and landing with a thump onto the next boat over. Seaton chased the other man across the deck and onto the next boat until Hart could no longer see them.

Getting onto his feet, Hart reached down to scoop Lucy from the deck floor. She snuggled into his shoulder and sighed. "You're making a habit of rescuing me."

"You're making a habit of getting into dangerous situations."

"I didn't want to go with him. He choked me unconscious."

Hart growled low as he carried her down the dock to where Thomas Kent waited with the carriage. He was going to kill Perrin with his bare hands. When they reached the carriage, the relief etched across the coachman's face was evident.

"Take her." He handed Lucy over to the coachman. "I have to take care of Griffen."

"No! Don't go back onto that boat," Lucy said.

He ran his fingers down her cheek. "I'll be right back." He turned and started back to the boat. His rage was at full throttle. The man who killed his family would pay. He was going to tear him apart limb from limb.

"Alex!" Lucy's voice cried out.

Hearing his given name pierced through his anger. He

swung around. No one had called him Alex in years. Only his father and brother had ever used his given name. Christ, he missed being Alex. Back when his biggest decision had been to choose his entertainments for the night or which brandy to consume. That Alex had simply enjoyed life to the fullest. He hadn't been afraid of anything.

Lucy raced to him and grabbed hold of the lapels of his jacket. "Listen to me. Killing Griffen will not change the past. You succeeded. You found the culprit. And he will be punished."

Her words hardly registered. All he wanted was for his name to spill from her lips again. "Say my name."

"Alex." Her lips curved up into a smile. Lucy placed a hand on his heart. "Tomorrow, we will go to the magistrate and tell him everything we know. Even if they do not hang him, it will ruin him. But tonight, I want you to come home with me. I want you to climb into our bed and make love to me. I need you to hold me in your arms all night long."

Hart slid his arms around his wife. Dipping his head to bury his face in her hair, he sucked in her unique scent that had come to mean, more than any brick-and-mortar house, home to him.

He let out a shaky exhale. "But he took you from me. He harmed you. I just want to make sure he can never threaten you again."

"Unlike him, you are not a murderer," she said. "He won't be able to hurt us anymore. You told me on our wedding day that I should always tell you what I need from you."

Hart raised his head to look down at her.

Lucy's hand cupped his scarred cheek. Her thumb brushed over one of the long scars as she snared his gaze. "I need you to look forward to our future together. Come, love, let us leave these ghosts behind."

"I hate it when you're right."

Lucy laughed, and the sound swept over him like a balm to his battered soul. He grasped her chin between his thumb and fingers. Those gorgeous eyes sparkled with humor. His feelings for her caught him like a vise around the throat. He couldn't breathe. "Lucy—"

A great boom echoed through the night as a large ball of orange flames exploded through the deck of Griffen's schooner. Flaming debris hurled through the air. Hart curled his body around Lucy. *Christ, why were things always blowing up around me?* His last thought before the world went black.

CHAPTER THIRTY-EIGHT

LUCY STARED DOWN at her husband as he lay in bed. She laid another cool, damp cloth on his head. He stirred.

His eyes fluttered open. "Lucy? Where am I?"

"Home." This was the third time he'd woken and asked the same question.

"Are you alright?"

"Yes, love. I'm fine. You saved me." By being reckless and blocking the flaming debris with his own body.

His fingers reached out to grip hers. "No, you saved me." Then his eyes closed, and he fell back to sleep.

Lucy sighed. What was she going to do about her heart? Her love for him was so big it scared her. To love someone this much and then lose them? Could she bear it?

"You haven't lost me yet." Hart's voice startled her.

Had she said that out loud? Looking down at her husband, she found his eyes were open and filled with emotion. "I thought you were asleep."

"I'm not going anywhere. I'm like a cat, nine lives." He smiled wickedly.

She removed the cloth from his forehead and placed a kiss on the lump that marred his right temple. "Even so, you have used up half of them. I will need you to be more careful from now on. My heart can't take any more close calls."

"I promise. Now, come to bed. You look dead on your feet. Come let me hold you all night long, as requested."

———— ~~~ ————

MORNING LIGHT SLANTED through the room. Lucy pushed her face against her husband's chest, trying to avoid the sunshine. His arm wrapped tightly around her, and she felt his lips brush against her hair. He was awake. She scooted up to sitting.

Pushing her hair away from her face, Lucy looked down at Hart. "How does your head feel?"

"Sore, I guess. But it doesn't pound like it did last night." He reached up and lazily wrapped a piece of her hair around his finger. "And you, were you hurt in any way by the blast?"

"No. You took all the hits. You saved me." She repeated her words from the night before.

Hart sat up with only a small wince. He pulled her onto his lap and nuzzled her earlobe. "No, you saved me."

"We saved each other." She furrowed her brow. "I didn't think he would do it."

"What do you mean?"

"Earlier in the evening, they had me tied to a chair below deck. I saw Lord Perrin attach a long length of fuse to a small barrel, which I assumed was black powder. He told me not to worry; it was not meant for me. Do you think he planned to kill his father this whole time? Or did he set it off in desperation after you found us?"

"I don't know. But Griffen is certainly dead. No one could have survived that blast." He stroked his thumb over her bruised throat gently. "Strangely, no sense of satisfaction comes from knowing he is dead. I guess I thought that was what I needed, to know that the man who killed my father would get his comeuppance." His gaze rose to meet hers. "But you were right. I don't need to dwell on the ghosts of the past. The only thing I need is you. And our future together. Wait here."

Hart got out of bed and crossed to where his clothes sat in a pile on the floor. Lucy admired his broad, strong shoulders and his taut backside as he bent over. After a moment of digging around, he came back with a small square box in his hand. He held it out on one palm. "I hope I did a good job with my first husbandly task. Take a look."

Lucy scrambled up to her knees, snatched up the box, and lifted the lid. Inside, against a white silk background, was the most beautiful ring she had ever seen. An enormous square sapphire framed by small diamonds on all sides winked and gleamed in the sunlight. "Oh, Hart, it's beautiful." She sighed in feminine appreciation. When she looked up at her husband, his eyes glowed with a soft emotion her mind scrambled to identify. Soft was not an adjective she would normally use to describe Hart.

His hand cupped her cheek. "Lucy, you are everything I

never knew I needed in my life. More laughter, more tenderness, more hope for what the future can be." He leaned down to kiss her lips soft and reverent. Lucy's breath hitched. "I feel like the luckiest man on earth that Fitzwilliam punched you in the eye."

A hoarse laugh escaped her chest, and the wet path of a tear rolled down her cheek. Damn the man and his unexpected declarations. More tears filled her eyes.

"Sweet, I'm sorry." Hart looked stricken. "It's too soon for such big emotions. I promised to give you time to get used to this marriage. I'm skipping ahead..."

She put a finger across his lips. "It's not that. These are happy tears."

"Women cry when they are happy?"

"Yes." She nodded and wiped at one eye. "I love you, you moody bastard. I always have."

He leaned his forehead against hers. "Still? Even with all this?" He motioned down his body.

What a fool. She brushed a feather-soft kiss against his lips. "Yes. Still. Always."

His chest rose and fell as he sucked in a long breath. "I don't deserve your love. The old me definitely did not. He did not realize how precious of a gift you were offering that day. But I am working to remake the man inside this ruined body. Perhaps I can become the man you need."

Another tear slipped down her face. She couldn't help it. His words spread through her like sunshine warming the part of her heart that hoped someday he would love her back. That he would look at her the way he was now, his expression one of quiet awe, like he couldn't believe she was his.

He brushed at her tears with his thumb. "Lucy, I love you. You are the reason that I want to rise from the ashes of my old life. You are my future, my family."

Lucy threw her arms around his neck. "I knew you could come back to life. You only had to stop feeling sorry for yourself," she teased him with a watery chuckle. His arms banded around her, and she leaned back to smirk at him. "I hope you don't remake everything. I rather liked the wicked rogue."

"Is that a challenge, wife?" Hart tossed her onto the middle of the bed. "Lay back my lady, I will show you just how wicked I can be."

CHAPTER THIRTY-NINE

H ART AND LUCY sat together on the settee across from Trudy and filled her in on all that they had discovered. After all that had happened, they had decided Trudy needed to know the truth, and hoped it would not shock her into an early grave. Trudy took all the news with surprising aplomb. In fact, she was non-plussed to hear about his father's affairs.

"My dears, I was one of your mother's confidants. She knew about Henry's affairs. She told him straight out that as long as he was discreet, he could keep his mistresses."

Lucy gasped in shock.

Hart chuckled at her outraged look. But regretted it in the next moment when she turned to glare at him.

Quickly, he grasped her hand and brought it to his lips for a kiss. "I was only laughing at your outrage on my mother's behalf. You never have to worry about being in a similar situation. No one compares to you, my love."

Trudy smiled at the two of them. "You have to understand that many wives of the ton are in similar positions as your mother. Though, I did not know that your father had sired another child. And you have met this man?"

"Yes, he is a hard man to describe. He is certainly a criminal of some sort but also a legitimate businessman, and he helped me to find Lucy when she was taken, even though he barely knows us. I couldn't tell you his motivations for the things he does, even if I tried."

A knock sounded at the drawing-room door. "Come in."

Townson entered the room. "Pardon, a Miss Elizabeth Harper, and her son are at the door."

"Show them in," Lucy said. "Trudy, this is Robert's fiancée and his son. I cannot think why they are here. Please be nice."

"Why would you think I wouldn't be nice?" Trudy looked positively affronted. "The child is family, is he not?"

"Miss Elizabeth Harper and Robert Harper." Townson intoned from the doorway.

The lady and her son cautiously entered the room. "I hope we are not intruding. I heard what happened to Lord Griffen, and I wanted to make sure that you knew about his demise."

Hart crossed to her. "Won't you both come in?" He gave a friendly smile to the boy, hoping that his scarred face wasn't too scary.

Robert grinned back at him and dug into his pocket. Pulling out a toy soldier, who rode atop a horse, he handed it up to Hart. "This is for you. He is my best commander."

"Thank you." Hart solemnly accepted the gift. "Would you like a biscuit? There are some here on the table."

Robert looked up at his mother, who nodded. Then he

hurried over to the table to peer at the selection of biscuits laid out next to the tea service.

Miss Harper followed Hart over to the seating area.

Lucy immediately embraced her. "We are glad to see you." She turned to Trudy. "May I introduce you to Miss Harper? Miss Harper, this is Hart's great aunt, Lady Weatherby."

"It's nice to meet you," Miss Harper said.

"You as well, my dear. He certainly looks like a Hartwick." She nodded her head to the boy.

Miss Harper looked taken aback at first, but then she glanced over at her son with a soft look of pride. "Yes, he reminds me of his father every day."

Hart thought it prudent to change the subject before Trudy really got to interrogating the poor woman. "Miss Harper, we already know about Griffen's death because we were there."

"You were? What happened?"

"He kidnapped my wife from the Covent Garden market with the intention of using her as ransom for this mysterious journal that my father kept."

"I heard there was an explosion, and several boats were set on fire. Are you unharmed?"

"Hart was hit by flying debris," Lucy said. "Luckily, he has a hard head."

"Well, that is good to hear. The other reason I came by to see you is because I did some research in my father's files. You see, he kept meticulous records of the headlines for every edition of the paper. Cross-referenced names and dates, it took a little searching, but I found this article from years ago." She pulled out a piece of folded newsprint and handed it to him. Halfway down the page, the headline read, "Aristocratic Sons Get Expelled from Eton."

"Well, what does it say?" Trudy asked.

Miss Harper answered for him. "It is an article about how a group of aristocratic sons were expelled from Eton for beating a teacher almost to death."

Trudy nodded. "Oh, yes, I remember when Henry got expelled. What trouble that boy was when he was young. My brother caned his backside in front of the whole family as punishment. The incident was quite embarrassing."

Hart read the whole article out loud. A group of boys were all expelled from the school after beating one of the arithmetic teachers so badly he was not expected to be able to walk again. The boy's names were all listed. The Duke of Hartwick's son, the Duke of Lavensham's son, the Duke of Fleming's son, the Earl of Blackpool's son, The Earl of Rawlings's son, Viscount Galey's son, and Viscount Griffen's son. All his father's cronies, in black and white.

"Did this group of boys comprise their club?" Miss Harper asked.

"Yes, and that incident was the genesis of our bond of friendship. One that's lasted forty years." A deep voice came from the doorway.

Everyone turned in their seats.

"The Duke of Fleming and Mr. Seaton," Townson announced.

Hart stood. He looked between the two men, and their connection clicked into place. "You are the one who hired Seaton to watch over me."

The duke nodded. "There have been too many lives sacrificed needlessly. My regrets are large. Protecting you was the least I could do for Henry."

"Please come in." Hart motioned for Fleming to take a seat.

The duke crossed to the seating area and gave a short bow to the ladies. "Lady Weatherby, Lady Hartwick." He turned to Miss Harper and her son. His eyes grew wide as his gaze roamed over them. "You are she. The one he wanted to marry."

Miss Harper gathered her son close to her side, her expression fierce. She nodded.

Hart stepped forward. "Please sit. Can you tell us what happened to Robert?"

Fleming sighed as he took a seat. "It happened so quickly. There was no time to stop it. I don't think any of us thought Griffen would shoot Henry." He shook his head. "And when he did, Robert was distraught as he knelt next to his father. He looked up, and I can still recall the rage that burned in his eyes. Then he was screaming at all of us. Said he'd seen the journal, that he knew all our secrets, that he would ruin all of us for allowing this to happen. Someone pulled out a gun and shot him. The moment is still seared into my memory. So rash, so reckless."

The silence in the room was broken by a choked sob from Miss Harper. Lucy crossed to sit next to her, enveloping her hand in both of hers.

Hart stood frozen for a long moment. Finally having the answer to his brother's death did not assuage his pain or his anger. Both still roiled in his gut. Perhaps nothing would. Grief, it seemed was not something that could be erased. It could only be grappled with, like his anxiety from the carriage explosion. He would have to find a way to live with it. He glanced over at Lucy where she comforted Miss Harper. So fierce, so loving. He knew that with Lucy by his side he could manage anything life brought them. There was just one more loose end.

"Who shot Robert?" he asked.

Fleming shook his head. "I can't tell you."

"You mean, you won't."

"Yes, I won't. These men are my family. They mean everything to me." Fleming ran a hand down over his face. "That year at Eton, the teacher, the one who they beat, he was—" Fleming glanced at the ladies. "Taking advantage of me in the most inappropriate way. I was smaller, weaker, and too ashamed to tell anyone what was happening to me. Henry came in quite by accident one day after classes to ask the teacher some questions and saw firsthand the abuse I was subject to. Later, when he told the others, I felt so betrayed. But he didn't tell them to make fun of me but to gather them together to make a plan for revenge. You see, they saved me from further abuse, and they stood by me when I needed it the most."

Hart didn't know what to say to Fleming's confession. It explained so much about the bond these boys had forged, but it did not excuse the actions of grown men. His heart ached at the senseless death of his brother. Not for the first time did he wish it could have been him instead that day.

Seaton stepped forward. Hart had almost forgotten the man was there; he had been so silent.

"I have something for you." Seaton reached under his jacket behind his back and pulled out a slim black journal.

Fleming's gaze snapped to Seaton. "You had it this whole time. Why does that not surprise me at all."

Seaton shrugged. He handed it to Hart. "Seemed prudent to hold onto something that contained so many secrets. You never know when you could need the information."

Hart opened the book and flipped through the pages. Each page had a name at the top. It was filled with information, not just of the six other men but others Hart recognized, men and women alike. It seemed his father had kept a record of all the gossip and knowledge he'd learned at court and in his dealings within the ton.

Seaton nodded to the journal. "Our father knew that information was power."

Hart snapped the journal shut. He turned to Fleming. "You may go tell the others that I have their secrets. I will keep it somewhere safe. If they threaten or harm anyone in my family"—he swept his arm wide over his people gathered in the room—"then I will not hesitate to use it. And if they make another attempt on my life, I will have my firm send it directly to the press."

Miss Harper nodded at him, her mouth set in a firm line.

Fleming stood with a sigh. "I will give them your message. I have lost three friends now. I do not want any more lives sacrificed. I will do my best to keep the others in check." He bowed. "Good day."

Once Fleming left, Lucy came over and wrapped her arms around his waist. "How are you feeling?"

"For the first time in a long time, I feel at peace with the past. I don't think I am going to read this unless it becomes necessary." He held up the journal. "It's time to focus on our future." Hart kissed the top of her head. "I love you."

Lucy lifted her face and kissed him. "I love you, too."

Hart looked around the room. Seaton had crossed to crouch down in front of little Robert. He held a hand up and then, quick as a wink, pulled a coin from behind the boy's ear. Robert giggled, and Miss Harper smiled.

Trudy rose from her seat. "Well, that was a lot of information to take in for one afternoon. We are going to need more tea. I still have questions, many, many questions." She crossed to ring for a servant.

Lucy laid her head against his chest with a sigh. "I think perhaps this means it's over."

Hart wasn't so sure. Perrin was still an unpredictable question mark. Seaton hadn't been able to catch him, and Hart had decided it would be safer for Lucy to not tell the authorities that they had been at the scene of the explosion.

Perrin certainly wouldn't be admitting that he was there that night either.

After losing everything he held dear, Hart understood how precious it was to be given a second chance to rebuild his life, to rebuild himself. He would not take for granted the people that had come into his life. He squeezed his wife tight. He would use everything in his power to protect his newfound family.

The End

EPILOGUE

"LEFT, THEN RIGHT. Left, right…yes that's it. Find the rhythm that works for you." Lucy laid a hand on Hart's back. "Slow, let your shoulder warm up." She smoothed her hand down over the firm muscles as they shifted underneath warm skin. Her husband stood with his feet positioned in warrior stance, in just his trousers. His shirt lay discarded on the settee.

"You are distracting me," Hart grumbled. But the staff he was working through the air in graceful arcs never stopped moving. He was a natural at manipulating the quarterstaff. Not that she was surprised. If he put his mind to it Hart could master just about anything. "We can switch activities if you are wanting to touch me," he teased.

"Not a chance. Always trying to cry off your exercises." Lucy tutted. She stepped back and crossed to the wall where her staff was propped. Grabbing it up she went to stand a short distance in front of Hart with her back to him. She widened her stance and raised the staff in front of her. "Alright, follow me. First, attack right. Then slide the left hand down and thrust."

She demonstrated once through and then turned to

watch Hart copy the motion. He looked magnificent wielding the staff. His brows lowered in concentration and his chest was beginning to glisten with sweat. Her whole body heated as she watched a drop of sweat slide down the center of his chest. Lucy quickly turned to face to the front before she took him up on his suggestion to switch activities.

"Next, let's add the additional block. After the thrust, take a step back into ready position. Keep your posture straight. And swing the staff around to counter your opponent's downward blow. All your power should be in your arms, your knees should be soft to absorb the blow."

She ran through the three movements altogether, ending in a crouch. Then suddenly a strong arm snaked around her waist from behind and lifted her off her feet. Her staff clattered to the floor as she shrieked. "Hart!"

His warm breath tickled her ear. "Come now, you can't expect me to pay attention when your arse looks so lovely in these trousers. You are far too tempting, sweetness." His staff fell to the floor with a thunk.

Lucy laid her head back against his shoulder. "You are incorrigible." She sighed contentedly as he began to nibble on her neck. Hart carried her over to the settee and pulled her onto his lap. "These exercises are meant to increase the range of motion in your shoulder. They are good for you," she admonished.

"You are good for me." He brushed his lips against hers.

Wrapping her arms around his neck she indulged her husband. Truth was she still couldn't get enough of his affection. She soaked up every kiss, every touch, still hardly believing that this man was hers to keep.

"I'm yours. I adore you my fierce warrior. You'll never be rid of me now." He murmured.

As usual his kisses scrambled her wits so easily she said even her inner thoughts out loud. No matter. Gone were the days when she had to keep her feeling to herself. Lucy brushed back his hair from his brow, he needed another trim. "I never will want to be rid of you. I love you."

A knock sounded. Lucy slid off his lap to go answer it. Townson stood on the other side when she cracked the door open.

"Your Grace, a note arrived for you. From Lady Amberley."

"Thank you, Townson." Lucy accepted the note. After closing the door, she unfolded the missive and read it. Oh dear.

My father announced that Ambassador Bellamy has offered for me. My brother protested on my behalf as the ambassador is three times my age. Father has reluctantly given me until Christmastide to find another offer. I need your help. Care to start some rumors? I am done being invisible.

Adeline

In book two of *The Lost Lords* series, Naval Commander Malcolm Iveson returns to London with a new assignment to discover missing artifacts smuggled into England. Falling head over heels for the daughter of his main suspect is not the plan! At the mercy of her cruel father, wallflower Adeline Amberly is trying desperately to find a way to save her family from scandal. Malcolm kidnaps his damsel in distress to keep her safe but will his desire for her overpower his duty to do his job and force him to set a new course for his life?

Scandal, Secrets and The Marquess is coming soon!

More Books by Karla Kratovil

The Maidens of Marbury series

Book 1: *A Perfect Engagement*

Book 2: *Saving a Scoundrel*

Book 3: *Christmas at Belhaven Hall*

Book 4: *Making the Marquess Mine*

Available now at your favorite online retailer!

About the Author

From the time she read fairytales as a child, Karla Kratovil was hooked on stories that ended in Happily Ever After. Now as an author of sexy historical romance she gets to craft her own happy endings. Karla lives right on the edge of Northern Virginia's wine country with her college sweetheart, two terrific teenagers, and two blond terriers. She is a Taurus. Like any good earth sign she loves good food, good wine, and getting her hands dirty growing things in her garden.

Thank you for reading

Rumors, Ruin and the Duke

If you enjoyed this book, you can find more from all our great authors at TulePublishing.com, or from your favorite online retailer.

TULE
PUBLISHING

www.ingramcontent.com/pod-product-compliance
Lightning Source LLC
Chambersburg PA
CBHW030639020726
47493CB00006B/1788